#HUNTEDLIVES

KADY HINOJOSA

Visit the author's website at www.kadyhinojosa.com

Note: This story is not suitable for persons under the age of 18.

Cover Design: Damonza.com

Editorial Services: Beth Dorward. Visit the editor's page on Reedsy at
https://reedsy.com/#/freelancers/beth-d

E-book ISBN-13: 978-1-7354976-0-0

Paperback ISBN-13: 978-1-7354976-1-7

To my husband, Jose:
Thank you for always loving and supporting
me, for believing in me, and for being my
sounding board for this story. I love you.

CHAPTER ONE

New York City
Thursday, March 5, 3:10 a.m.

SHE COWERED IN the corner of the stone cottage ladies restroom near the open-air Delacorte Theater in Central Park, crying and depleted by hunger, exhaustion, and fear. Her long blond hair was matted and tangled. She wore only a dirty black 'I love New York' sweatshirt, no bra, baggy black exercise pants, and frayed red tennis shoes.

A light snow blanketed the park in fairy tale beauty making this run for her life all the more surreal. Shivering uncontrollably, her bones ached from the cold. Shallow breathing matched the pounding in her head and racing heartbeat. Terrified eyes, ringed black by fatigue, dominated an ashen face.

Grabbing onto the wall for support and inching her way up, she limped to the sink. Hoping to steal some warmth from the water, she turned on the faucet and splashed her face. No luck. Gasping for air and teeth chattering, she wiped her eyes on the sleeve of the sweat-shirt.

Her nightmare began three days ago when she was abducted.

She had popped over to the grocery store near her home in Newark, New Jersey, to buy a special treat for her older daughter who was home sick with the flu. Returning to the parking lot, she noticed an older gentleman in his sixties leaning against a black, windowless van gripping his chest, grimacing and wheezing. Alarmed, she rushed over to ask if he was all right. He shook his head. As she reached for her cellphone to call 911, the van's sliding door opened and a large muscular man grabbed her while the man outside shoved her in, slamming the door and disappearing as the van raced away. On the floor of the van, the man knelt on her legs, reached for a syringe on the console between the front and passenger seats, and plunged it into the base of her neck. That was the last thing she remembered.

Awareness came slowly to her, a musty, stale smell bringing her fully awake. She was lying on her back on a lumpy sofa in her underclothes. Turning her head toward a squeaking sound, she shrieked and pushed herself into a sitting position as a rat scurried away. Groaning in pain, her fingers gingerly probed the area behind her ear. Feeling a sticky wetness, she pulled her hand back and observed with horror the blood staining her fingers. She raised her hand to her head again and touched what felt like stitches. The wound was about three fingers wide and blood was oozing out. What had happened?

Looking cautiously around, she assessed her surroundings. The sofa was the single piece of furniture in the room, barely fitting. Standing up and stretching her arms out shoulder height, her fingers almost touched the walls on each side. There were no windows and the only light was a thin beam of sunlight shining in from an opening at one end. She crept to the opening and peeked outside.

Shock crossed her face, her mouth dropping open slightly. She was in a shipping container in a yard full of containers. Pushing the door wider for light, she turned back to the interior, noticing, for the first time, the filthy clothes lying next to a note and picture of her family on the floor.

In disbelief and with a growing sense of panic, she had read the note, alternately staring at the picture of her family. Without wasting any time, she had dressed and fled. On the run now for sixteen hours, could she make it another fifty-six?

She thought about her girls now, picturing their sweet smiles. She and her husband, Joe, had started their family later in life. At the age of forty-two, six short years ago, her precious Becky was born. Jamie followed three years later. They were her pride and joy—her life. Thinking of them gave her the impetus to keep going. She had to survive, for them.

She took a drink of water from the faucet and closed her eyes, filling her lungs with air to try to calm herself with the breathing exercises she had learned in yoga. It didn't work. It felt as though an elephant sat on her chest, every breath a struggle, the pressure immobilizing her.

I can do this. I have to do this. I can survive seventy-two hours for my girls. Preparing to leave, she chanted this mantra over and over in her head, determination giving her focus and strength.

She peered out the restroom door and skimmed the area looking for movement, straining to hear any noise out of the ordinary. It was still and quiet. Time to make a move.

Trembling, she stepped outside the restroom and over the black rail lining the pathway, then crept to the corner of the building. A bitter breeze hit her in the face as she looked around the corner. A few snow flurries were drifting down from the sky. Sunrise was still a few hours away but she'd have more protection on West Drive where traffic was picking up.

Not seeing anyone or hearing anything, she crouched low and tiptoed through the brush to the path that would take her to the street. Stepping over another black rail onto the path, she took a deep breath then half-limped and half-ran toward the street.

She didn't make it ten steps. The bolt slammed into her chest, a direct hit to her heart, the force of it sending her sprawling onto her back. She was dead before she hit the ground.

* * *

FBI Field Office, Federal Plaza, New York City
Tuesday, March 10, 6:42 a.m.

"GOOD MORNING, MALI Hooper speaking."

"Now, how did I know you'd be in the office already?" teased Mali's best friend, Kirsten Bellows, an IT FBI agent, not an intelligence analyst like Mali.

"Same reason you're here, my friend. You love your job as much as I love mine." Mali smiled as she clamped the phone against her ear and continued responding to her e-mail. "I wanted to get an early jump on my inbox. How was your long weekend at Niagara Falls?"

"You are a workaholic! I bet you came in this weekend too, right? Our weekend was amazing! I never tire of listening to that rush of falling water and watching it cascade over the edge to the rocks below. The power of all that water is mesmerizing. You should have gone with us."

"Yeah right." Mali laughed. "Two is company, three is definitely a crowd. And, no, I didn't come in this weekend although I did work on my analysis of the Rodriguez case yesterday from home. Made good progress too."

"I knew it!" Kirsten crowed. "Our weekend was rather romantic. Ok, so I'm glad you didn't go."

The friends shared a laugh.

Kirsten continued, "And in case I haven't told you lately, thanks again for introducing me to Jennifer three years ago. Best thing that ever happened to me. Hey, if you're not too busy today, let's do lunch and catch up."

"You tell me all the time. I had a feeling about you

and my college roomie. Lunch sounds good. I want to hear more about your weekend. How about eleven thirty? I'll meet you in the lobby."

"Great. Later, friend."

Mali turned on the WABC live stream on her second monitor, reading her e-mail displayed on the first one. She loved coming into the office early to knock out some work, listen to the news, and prepare for the day without interruption, Kirsten being the regular exception.

"An update on the Central Park murder we reported on yesterday," said the local reporter on the live stream. "The woman has been identified as Margie Thornburg, forty-eight years of age, a wife and a mother of two young girls. She was found near the Delacorte Theater yesterday morning at five fifteen by a jogger. Her husband says she disappeared three days ago; a police report confirms that. Cause of death, a puncture wound to the heart. The police believe it was an arrow of some kind. They also report that there was a small cut behind her right ear. An autopsy will be performed. No further details were provided. The investigation is on-going and we will update you with more information as soon as we have it. Now to Gina Smith and our weather forecast for today . . . Gina?"

Sitting in her cubicle on the twenty-third floor, Mali was saddened to learn about what was just reported and the heartbreak that family was now living, details of the warming trend in the weather totally lost on her. She remembered hearing about the death yesterday. Such a senseless murder. Looking out the window at the New

York City skyline, Mali marveled that she lived and worked here. New York was bustling and alive. She loved the noise of the taxi horns blaring, the delivery trucks screeching to a stop, the clip-clop of the horses as they pulled young lovers in pristine white carriages through Central Park. And then there were the various odors (good and not-so-good) that drifted down most streets. From the many off-Broadway and Broadway shows to picnicking in Central Park, to the incredible shopping or the many museums and sights, there was something for everyone in this beautiful metropolis.

Her friends laughed at her clichéd descriptions, but having lived in the city only two years, it was all still new and magical to her. Mali loved it all.

Even with all its beauty and diversity, there was a dark side to the city, and stories like the woman in Central Park always troubled her. Whether local news like this most recent murder or national news of murder, rape, or vicious attacks, the papers and media reported these stories for a five-minute segment and sometimes there was a candle vigil but it rarely went further than that. Her death was tragic, of course, but it troubled her that the murder of a suburban housewife generated more viewers to the news channel than that of a youth from a poor neighborhood, and both were forgotten in the blink of an eye, the latter almost as soon as it was reported. Why? Why was one murder more disturbing than another? Did people try to affect change after hearing stories like this or did they just go on about their day? This didn't apply to everyone, of course, but the masses were too busy texting, posting selfies and videos to social media, and hustling here and there to care when death stained the city or nation.

Growing up in Philadelphia as a member of the Hooper dynasty, Mali had led a sheltered life. She didn't experience hardship of any kind, much less death, while growing up. Her parents' idea of helping others was to write a check to various charities. Not that there was anything wrong with that. But Mali had always wanted to help people face to face. At seventeen, she volunteered to work at the local soup kitchen. When her father found out where she was one Saturday, he had raced to the kitchen and yanked her out, taking her home then and there. She was mortified. She didn't talk to her father for two days.

Her parents expected their youngest daughter to marry into the 'right' family and be a dutiful wife, as her two older sisters had. They were shocked and disappointed when Mali eloped with Daniel Matthews, a football player she met in college. They were appalled when she divorced him less than four months later. And they threatened to disown her when she took a job at the FBI right out of university.

Her first job, where she honed her skills and paid her dues, was in Chicago. She worked like a dog, feeling as though she had to work twice as hard as the men to prove herself. Despite that, Mali enjoyed her time there and learned a lot. But New York City was always where she wanted to be. It took her close to three years to get transferred and she had not looked back.

Her mother didn't talk to her for two months when she moved to Chicago, had never visited her there, and still had not traveled to New York City for a visit. She lived for the day Mali regained her senses and returned home to marry the right man. *Like that will happen.* Mali shrugged, admitting to herself that she joined the FBI initially to rebel against her parents but discovering that she loved the work, loved the FBI, and wouldn't trade her life for anything.

With a deep sigh and forcefully shifting the direction of her thoughts, Mali turned her attention back to her computer and her work.

"I'm glad you could get away for lunch," Kirsten said as they left the lobby and headed to their favorite deli, Corte Cafe on Lafayette. They stepped into the street to cross but had to jump back when a horn blared and someone yelled an obscenity, flipping the bird as he drove past.

"Hey, watch it moron!" shouted Kirsten. They walked across the street to the deli. "You don't do it often enough," she continued, as if there had been no interruption.

"Things are busy at work so I prefer to eat in. But this is a great break. Thanks for the suggestion. And you know how much I love my meatball parmigiana hero. It's my absolute favorite."

"How can you put that away time and time again?"

With her unusual gray almond-shaped eyes, high

cheekbones, perfect Big Apple red-colored nails with matching lipstick, and toned body, Mali could have been a model.

"I exercise to eat, my friend. Hey Johnny," Mali waved hello to the cafe owner's son as she strode inside.

"Hi, Ms. Hooper. Good to see you today. The usual?"

"Yes, please. And a Diet Coke." Glancing at Kirsten, she said, "Let's eat inside today, okay? It's still cold out." At Kirsten's nod, Mali turned back to Johnny. "We're eating in today."

"Actually, I'm not surprised." Kirsten placed her order then picked up the conversation where she left off. "I remember the first time we met at Quantico during training. You were eating a fully loaded pizza."

"That's not the first time we met," Mali said absently as she looked around for an open table. It was crowded but she spotted one in the back. She waved to a few people she knew as they wound their way around the tables to the rear.

"What do you mean?" Kirsten asked as they sat down. Placing her elbows on the table, she leaned forward so Mali could hear her over the din of the surrounding conversations.

"The second day of training, you fell down a steep hill during our five-mile run."

"I had forgotten about that." She paused. "That hurt like the dickens. I climbed up the hill and someone helped me up . . . Wait, that was you?"

"Yep."

"Why haven't you ever said anything?"

Mali shrugged. "At the time, we were so focused on catching up to the others, there was no time for talk. And then I didn't see you again until a few days later in the cafeteria. It didn't seem important then, or since."

Grinning, Kirsten said, "Wow. Well thank you for helping me all those years ago. I guess I'm not surprised. You have always been willing to help me, Jen too. She told me about the phone call you made on her behalf last week. That was really nice of you."

"That's what friends do. I hope some jobs are sent her way. She's really good at event planning," Mali stated, shrugging.

The conversation moved to Niagara Falls as they waited for their lunch to arrive.

As soon as her plate was placed before her, Kirsten grabbed her sandwich and bit into it with gusto.

Taking a sip of her Diet Coke, Mali watched her friend eat. What you saw was what you got with Kirsten, something Mali always appreciated. Her thoughts were interrupted by her grumbling stomach when the aromatic scent of the meatball sandwich assailed her. She picked it up and attacked it with the same enthusiasm as her friend. There was very little conversation while they ate.

After demolishing her meal, Kirsten patted her midsection and leaned back in her seat, studying Mali. Out of the blue, she blurted, "You need a man."

Choking on the last sip of her drink, Mali went into a coughing fit. When she could speak again, she gasped, "Are you kidding me? Where in the world is this coming from? I'm happy in my life and don't need a man. You're nuts!"

"Methinks you protest too much! And I'm not nuts. Jen and I were talking about it this weekend at the Falls. We just want you to be as happy as we are."

"Kirsten, you remember what happened with Daniel. And, hello! My parents? Those are two solid reasons why I love being on my own. Besides, the last thing you should do on a romantic weekend is talk about me. Now, finish your drink, I have to get back to the office."

Kirsten grimaced. "I'm sorry if I made you angry."

"Just tired of the same ol', same ol', my friend." She gave Kirsten a quick hug as they took their leave.

* * *

Monday, March 16, 8:30 a.m.

"Settle down people," Frank Grant, Special Agent in Charge, said as everyone filed into the conference room.

"What's going on, Mali?" Kirsten whispered as she walked up to Mali, who was looking out the window watching the rain fall.

"I have no idea." Mali turned toward the front of the room and observed Frank. Because of his balding head and slight paunch, probably from one too many of the Dos Equis beers he favored, many people underestimated him. Her boss for the past two years, Mali knew him to be a hard-hitter, no-holds-barred kind of agent, fair, and one who stopped at nothing for the truth. She admired Frank. Jovial by nature, today the grim look on his face told a different story.

"We received word that fellow agent, Ken Miller, was killed late last night while working undercover on special assignment in San Francisco. We don't have many details yet on what happened. Special Agent Jacob Black flew out earlier this morning to assist in the investigation and also to bring Ken home. Many of you have worked with Ken on prior cases, including this current one. You may be called upon to assist, so be ready. This is a priority for us. Let's quickly find the bastard who did this!" Frank looked out the window then turned back to the team. "We'll provide specifics on funeral services when we have them. That's all, people, back to work." His eyes roamed the room until they landed on Mali. "Hoop, in my office."

Mali and Kirsten looked at each other before they quietly left the conference room. No one spoke as they shuffled back to their cubicles.

Mali walked into Frank's office and sat down, still in a state of shock. She had met Ken and his wife, Sally, a few times at various functions, spending more than an hour with Sally at the Christmas party last year. Ken was on assignment in San Francisco at the time, sent there last fall after her analysis showed a clear and present danger of an impending terrorist attack, so Sally had attended the party alone. She had wanted to represent the Miller family. Mali's lips turned down as she remembered Ken. She was broken-hearted for Sally and their eleven-year-old son, Jimmy.

"What the hell happened, Frank?"

"We don't know. His last communication was on Wednesday. He was confident that he had gained their trust and was moving forward with our plan. According to his undercover wife, local agent Tina White, Ken was supposed to meet with the leader of the cell two days ago and make the offer for them to join forces with New York and carry out a joint coordinated attack. He didn't return at the appointed time and we never heard from him again. Damn it! I sent him there because of his undercover work with the Hermes terrorist cell here in New York. That, combined with his local knowledge of the City, were ideal in terms of believability." He rubbed his forehead.

"How are Sally and Jimmy?"

"They're both devastated, as you would expect. Ken was a good man and an outstanding agent."

"How did he die?"

"Shot in the head from behind with a Glock 43. A small cut was found above his right ear although it was not a contributing factor in his death. They estimate time of death to be yesterday morning sometime before four. Agent Black will work with local agents to gather more information. We're meeting with them via secure satellite video tomorrow morning at ten to discuss their findings. I want you at the meeting and I want you to work with Jake to find Ken's killer."

"Yes sir."

Back at her office, Mali spent the remainder of the day reviewing her original analysis of the suspected terrorist cell in San Francisco. She pulled up the latest intel but nothing significant had changed. As she read through the information, she felt something wasn't right. The manner in which Ken was killed was not how this cell operated. What kind of message were they trying to send? How did they find out about Ken? And why that method of execution? It didn't make sense.

"Go home, Hoop," Frank sighed, rubbing his neck. "It's almost eight and tomorrow is going to be a long day. I'll walk you down." To argue with him would be pointless, so Mali logged off her computer, grabbed her things, and walked out with him.

Picking up the metro on Franklin Street, it was a short ride to her stop on Christopher Street and a quick walk to her apartment on Perry. Arriving home, Mali took in a deep breath and let it out, decompressing. Her home always had that effect on her. Her one bedroom, one-and-a-half bath apartment was on the ninth floor of a wonderful complex, right on the Hudson River. Every time she stepped inside, she gave thanks to her grand-mother for her trust fund, which had allowed her to purchase it. Her friends often told her that her place was warm and inviting, a peaceful rustic appeal they said. She loved the open concept main room with her cozy and comfortable light brown overstuffed sofa, the oak table and chairs, the cow hide stools, and the multiple earth-tone rugs on the hardwood floors. The large canvas paintings on the walls were by different artists but with a common theme of warm countryside landscapes painted with the most minute detail. Muscles rippled on the horses and dew dripped from roses and wild flowers. No abstract art for her; she wasn't the Picasso type like her mother. Studying the space with a critical eye, she knew that her mother would not like her home at all. While it offered the security and views her mother would approve of and appreciate, her mother would wrinkle her nose in distaste at the small size and non-contemporary style, not to mention the cow hides. Lucky for her that her mother had not deigned to visit her in New York since she moved here two years ago.

Mali changed into yoga pants and a sweatshirt, and pinned up her hair in a loose bun. She made a mug of hot tea and stepped out onto her balcony. Sitting down, she lost herself in the Hudson. The moonlight reflected off the ripples in the wake of a pontoon chugging down the river, the small waves brushing the grass on the side a mere whisper of sound. The Hudson had the power to relax and calm her, and tonight was no exception. It was exactly what Mali needed. Stretching out her legs in front of her, she cupped the mug between her hands as she leaned back in the chair. The peace and serenity lulled her into drowsiness and it was not long before she went inside. Crawling into bed, she was asleep before her head hit the pillow.

CHAPTER TWO

FBI Field Office, New York City
Tuesday, March 17, 9:58 a.m.

". . . AND THE INTEL that was provided to Ken was crap!"

Mali hesitated at the entrance to the Frank's office when that comment registered. She couldn't view the person on the video monitor who made the remark since the monitor was facing away from her. Frank glanced her way and grimaced.

He waved her in and Mali seated herself. She opened her mouth to respond but froze as she looked at the monitor. Staring back at her was the most gorgeous face she had ever seen, despite the scowl. With jet black hair curling over his collar, piercing blue eyes that bored into hers, and a thin jagged scar trailing from his left eyebrow to his ear, Jacob Black was intense.

Introductions on both sides gave Mali time to school herself. "The intel I provided was sound. I reviewed everything I had provided to Ken and checked current information about that cell. Nothing has changed."

"Well, something sure as hell changed. You're the Intel Analyst, Agent Hooper. How reliable were your sources that got him 'in' with this cell in the first place? They're nowhere to be found. Ken's last report indicated that an attack was imminent. Your report mentioned nothing of the sort. What's with the cut behind his ear? And why that method of execution?" Jake rattled off each question, staccato style.

"Slow down, Jake. We all want answers. Mali is one of the best tactical intelligence analysts we have and I've reviewed her intel myself. It's sound. Let's start with what you found out on your end."

Mali simmered as she listened to Jake and the local team detail their findings thus far. Evidently, the plan to infiltrate the cell had worked after months of preparation and effort by Ken and the team. Ken had convinced the leaders that they could go national by initially joining forces with the New York cell and expanding from there. They were to meet to discuss specifics and to plan a coordinated attack in San Francisco and New York, as a kick-off of sorts. According to Ken's last message, the attack was on a large scale involving multiple suicide bombers. Once he had the details of the plan, the team could thwart the attack and capture or kill most, if not all, of the cell.

"Our team is not sure if the meeting took place and Ken was killed at that time or if something happened after the meeting to tip them off. We're searching for our sources and hope to have answers soon, both about Ken's death as well as the attack," added Tom Hanson, the local Special Agent in Charge. "We're also trying to figure out the meaning of the card found on Ken."

That comment jolted Mali back into the conversation. "What card?"

Jake watched her as Tom replied, "A card was placed on Ken's chest. It had a silhouette of San Francisco and a Glock 43. On the back was a number, thirty-six."

"What is the significance of the cut behind his right ear?" Mali asked, on full alert now, recalling Agent Black's earlier question.

"Where are you going with this, Mali?" asked Frank.

"Things are not adding up. In the first place, Glocks are not this cell's weapon of choice, the AK-47 is their preferred weapon, or machetes. Secondly, their kills are well publicized, as is typical with this terrorist group. That would certainly be the case if they had found out that Ken was FBI. Remember what happened to Blair White of the U.K.? And lastly, they don't leave calling cards. Elements of this are ringing a bell with me that I need to check. Mind if I bring Kirsten Bellows in to help, Frank?" Mali glanced at Jake and found him studying her. She blinked, a little startled, then turned to Frank.

Frank shook his head. "It looks like we have a few things on our end to check. Mali and Jake, exchange your contact information and plan to talk tomorrow morning. Follow all leads, no matter how small, and keep me posted on your findings. We need to work quickly; it sounds like time is running out for us on this attack and we can't assume that they'll delay their plans if New York is out of the picture. They may move forward with just San Francisco. When are you bringing Ken home, Jake?"

"We're on a flight in a few hours. I spoke with Sally and his Rosary is Friday evening with the funeral on Saturday morning. Although it's open to all, Sally prefers that only family and close friends attend the Rosary. I'll send you the information. The funeral is at ten in the morning at the Parish of Most Holy Trinity in Williamsburg, Brooklyn, with burial following in their cemetery."

"Thanks Jake. Carol and I will attend both. The Parish is a beautiful church and the grounds are peaceful. A good resting place for Ken. He was a good friend of yours, Jake. I'm grateful you're there to bring him home."

"So am I, Frank."

Mali returned to her cubicle, left a quick message for Kirsten to call, then went over everything she had learned, especially the cut behind his ear and the calling card. Why cut him after he'd been shot? Or was it before he was shot? Why cut him at all? What does that calling card mean? Was it something new for the cell? What was the significance of the number on the back of the card? Feeling that there was an important point on the edge of her memory, Mali turned to the computer and the internet.

She spent the rest of the day searching San Francisco public records for murders with an M.O. of using a Glock 43 as the weapon or cutting the victim behind the ear. She also expanded her search to members of the terrorist cell, maybe they had used this M.O. before they joined the cell. Nothing popped in public records or with members of the cell about a Glock 43 that sounded remotely familiar to this M.O. and no cuts behind the ear except for a prostitute, but she was cut from ear to ear. Not the same thing.

Frustrated, Mali stood and stretched, rolling her neck from side to side to work out the kinks. Not hearing anything, her eyes roamed the office. She was alone and it was dark outside. It was ten minutes after seven. *Where did the time go?* Her stomach growled. Time to go home.

Later that evening, Mali walked out to her balcony. It was a chilly, clear night. She leaned on the rail and stared at the Hudson, looking for answers in its murky waters and thinking of Ken's wife and son. She, like everyone else on the force, recognized the risks of the job. Some jobs required more risk than others, of course, and families knew this as well. Knowing that didn't make it easier for them, though.

Mali stepped back into her apartment and into her bedroom. The walls were painted a pale rose and her bed was covered with a white quilt, small red roses embroidered along the hem. She sat down on her bed and leaned back against the pillowed headboard. It was the only 'girly' area in the apartment and it would probably be the only room her mother liked. Her eyes crinkled at the corners at that thought.

Mali reached for her laptop and logged in to the secure server expanding her web search for the killer's

M.O. to all of the states, starting with New York. There was a recent murder in the city that was vaguely similar to Ken's. Nothing from the *New York Times*. She moved on to public records. No one with a cut behind the ear. Multiple deaths with a Glock.

Nothing. At one a.m., she logged off and closed her laptop, setting the alarm for five thirty in the morning. She turned off the light, scrunched down under the covers, and rolled onto her side. Sleep did not come easily.

* * *

Friday, March 20, 7:00 a.m.

IT WAS A brisk clear morning as Mali walked into the Federal building. Dressed smartly in the standard FBI 'uniform,' a dark suit with a white blouse and black pumps, Mali walked into the conference room assigned for the case that she and Jake, and anyone else they needed, would be using. Her computer and two monitors were already set up on one side of the rectangular table with a telephone, as requested, and there were two other telephones sitting on the table. A white board was hanging on the far wall and a forty-six-inch plasma television was positioned above it.

Mali left a message for Kirsten to join her when she arrived and turned the television on to her favorite news station, KABC News. Flipping on her computer to continue her research, Mali began on the KABC website systematically reading through news articles working from today's news backward in time.

Suddenly there it was, a picture of Margie Thornburg, forty-eight years of age, murdered in Central Park on March 5th. She had the cut behind the ear but was killed by a puncture wound not a Glock. Could this possibly be related to Ken's murder? A housewife and an FBI agent? New York and San Francisco? The only similarity was the cut.

Mali called the Office of the Chief Medical Examiner in New York and requested information on Margie Thornburg's murder. The Chief Medical Examiner agreed to meet with her at ten. Next, she contacted the Central Park Police Precinct and requested a meeting at eleven with the detectives in charge of Margie's murder investigation. She made a note to contact the Chief Medical Examiner in San Francisco after lunch to request Ken's autopsy and any information related to his death.

"So, you are supposedly the best tactical intelligence analyst in the New York office."

Mali jumped, startled, and looked up from her computer. Jake Black leaned against the doorway, studying her. His intensity through a monitor was nothing compared to experiencing him in person. By his stance, he looked relaxed; he was anything but. Dressed in a black suit with a white shirt and black tie, he exuded strength and looked like a panther ready to strike. Jake Black was all male.

"So Frank says." She stood and walked over to him, extending her hand.

Taking a few steps into the room, Jake stopped and waited for her to reach him.

Standing in front of him now, Mali held his gaze, her eyebrow arching as she challenged him to continue his rudeness by not shaking her hand.

He looked from her hand up to her face, a small smile playing on his mouth. Just when she was about to drop her hand, he shook it.

Mali blinked when his hand touched hers, jolted but trying not to show it. She pulled her hand away, turned, and walked back to her computer.

"There was a murder here in New York two weeks ago, same cut behind the ear."

"Shot with a Glock, card left on the chest?"

"Not shot with a Glock. I'm not sure about the card. In fact, the cut behind her ear is the only common tie between this murder and Ken's at this point. But I'm meeting with the M.E. as well as the detectives in charge of that murder for more information to see if there's a connection. I am also checking San Francisco for similar M.O.s."

"You're blowing smoke, Hooper. You believe that the terrorist cell had nothing to do with Ken's death because the M.O. is not their standard method, but terrorists change their M.O.s to suit their needs. Believe me, I know. So do us both a favor and take your little arse back to Philadelphia, get married, and have a dozen kids as I'm sure your parents want. We need real experts working on this case."

Mali gasped. That statement was more accurate

than he realized. Narrowing her eyes, she glared at Jake. "Don't think that reading my bio makes you an expert on me. You don't know the first thing about me." Mali took a calming breath. "I am going to write your rudeness off to the loss of your good friend, and—"

"Excuse me, Mali?" Kirsten interrupted, walking into the room and looking from Mali to Jake.

Glancing at Kirsten, Mali smiled stiffly. "Kirsten Bellows, Jacob Black. Jake, Kirsten." Kirsten shook Jake's hand while Mali sat down at her computer. "Kirsten, Frank gave you approval to help on the case. I could use your eyes and expertise."

"I'm sorry for your loss, Jake," said Kirsten. He nodded and Kirsten stepped past him and sat down next to Mali. "Absolutely. I'm sorry I didn't call yesterday. I was on a tight deadline."

"Not a problem. I know you're in high demand."

"Okay. Bring me up to speed." They went over her findings to date. Mali was keenly aware of Jake setting up his laptop across the table from her as she spoke with Kirsten.

"So take over the search for similar M.O.s in New York and San Francisco and contact the Chief Medical Examiner in San Francisco," Mali instructed.

"Will do."

"I'm headed out to meet the M.E. and the detectives regarding Margie Thornburg's murder. Not sure when I'll be back given where they're located. I have my cell in case you need to reach me." She looked at Jake. "You're welcome to join me."

"I'm waiting to get some information from our San Francisco office so I might as well go with you. I'll get the keys to the company car and meet you at the elevator." He walked out of the room.

Kirsten opened her mouth but before uttering a word, Mali rolled her eyes. "Don't ask. I'll fill you in this weekend when we get together. You, Sara, Jen, and I are still going out for brunch on Sunday, right?"

"There's no way we're skipping our get-together. I'm positively bursting with questions about Mr. Gorgeous."

Mali laughed and shook her head as she headed out of the conference room.

"Thank you for meeting us, Mr. Weathers." Mali said as they sat down in the Chief Medical Examiner's office.

"Agent Hooper, Agent Black." He reached for a file. "I pulled up what information we have on the Thornburg murder. Results have not yet been released but she was killed with a crossbow, the bolt piercing her heart. There were a few abrasions on her arms and back as well as a cut on the back of the head, all consistent with being slammed to the ground by the force of the bolt."

"What about the cut behind her ear?" Jake asked.

"A small incision, and I use that word specifically because the cut was made with medical precision. There were minute traces of cyanide in the cut."

"Cyanide? From what?" Jake asked, surprised.

"Something was removed. That's all the information I have. We should finish the autopsy today or Monday and we will release the results and the body to the family after that. If I have more information for you, I'll call."

"One more question," Mali said. "Can you search your database for any other murders with the same characteristics as this one?"

Mr. Weathers studied Mali as if assessing her, opening his mouth to ask a question. He snapped his mouth closed and nodded. "I'll have my assistant look it up and send any information to you. Shall we go one year back?"

"Make it five years. Thanks."

"Thank you for your time, Mr. Weathers." Jake said. They stood and shook hands.

Jake and Mali were both quiet as they drove uptown to the Central Park Precinct. A siren wailed as it drove by them on the opposite side of the street and a delivery truck beeped as it backed up in a side alley they passed. Masses of people strode down the sidewalks, some in the latest fashion styles and others in jeans. Many were either talking or texting on their cell phones, oblivious to everyone and everything, occasionally bumping into other people or inanimate objects like trash cans.

All was lost on Mali as she considered everything they had learned. Cyanide. A crossbow. A medical incision behind the ear. Some sort of implant. Nothing was making sense. One thing for sure, though, they needed Ken's autopsy report as soon as possible.

"We need Ken's autopsy report," Jake stated.

"I was thinking the same thing. Kirsten is working on that as we speak."

They marched into the waiting area of a bustling precinct and Jake asked for detectives Smith and Stark. The room was separated by a wooden counter that ran the length of the room, separating the inner workings of the station from the waiting area. The room was a cacophony of noise. People shifted about while waiting, doors buzzed, dispatchers were speaking into headsets, keyboards clicked, officers chatted, someone slurped water from the drinking fountain.

After waiting a few minutes, two men ambled through a secure door toward them.

"I'm Agent Jacob Black and this is Agent Mali Hooper," said Jake, showing his credentials then shaking hands with both detectives.

"Nice to meet you both. This is detective Stark and I'm detective Smith."

The detectives guided Mali and Jake to the back offices and asked them to take a seat in front of Smith's desk. Smith also sat, placed his arms on his desk, and looked at them with kind, if tired, brown eyes. Detective Stark, a burly man in his mid-thirties, stood behind Detective Smith, his square chin jutting out, arms crossed, a scowl on his face.

"How can we help the FBI today?" Stark snarled.

Smith, an older man in his late fifties, looked at his partner then back at Mali and Jake. "Don't mind my partner. Stark got up on the wrong side of the bed today." He paused. "You had asked about the Thornburg murder. It's an on-going investigation."

"Yes, we are aware of that. What can you tell us about the crime scene and Mrs. Thornburg?" Mali asked.

Pulling out his black notebook and flipping through a couple of pages, Detective Smith said, "The vic was lying on her back on a concrete walking path, arms spread. No weapon but there was a hole in her chest and a cut behind her right ear. She was wearing an oversized, dirty sweatshirt, sweatpants, and tennis shoes that appeared to be too small, if the abrasions on her ankles were any indication." He opened a folder and slid a picture across his desk.

"That doesn't sound or look like the kind of clothing Margie Thornburg would wear," Mali stated as she leaned closer to Jake, who was holding the picture, to study the victim. All men looked at her, eyebrows raised. "She's from a middle-class family, by all reports living an ideal family life. Why would she wear shoes that are too small for her? Why would she be dressed in so little when there was snow that night?"

"Is there anything else you can tell us," Jake asked, ignoring Mali's comments and looking back at the detectives.

"Yes. We found a card on her chest. It has the New York City skyline on the front with a crossbow. The number sixteen is written on the back."

CHAPTER THREE

"WHAT THE HELL is going on?" Mali asked as they walked out of the precinct.

Jake's cell phone rang. It was a call from San Francisco. As Jake paused to talk, Mali walked down the steps to the food truck sitting at the curb and grabbed a cup of coffee, distracted with thoughts about the bombshell the detectives unwittingly dropped on them. Calling cards on both of them? The specifics of the cards were different but they were too similar to ignore. The murders had to be related. There was no question about that in her mind. But how? And what did it mean?

"Another operative in the cell, at a much lower level than Ken was, confirmed that the cell is in a state of disarray right now. Apparently, the leaders are trying to figure out why Ken didn't show, why he's not returning calls, and how it affects their timeline. Our second man is trying to position himself in such a way that the leaders begin to trust him," said Jake, walking up to Mali. He ordered a coffee before they walked to the car.

"So it doesn't sound like the cell is responsible for Ken's murder."

"I'm not willing to concede that yet. The leaders of the cell could be proceeding cautiously and being careful what they say around those not in their inner circle. Our operative is working his way up but is not yet fully trusted. He has no idea if the San Francisco attack will be delayed."

They got in the car and Jake started the ignition, hesitating before turning toward Mali. "I am willing to admit that there might be a connection between Ken and the Thornburg murder. We need to delve into her past to determine if she was all she appeared to be. Did she have any connection to that terrorist cell? We need to find out."

"I agree. We also need to determine if they knew each other here." Sipping her coffee to steady herself, Mali's mind whirled with all of the latest information.

Jake nodded as he pulled into traffic.

Forty-five minutes later, they arrived back at the office and made their way to the conference room. Kirsten joined them. Her hand grasped a manila file folder.

"What did you find out?" she asked.

"The CMA indicated cause of death to be a crossbow bolt to the heart. The cut behind her ear was surgical and contained traces of cyanide."

"Cyanide? Hmmmm." interrupted Kirsten.

"Yes." Jake continued. "And something was removed, although he could not say what. The most intriguing news from the detectives was that a calling card was found on the body, with the New York skyline and crossbow on the front and the number sixteen written on the back."

"Similar to the card found on Ken," interjected Mali. "I am a visual person and want to write some of this down." She walked over to the white board.

On the left side of the board at the top, she wrote 'NYC,' the date of Margie Thornburg's death and her name. Mali also taped a copy of her picture and the calling card, that the detectives gave them, beside her name. Below that, she wrote 'crossbow, trace of cyanide, 16'.

"What have you discovered about Ken's death?" Jake asked, sitting down in front of his laptop and turning to face Kirsten who had joined Mali at the white board.

"Ken was shot point blank with a Glock 43 and a calling card was left on his chest." She opened the folder that was still in her hand and handed pictures of Ken and the calling card to Mali. To the right of Margie Thornburg's information, Mali wrote 'SF' with the date of Ken's death and his name next to it. She taped his picture and the calling card next to his name, and below that, wrote 'Glock 43,'.

She turned to Kirsten who, reading from the file, said "According to the coroner's preliminary report, the cut behind his ear was a medical incision and minute traces of cyanide were found inside." No one said a word as Mali added 'trace of cyanide, 36' next to 'Glock 43,'.

Jake stood and walked over to Mali. Taking the pen from her hand, he drew a straight dotted line between the Thornburg death and Ken's information, and wrote 'tied to SF cell?' above the dotted line. Standing back, they all looked at the board.

"Kirsten, run a background check on Margie Thornburg." Jake said. "I want to know everything about her—her parents, who her friends were in school, who they are today, what her husband does, how she spends her day—everything. This takes precedence over the other research."

"I have a couple of hot issues downstairs that I need to take care of but I'll jump on it as soon as I return."

Nodding, he glanced at Mali. "I'll be out the rest of the day. I need to be with Sally and Jimmy." He walked out the door without waiting for a response.

Mali grumbled as she walked to her computer to continue the research.

"What was that?" Kirsten asked, laughter in her voice.

"Never mind. Tell me where you left off in your M.O. research and I'll continue with it while you take care of your business. I'll let you handle the research on Margie Thornburg."

Promising to meet at Mali's apartment on Sunday morning at nine thirty, Kirsten left.

Mali spent the rest of the day on the computer.

Frank stopped by on his way out, just after six, for an update.

"Thanks, Mali." Frank said, studying the white board. "The possible connection is concerning. Keep me posted."

"Yes sir."

"And don't stay too late."

* * *

Parish of Most Holy Trinity in Williamsburg, Brooklyn
Saturday, March 21, 9:50 a.m.

IT WAS A crisp, cool morning when Mali arrived at the church for the funeral. Standing outside, she tipped her head back to admire it. Completed in eighteen eighty-five, it was modeled after the French Gothic of the thirteenth century style that was popular in the United States, and it was one of the largest churches in Brooklyn and New York City, at that time. The church boasted majestic twin spires reaching twenty stories into the sky, a dominating feature seen for miles back then. While still impressive, the church was now sandwiched between brick buildings and had lost some of its glory. What made Mali gasp in awe, however, when she walked inside the main doors, were the exquisite stained-glass windows. They lined the upper tier of the church on both sides all the way to the back as if to draw the eye to the stunning altar. The sun sparkled through the windows creating a colorful masterpiece inside.

A growing sea of black filled the pews as friends and family filed in. Many were praying or speaking to each other in hushed tones. Sally stood next to the closed coffin near the altar, hand gently resting on the casket, head bowed in prayer. Jacob Black stood next to her in silent support.

As Mali walked down the main aisle toward the altar, she saw Frank and his wife, Carol, a few rows from the front. She was headed toward them when Sally turned around to return to the front pew where her son was sitting.

When Sally recognized Mali, she stopped, her demeanor changing, becoming rigid. She turned her head to Jake and whispered something. He frowned and his eyes darted to Mali, before turning his attention back to Sally to respond to her. Without giving him a second glance, she pushed past him and barreled up the aisle, hands clenching and unclenching at her sides. She stopped only when she was nose to nose with Mali.

Startled, Mali retreated two steps, her head flinching back slightly.

"What are you doing here?" she barked out, lips curled back in a snarl.

The hushed conversations in the pews near them ceased as people looked their way and strained to understand what was being said.

"I-I-I came to pay my respects to Ken, Sally."

"Get out."

Mali paled and her breath caught in her throat. Her mind struggled to comprehend what was happening. "Sally, I'm so—"

"I don't want your sympathy. I don't want your prayers. I don't want anything from you. My husband died because of you and your bad intel."

Mali gasped in shock and dismay, looking at Jake, who had quietly approached, in disbelief.

"Get her out of here, Jake. She's not welcome." Without waiting for a response, Sally turned and walked up the aisle. She sat down next to her son and gazed at the large picture of her husband.

Stiffening her spine and curling her hands around her middle, Mali cleared her throat. "No need to escort me out, Jake. I'll leave. Tell Sally I'm sorry for her loss."

Not waiting for a response and head held high, Mali turned and walked out of the church. She didn't let herself react, she didn't get upset, she didn't analyze what had just happened. Her only focus was to get home.

It wasn't until Mali walked into her apartment and sat down on her sofa that the tears flowed.

* * *

Mali's apartment
Sunday, March 22, 9:25 a.m.

"HEY THERE, GIRL. How are you?" Jen asked as she and Kirsten walked into Mali's apartment and gave her a hug.

"I'm okay. How are you?"

"We're great but you sound tired."

"I didn't get much sleep last night," was Mali's only reply.

Kirsten and Jen looked at each other before they draped their coats on one of Mali's dining room chairs. The three walked into Mali's living room. Jen sat on the sofa and Kirsten sat Indian style on the floor next to Jen, leaning her back against the sofa.

"Jen, Kirsten told me you're working on a huge event coming up this fall."

"An incredible opportunity landed in my lap, thanks to your phone call. The event is a charity fundraiser for the city's police department. The foundation is dedicated to assisting the families of slain officers. They hold an event every year but this is the twenty-fifth anniversary so they want to go big. We're having a sit-down dinner, at a mere twenty-five hundred per plate, and live entertainment. I'm trying to book a big name but no luck so far. Our goal is to sell five hundred tickets."

"Wow! I'm impressed." Mali had always admired Jennifer for her bubbly personality. Jen had found her niche in event planning and it suited her disposition and skills perfectly.

"Thanks. Dan Everly and Kyle Owens have already booked a table. They've invited two families of slain officers to join them. They are so hot on New York radio right now. They've even discussed the event on their show. They're trendsetters, and I know we'll see more celebrities buy tables and invite families of fallen officers. I'm so thrilled," Jen enthused.

The doorbell rang. "You've earned this, Jen," said Mali over her shoulder as she walked to the door. "Hi Sara, you look fabulous."

"Thanks Mali. You're so sweet." Sara hugged her and bounced over to her other friends, greeting them with hugs.

Mali followed Sara with her eyes and smiled, trailing after her into the living room. Sara was her oldest best friend. They'd known each other since they met at summer camp when they were ten years old. Sara was the only gal in their circle who was married, and happily so. She was also the most centered of them all. She had a loving husband who adored her and their three kids, two boys and a girl. Mali was the godmother of all three, for which she counted her blessings every day. Her BFF was self-conscious about her weight and said her frizzy red hair made her look like a female version of Richard Simmons but Mali thought Sara was beautiful. Yes, her hair was frizzy but only because Sara was too busy to work on it. She had the most incredible green eyes Mali had ever seen and her kind heart, positive outlook on life, and down-to-earth views had meant the world to Mali over the years.

"Now tell me how my adorable godchildren are doing," Mali said.

After the four friends caught up on each others' lives, they headed down to the street where a car was waiting for them.

"Mali, where are we going today?" asked Kirsten.

"I made a reservation at Agave's. I love that place."

"So do I," piped Sara.

"I love their margaritas," Jen said.

The chatter was non-stop and light-hearted as the car made its way to Seventh Avenue.

Once they were seated inside and had ordered drinks,

Kirsten said, "So, ladies, has Mali told you about the gorgeous agent she's working with on a new case?"

Mali frowned then rolled her eyes. Sara looked at Mali with wide eyes and her mouth formed a perfect 'O'.

Jen squealed in delight. "Fess up, Mali. We want all the details!"

Before Mali could answer, Kirsten added, "Sparks positively fly whenever they're in the same room."

"Oooooooh," Sara cooed. "Details, now." She parked her elbow on the table and placed her chin in her palm, focusing all her attention on Mali. Jen did the same.

Resigning herself to talking about Jacob Black, Mali opened her mouth to answer when the waitress returned with their drinks. "Saved by the mimosa," she muttered to herself. After the waitress took their order and left, three pairs of eyes returned to Mali.

Eyebrow raised, Mali shrugged and then sighed. "You guys are relentless. There's not much to say, actually. There are no sparks, as Kirsten insists. What she sees are daggers being thrown from my eyes. He is annoying,"

"And gorgeous," Kirsten added with a smile.

Mali made a face at Kirsten and continued, "arrogant, opinionated—"

"Did I say gorgeous?" Kirsten said, with a laugh.

"Stop, Kirsten!" said Mali, smiling in spite of herself.

"Is that a blush, Mali?" Jen teased.

"Okay you two, enough ganging up on our Mali,"

Sara, the pacifier of the group, said. She turned to Mali. "Will you be able to work with him?"

"I have to. And, yes, Kirsten, I will admit that he's attractive, well . . . gorgeous. But after yesterday, I want nothing to do with him other than work. My focus is the case we're working on. Do you remember hearing about the murder of a woman in Central Park? It was on the news a couple of weeks ago." Her friends nodded. "Our case may tie to that murder. That's all I can say about it."

"Such a tragic death," Sara said, shaking her head. "She had two young children, if I recall."

"So, given what you just said, something must have happened at the funeral yesterday." Kirsten said, changing the subject as she watched Mali closely. Kirsten turned to Jen and Sara. "An agent was killed last week. His funeral was in Brooklyn."

"I provided the analysis on a case he was involved in," Mali said. "The church was lovely. Other than that, there's nothing I can say. I was kicked out."

"What!?!" The three exclaimed simultaneously.

"Yep. I was walking up the aisle and when Sally saw me, she marched over and told me to leave. Said I wasn't welcome. Also told me that I was the one to blame for Ken's death because of bad intel I provided."

"You're kidding. Where would she even get an idea like that?" asked Sara.

"Jacob Black, that's who." Mali responded, lips thinning in distaste. "He said as much during that first video conference call we had when he was in San Francisco picking up Ken's body. I told him my intel was sound, so did Frank. He obviously didn't believe either of us."

"He wouldn't tell Sally that, would he? I'm shocked," said Kirsten.

"Yes, well," Mali paused and gave herself a mental shake. "Enough about him. We're here to have a good time."

The restaurant was bustling, as usual, Mali noted as she perused the patrons, not noticing the concern on her friends' faces. She was glad that they were inside today. The weather was clear but crisp and cold. A few brave souls were dining at Agave's outdoor tables, coats buttoned and collars up. Some wore hats and scarves as well. *Better them than us.* Mali took another bite of her savory grilled asparagus.

"The absolute best Mexican restaurant ever!" Kirsten exclaimed, leaning back in her chair with a sigh of satisfaction and patting her stomach. There was quick acquiescence by the rest as they finished their meals and raised a glass to their friendship before paying their bills and leaving with the promise of getting together again soon.

When Mali arrived home, she hung up her jacket and pulled her phone out of her purse, noticing that her mother had called. Willow Hooper was a force to be reckoned with and not one to be ignored. Her mother was every inch the socialite, always concerned about their standing in Philadelphia 'society,' and never ever went out in public without her war paint on, as she called it, and dressed to the nines. She was probably calling about her parents' fortieth wedding anniversary in early April. No doubt her mother was throwing a massive party with three hundred of their 'closest' friends and it was sure to be the event of the year. They had to keep up appearances, after all, a reality that put Mali into a melancholy mood. Her parents' arranged marriage was a sham, had been for years. Mali doubted there was ever any love between them. If so, it was long gone. The marriages of her two older sisters, Rose and Lilly, had also been arranged and it was pretty obvious that her sisters were not content in their lives either. Her dysfunctional family was the mold from which all others were created.

Grabbing her jacket, Mali went on the balcony to enjoy the brisk spring afternoon. The sun was shining down on the Hudson and it sparkled like stars. Feeling calmer, Mali called her mother.

CHAPTER FOUR

FBI Field Office, New York City
Monday, March 23, 9:15 a.m.

"Hey. I'm sorry I didn't make it back here sooner but things in the cave came to a head and I had to deal with the issues. Jen and I sure enjoyed our brunch yesterday," Kirsten said as she walked into the conference room. The IT team affectionately called their computer control center the cave. The room had no windows, was always dark, and the temperature never reached above sixty-five degrees.

Glancing up from her computer, Mali smiled at her friend. "Same here, and there's no need to apologize. You're in high demand. I just received the additional information from the Chief Medical Examiner and will go through it."

"Great. I'll take the Thornburg background check."

They worked silently, each focused on their tasks. Both jumped when Frank and Jake walked into the conference room a short time later.

Frank cleared his throat. "Jake and I just finished a conference call with the San Francisco office."

"That's an early call for them," Mali replied. She ignored Jake as she focused on Frank.

"They updated us on the terrorist cell but they were unable to provide more information related to Ken's murder."

"So Ken's murder was not tied to the cell?" Mali asked.

Jake looked at her, his face a mask hiding any emotion. "We'll continue to pursue both theories until one or the other is disproven, or another one materializes." He sat down in front of his laptop as Frank left.

What an arrogant . . . Mali took a deep breath and turned back to the report.

Starting from the oldest year and working toward the present, Mali found nothing in the first three years. Most of the murders were similar in the weapon used, plenty of Glock deaths and even one with a crossbow. But none with a cut behind the ear. She had finished the third year and was starting on the fourth, when something caught her eye. Looking closer, Mali read about a murder by cyanide poisoning. Studying the rest of the report, a chill went down her spine.

"Listen to this," she said and read out loud. "Victim had high dose of methamphetamine in his bloodstream, not significant enough to cause death. A cut was found behind the right ear, approximately one inch long and made with medical precision. Heavy dose of cyanide found around and inside the cut. No other injury found on the body. Cause of death: cyanide poisoning."

Jake looked up from his computer and focused on Mali as she read from the report. "Who was the victim and where was he killed?"

"John Doe, homeless, approximate age twenty-four. We'll need to contact the police for the rest of the information. There's more. Eight months later, this past November, there was another murder, Glenn Marker, age forty-nine, killed point-blank by a gun. The report doesn't indicate what type. The victim had a small cut behind the right ear, same as the others, a medically precise incision with a trace of cyanide."

Kirsten, Jake, and Mali looked at each other.

"Excuse my French," Kirsten said, "but shit."

Mali walked over to the white board, moved the Thornburg information lower in order to add the new information, and wrote 'NYC Mar2014 John Doe' and beneath it 'cyanide' and 'NYC Nov2014 Glenn Marker' with 'gun, trace of cyanide' below it.

The three of them studied the board then Jake walked over and erased the dashed lines representing the theory of the murders being tied to the terrorist cell. He looked from Mali to Kirsten. "There's no need to continue with the background check on Margie Thornburg, Kirsten. We need the police reports related to these two deaths."

"I'm on it."

A serial killer in New York City? Copycat killer in San Francisco? How could that be when there had been no media coverage? Perhaps the media had not connected any dots yet. Multiple killers working together? To what end? Were the victims connected in some way? By all appearances, that wasn't the case. What was going on? So many questions, too few answers.

Jake left to update Frank as Mali sat down to continue her research.

Twenty minutes later, her phone rang.

"Hoop, I need to see you in my office," Frank said.

* * *

MALI WALKED INTO Frank's office and looked at him in surprise. Frank was sitting behind his desk, nostrils flared and a vein pulsing in his neck. His lips were thinned, his body rigid. Mali glanced at Jake, who looked equally the same, and would not look at her as she sat down in the chair next to him.

"What's going on, Frank?"

"Jake just updated me on the two cases and the fact that Ken's death is clearly not related to the terrorist cell."

"Yes, beyond that, we're in the dark."

"He believes that since you were brought in to help find Ken's killer because of your intel on the terrorist cell, and since that cell is no longer the reason for Ken's death, you are no longer needed on this case."

"What!?! That's ridiculous. I was the one who found the connection between Ken's murder and the Thornburg and other New York murders." Her heartbeat pounded through her veins and the heat rose to her face as she sat forward in her chair. "And, by the way, my intel on Ken's case was not bad and I was not responsible for his death." She glared at Jake, who grimaced and cleared his throat.

"We know you weren't responsible for his death, Hoop, and I don't agree that you should be removed. I just informed Jake that you're still on this case." Frank said, holding up a conciliatory hand.

Jake spoke for the first time since Mali entered the room. "This case is much more involved than just providing simple analysis. I need a seasoned field agent to work with me."

"I've proven in just the past few days that I can go out in the field and get answers that we need." Her eyes narrowed as she continued to scowl at Jake. "If you have a problem with me, Jake, then it has nothing to do with my abilities. Maybe YOU should be reassigned."

"Enough!" Frank roared. "Hoop, I brought you in here for full disclosure, not to question your ability. I know you can handle the job. Jake, the two of you will work together on this case. Period. Both of you have the skills needed to figure out what's going on and put an end to the murders. Find a way to work together." He calmed himself with a deep breath. "Understood?"

Both nodded.

"Good. One more thing, on another subject, I expect both of you at my house for dinner this Friday, six o'clock. Now, out of my office and back to work."

Jake's phone rang as they walked out of Frank's office. Glancing at the screen, he excused himself and headed away as Mali returned to the conference room. Kirsten was on the phone when Mali strode into the room and sat down in front of her laptop, seething.

"What happened?" Kirsten asked as her call ended.

Mali held up her hand, shaking her head. "Later."

The room was quiet as both continued their work.

An hour passed before Jake walked back into the room.

"Kirsten, can you give Jake and I a few minutes alone, please?" Mali asked as she stood up to face Jake.

Kirsten raised her eyes, took one look at them, and logged out of her computer. "I'll be back in a few minutes," she said as she walked out the door, closing it behind her.

"What the hell was that all about?" Mali asked as soon as Kirsten closed the door.

Jake was standing in front of his laptop across the table from Mali.

Staring at him, jaw tight and hands fisted at her sides, she continued, "And how could you tell Sally that I provided bad intel? Not only was that not true but you had no right."

Jake sighed and rubbed the back of his neck. "I didn't. She must have overheard me when I was venting to Frank on the phone. Your intel was sound and I told her as much after the funeral and burial when she was less distraught."

Mali continued to stare at him, waiting.

He paused and hung his head, eyes closed, before taking a deep breath and looking up at Mali. "I apologize for my behavior and for what happened at the funeral. I guess I've been looking for someone to blame and you were conveniently there."

The air left Mali's lungs in a whoosh as the anger drained out of her. "I appreciate your apology, Jake, but don't ever do anything like that to me again."

He nodded and they stared at each other for an eternity, one pair of eyes filled with disappointment and hurt, the other with regret.

Kirsten knocked and opened the door. "Coast clear?" At Jake's nod, she walked in as Mali sat down.

"I'm going to look for connections between the four victims. I don't expect to find any but I want to verify it," said Jake, picking up his phone to make some calls.

Mali decided to execute a search on the first victim, Margie Thornburg. Perhaps she was a fan of social media and had posted things on Facebook, YouTube, or other sources that could shed some light.

Lunch was brought in and the trio spent the rest of the day on research. Kirsten obtained the police reports of the two victims and they learned that John Doe was found in Battery Park and Glenn Parker was killed with a Colt 45 in the Upper East Side. No card was found on or near either victim. The white board was updated.

After finding no connection between the four victims, Jake left early to take care of personal business.

"What is going on between you and Jake?" asked Kirsten. "I could tell you were furious when you returned from Frank's office, and you could cut the tension with a knife when he walked back into the room."

Sighing, Mali looked over at Kirsten. "He wanted

me off the case, said he needed a seasoned field agent to work with."

"You're kidding!"

"Frank put the ka-bosh on that idea and said he expected the two of us to work together. Jake later apologized for his behavior. End of story."

In the ensuing silence, Mali caught Kirsten staring at her. "What?"

"Why is this case so important to you?"

"My professional abilities as an analyst have been questioned repeatedly over the last few days and I was accused of causing a fellow agent's death. This is personal. I thought my days of having to prove myself were over. Apparently, I was wrong."

"Anything I can do?"

Mali smiled. "You just did by letting me vent. Thank you."

Kirsten patted her shoulder and they both turned back to their work.

By the end of the day, Kirsten had not discovered any other murders with the same M.O. in eight states, she just had forty-two to go, and Mali had not found anything of value on Thornburg's Facebook page or that of her friends.

Later that evening at home, Mali was back on the computer. Taking a break from researching Margie Thornburg, she began searching for murders similar to Ken's in San Francisco instead. Hours passed with nothing of value. A headache was beginning in the back of her head working its way forward and her eyes were gritty as if sand were rubbing inside. Glancing at the clock, she groaned. Eleven-twenty. Standing up from the comfort of her bed and rolling her shoulders, Mali walked into the restroom, took two Advil, and placed a drop of Visine in each eye. She walked into the kitchen for a glass of water before settling herself back on the bed. Placing her glass next to the clock, she promised herself that she would only look for another fifteen to twenty minutes before hitting the sack.

Circling back to Margie Thornburg, Mali switched to YouTube and searched for videos of 'Margie.' There were many just none of Margie Thornburg. Likewise, she searched 'Thornburg' and found a few videos but, again, none of Margie Thornburg. Mali changed her search to 'Margie Thornburg murder in New York City.' Nothing. Sighing in frustration, she made the search more generic to 'murders in New York City.' The list was long. She scrolled down the list and perused the first twelve videos with titles like 'Streets of New York Documentary' and 'Bronx Surveillance Murder.' Scrolling to the thirteenth video, Mali froze.

Titled '#HuntedLives, Central Park,' Mali viewed a still shot of what looked like a person lying on a walkway in the video frame. With a sense of foreboding, she pressed the play icon and watched. Margie Thornburg's last seconds alive were played out on YouTube in living color. The vantage point must have been from the killer. Given how close to the ground the camera was positioned, he must have been crouched or lying down and was probably wearing a Go-Pro type camera on his forehead. No words were spoken on the video. The only sound was the steady and slow breathing of the killer. Mali watched as the victim peered around the corner of the Delacorte Theatre restroom and scanned the area before climbing over a rail, creeping through some bushes, and stepping over a second rail onto the trail. The crossbow bolt made a hissing sound as it left the bow. It slammed into the victim with brutal force. She didn't stand a chance. The killer stood and walked over to her, the crunch of snow with each step the only sound. The video ended with the killer looking at Margie Thornburg. The crossbow bolt was sticking out of her chest, her eyes were wide open, and blood trickled out of her mouth and dripped onto the ground. The look on her face was one of shock. The video lasted for two minutes and thirty-nine seconds.

CHAPTER FIVE

Tuesday, March 24, 2:40 a.m.

"Jacob Black, this damn well better be good," a tired and irritated voice said on the other end of her phone.

"Jake, this is Mali." She looked at the clock. Two forty in the morning. Crap. "I'm sorry it's so late but I found something. I'm headed to the office now."

"It can't wait until the sun comes up?"

"No."

"What did you find, Mali?"

"I found a video on YouTube of Margie Thornburg's murder."

Forty-five minutes later, Mali walked from the Chambers Street subway station to the office. Her hair was in a high ponytail and muffs covered her ears. The icy rain hit her face, and her hands and feet were cold and wet. She was numb inside. She walked into the FBI building and took the elevator up to her office after going through security. Despite the early hour, there was quite a bit of activity this frigid morning.

She removed her coat and sneakers and stepped into navy pumps that were pulled from her bag. She walked over to her computer and turned it on as Jake walked in. He hung his coat on the back of a chair and circled the table to Mali, looking like a panther on the prowl.

"Show me." They watched the video without saying a word. "Christ." Jake rubbed the back of his neck.

"That's not all. Look at the information below the video. There are more than two hundred and twenty THOUSAND views and counting. And check out some of these comments. 'Cool,' 'Great shot,' 'It looks so real.' What is wrong with these people?" Mali asked, shaking her head.

Kirsten walked in. "You won't believe what I found." She sat down next to Jake and opened her computer.

"Thanks for coming in so early, Kirsten," Mali said.

Kirsten nodded and continued, "I ran a search on multiple media outlets of '#huntedlives' and found countless comments on the video. I'm assuming that's the video of Margie Thornburg," she said, glancing at Mali's computer. Mali and Jake nodded. "Look at these comments on Twitter."

"Awesome!"

"Totally RAD man!!"

"Is it real?"

"The graphics of Central Park look so accurate."

"What a shot. What weapon was used?"

"Who's the broad?"

"She looks like an old maid, a dead old maid. Ha, Ha."

"There was a video similar to this but it looked like a lake or something was in the background."

"Love it!"

"Is that the Golden Gate bridge behind the guy who got whacked?"

Kirsten looked up from the computer. "The comments go on and on."

"Hold it," Jake said. "Golden Gate bridge?" He looked at Mali. By the look on his face, she knew he was thinking the same thing she was. "I'll search for a video on Ken."

"I'll do the search, Jake," Mali whispered.

"No. I need to." Settling in front of his laptop, his fingers moved swiftly as he typed in search keywords.

Mali looked at Kirsten, who had tears in her eyes. "Kirsten, track down the IP address of the originating twitter account and also find the name of the YouTube account owner. That might lead us to the killer or to an accomplice. Save the video and all the comments and YouTube user names as well as the tweets and associated twitter account names. We'll need to track them down. As soon as you've saved everything, contact YouTube and Twitter and have all of this removed."

Kirsten nodded and turned to her computer.

"No," escaped his mouth in a puff of air, but his whisper reached them. Jake was ashen-faced and staring at the screen. Mali and Kirsten rushed to his side of the table and Jake hit the play button. They watched as Ken turned briefly toward the killer, checking his surroundings. While it was dark out, there was a full moon and they could easily identify him. Mali noted that he looked tired and his clean-shaven face appeared scruffy with the early shadow of a beard. His hair looked unkempt. Ken was wearing jeans, a dark sweatshirt with rips in the left sleeve, and dirty light-colored tennis shoes with holes in the big toe of his left foot and on the side of his right foot.

The killer couldn't be more than fifty yards away from Ken unless his camera had a telescopic lens. *Why couldn't Ken spot the killer? And why was he in Lincoln Park?* They could see water in the background and the lights of the Golden Gate bridge. That part of the park had some large oak trees with grassy terrain. The killer would have to be hiding behind the trees. They watched as Ken turned away and slowly jogged across the grass toward the water. The killer was following Ken, moving from tree to tree, and getting closer. The only sound on the video was the quiet breathing of the killer. Stopping behind a tree, the killer looked down at a device on his wrist. All of a sudden, he moved forward. Just as Ken started turning his head to glance behind him, the killer raised the gun and shot him. The bullet slammed into Ken's head and he fell forward.

Kirsten gasped and raised her hand to her mouth, whether to hold in a scream or bile, only she knew. She looked away from the screen.

Mali and Jake continued to watch as the killer walked over to Ken and turned him over with his booted foot. Ken's lifeless face stared ahead, a dark pool of blood growing beneath his head and a trickle running down his forehead. The video was just over two minutes long.

Mali felt sick. She glanced at Jake who was staring at the screen, pale, his jaw tight. Mali placed her hand on his shoulder but it fell away unnoticed as he abruptly stood, his chair slamming to the ground. With a curt "Excuse me," he left the room.

"How horrible," Kirsten choked out.

Mali closed the browser window on Jake's laptop and returned to her computer. She brought up YouTube, finding the video. "Kirsten, what is the user name for the account that posted the Thornburg murder? Kirsten?" she asked again when there was no response.

Collecting herself, Kirsten walked back to her laptop and, after a quick search, replied "Sally Henderson."

"The name on this account is different. It's 'Henry Thorn.' There are more than seventy thousand views of this video, increasing by the minute, and look at all of the comments," she said, shaking her head in disgust, adding, "I will save all information related to this video, including the video itself."

"Good. I'll include it when I contact YouTube and Twitter."

"Thanks Kirsten. Let's get these videos off social media as quickly as possible."

They both continued to work, the only sound the tapping of fingers on computer keys. It was still dark outside, the sun not yet making its appearance.

Frank and Jake walked into the room just after eight. Frank was carrying coffee and donuts and he set them down on the table. Mali gratefully grabbed a donut and gobbled it down, her stomach had been growling for hours. Taking one of the cups of coffee, she added a packet of Splenda and stirred it before taking a much-needed sip.

For the next hour, they reviewed the white board, which now had "#HuntedLives" at the top, and discussed their findings and next steps. Kirsten's immediate task was to work with YouTube and Twitter to remove the videos, comments and all tweets and to obtain names and addresses for all users who commented or tweeted on the videos. Frank assigned two agents to search social media outlets—YouTube, Instagram, Facebook, and others—to ensure the videos had not been posted elsewhere, and to help with contacting the users.

Jake tracked down the addresses for the two YouTube users who posted the videos. One of the users lived in Miami, Florida, but the other lived in Brooklyn. They headed out just before lunch to track down the local user. Not a word was said as they rode the elevator down to the parking garage and walked to the car.

Mali buckled her seatbelt. "Jake."

"Mali, let it go. I don't want to talk about the video. I don't want to do anything except find the son-of-a-bitch who did this." He threw the car in gear and screeched out of the garage onto the busy street. The rain was still falling steadily, cold but no longer icy. Mali watched New Yorkers rushing down the sidewalk, umbrellas over their heads, determined to get wherever they were going as quickly as possible. Traffic was slower than usual because of the weather. The honking horns and lack of sleep and food were giving Mali a headache. Jake glanced at Mali, frowned, and reached into his jacket pocket. Pulling out a pop tart, he handed it to Mali saying, "You look like you could use something to eat. This is the best I can do. My daughter put it in my coat last night."

Whoa, Jake had a daughter?

"Yes, I do." Jake smiled as he glanced her way.

"I said that out loud? I'm sorry, Jake. It just never occurred to me that you had a daughter. And thanks for the pop tart. The donut I ate earlier wasn't enough."

"You're welcome." He paused. "I keep my private life private. Heather is six and quite a pistol."

Mali was dying to ask him about his wife. The file she read had no information on his family or marital status. He didn't wear a ring. *Stop it! You're not interested in him or his marital status. Focus on the job at hand.* Satisfied that she had successfully admonished herself and was not in any way interested in Jake, Mali glanced at him and found him staring at her with an enigmatic look.

"I can see the wheels turning in that head of yours."

"The light is green, Jake."

He returned his focus to the road and continued down the street.

Saying no more and frowning pensively, Mali dove into the pop tart, relishing every bite of the strawberry delight.

* * *

Bay Ridge, Brooklyn, Frank's house
Friday, March 27, 6:15 p.m.

"COME ON IN, Mali. Jake is already here," Frank said. Mali had been to Frank and Carol's home for dinner before and she loved the warmth within its four walls; it was different from her own home growing up. Frank's house was decorated in warm brown, beige, and yellow tones, and it had a wood-burning fireplace in the living room. The large mantel above the roaring fire was filled with pictures of Frank and his family. *This is a family that loves.* Mali smiled.

Carol approached Mali in the hall and gave her a big hug before ushering her into the living room. "Mali, I'm so glad you could come tonight. Frank says you and Jake have been working way too hard. I told him that a nice home-cooked meal is just the break you need." Carol was a jovial woman, a little plump, comfortable in her skin.

Mali nodded at Jake as she walked over to the mantle to admire the photos before turning to face the room, her back warming by the fire. "Thank you so much for the invitation, Carol. I always enjoy my time with you, Frank, and the kids. And, you're right, this is exactly what the doctor ordered. Can I help with anything?"

Carol shook her head. "Thanks for the offer but no. Everything is under control. Relax and have a drink." She excused herself and left the room.

Mali sat down on the sofa next to Jake, who was wearing the same suit he had on that day in the office although his jacket and tie were gone and three buttons of his shirt were unbuttoned. *Damn, how can anyone look so sexy?*

"What can I get for you to drink?" asked Frank. "I have a variety of sodas, water, white and red wine, and beer."

"I'll have a glass of white wine," said Mali.

"Just water for me, Frank, I'm driving," Jake responded.

Frank left for the kitchen, returning moments later with their drinks.

"Let me get the boys." Frank headed upstairs.

Jake murmured, "Much as I like the idea of a home-cooked meal, I would much rather be working."

"It's been a frustrating week, especially after all the dead-ends we've encountered. A break might do wonders for us."

The YouTube account user they had spoken to in Brooklyn, Sally Henderson, shed no light on the Thornburg video. She had not even accessed her YouTube account in a couple of months, which they were able to verify. The killer had hacked into her account and posted the video. Working with the Miami office, local agents discovered that Henry Thorn, the second YouTube account that posted Ken's video, had reported that his account had been hacked as well. The Miami agents were able to confirm that. The IP address found in the email header of the hacker for the Miami YouTube account was the same as the hacker for the other account. The hackers were the same person.

Unfortunately, the IP address was forged using TOR,

an open network that helps defend against traffic analysis, a form of network surveillance. It protects one's privacy and identity on the network by securing a connection with three layers of encryption and passing it through three voluntarily operated servers around the world, allowing people or organizations to communicate anonymously over the internet without identifying the user's location. The IP address lead was dead.

Every corner they turned just raised more questions, with no answers.

Frank walked back downstairs and it wasn't long before it sounded like a stampede pounding down the stairs as each boy fought for the lead. Frank's sons, Kevin and Josh, were twelve and eleven, boisterous and lanky pre-teens, always with smiles on their faces. Mali enjoyed seeing them and talking sports with Kevin and chess with Josh. Kevin was into baseball, loved playing first base, quite good too. Mali had attended one of his games last year and he played well. Josh, on the other hand, was more introspective. He wasn't interested in team sports, or any competitive sports, but loved to compete in chess. He won more often than not. Spending time with them was a treat for Mali.

Conversation was lively and before long, Carol called everyone into the dining room. The liveliness continued through a delicious meal of kale salad, lasagna with garlic bread, finishing with strawberry shortcake and coffee.

As soon as they were finished, the boys excused themselves to go upstairs with a promise from Mali that she would pop in before leaving to say goodbye.

"No doubt they're headed upstairs to play Kevin's new game on his Xbox. They can't get enough of it," Frank said with a sigh.

"What game is that?" Jake asked.

"It's called The Hunted Ones. It's been the hottest xbox game on the market for the past four years, according to Kevin. I resisted his pleas for the game ever since it was released. The deaths are too realistic to me. I was afraid the boys would become desensitized to real murders. There's even a phone app of the game. It's only a matter of time before a phone is going to be the next plea," Frank finished with a groan.

"So you finally buckled, huh?" Mali teased.

"Yeah, I said he could buy it with the birthday money he received two months ago. They've been playing it ever since."

"Actually, I convinced Frank to let them have their fun," Carol piped in. "It's just a game and the boys understand the difference between a game and what goes on in the real world." She moved closer to Frank.

"I am still not too sure about that game, Carol," Frank said as Mali and Jake headed into the living room and Frank relaxed into his favorite recliner. "It's all they want to do."

"Don't worry about Josh and Kevin, Frank. They are good boys and they're doing well in school since we moved here two and a half years ago. I'm so proud of them," she added, looking at Mali and Jake. "Josh made it into the Honor Academy this year and Kevin's progress and attitude are night and day from two years ago. You're as proud of them as I am," she said, reaching over to pat Frank's hand. "They've made some good friends who are a positive influence. Things are going well."

"Congratulations on their success in school. I imagine the extracurricular activities are also a positive influence," Jake said.

"Indeed they are, Jake," said Frank. "Our smartest decision was moving close to Carol's family. Fort Hamilton High School is a good school and the district is responsive and caring. Did you know that Carol graduated from Fort Hamilton? We love it here in Bay Ridge."

Just before nine, Mali stood up and prepared to leave.

"Why don't the two of you head upstairs to say goodnight to the boys? They're expecting you. Turn left at the top of the stairs. You can't miss them." Carol said.

Smiling, Mali and Jake stood and walked over to the stairs. Once they reached the top, they had no problem figuring out which room the boys were in. Kevin and Josh were obviously playing their game, if the hoots and hollers were any indication. Smiling at each other, they quietly stopped at the open door to watch the boys. They were able to view a small part of the monitor but their focus was primarily on the antics of the boys.

"You lose, sucker!" Josh teased his older brother, Kevin, the machete sticking out of his player's head a telltale sign. "Game over. You didn't stand a chance!" he hooted, falling off his brother's bed and onto the floor in glee.

"Shut up, punk." Kevin slammed a pillow down on

his brother's head as he sat up on the floor. "Man, I almost beat him. That assassin came out of nowhere."

Josh climbed back on the bed and looked at the Xbox 360 console, commiserating with his brother. "You'll make it next time. Detroit looks like a cool city. Let me have a turn now. I'm going to pick someplace new for the game." Playing their favorite game, the two boys took turns trying to outwit the assassin, not noticing that they had an audience.

"Duck into that building, Josh, before the assassin finds you," shouted Kevin. "Whew, that was close. Keep moving . . . go up those stairs . . . no, your best bet is to go out the back . . . you don't want to get trapped."

"I've got it, Kev, don't worry! I'm sure I fooled the assassin back there when I jumped off the bridge. That got me to level three. I only have to survive five more minutes and perform one more dodge and I'll move up to level four." A few seconds passed before, "No!! No!! Crap. I had it. How did the assassin find me?" he wailed. "Hey, a crossbow! Cool weapon for the assassin. Awesome the way it nailed the target between the eyes! I like that card. It's totally RAD, better than the last one. A few more gold coins and we can buy those cards. The New York City skyline is better than Detroit's too."

"Yeah but I'd still like to see Detroit. Maybe mom and dad can take us there for our next vacation!"

Alarmed, Mali looked at Jake, who was on full alert, shaking his head in disbelief. *Crossbow? Assassin? Card? Skyline? The Hunted Ones. #HuntedLives. Oh my God! The murders were copycatting a computer game!*

CHAPTER SIX

"Kevin, Josh," Mali said, stepping into the room. Jake headed downstairs to get Frank.

"Mali, we didn't know you were there," Kevin said, worried because they had been caught cussing.

"Kevin, you two are not in trouble. We just want to learn more about this game."

Frank and Jake walked into the room and sat on one of the beds as Kevin and Josh described the game to them. The player could select whether they were the target or the assassin and could specify the duration of time for the game. If the target stayed alive past the duration time, he won and received gold coins, the number of coins depending on the duration and other factors. If the target was assassinated prior to that designated time, the assassin won and a card was placed on the chest of the target. The player could select computer-generated faces for the target and assassin or upload pictures and customize them. The player also chose the weapon and location. As the game progressed, the player (if the target) moved to progressively more difficult levels by achieving certain goals.

". . .and you can play by yourself choosing to be the target or assassin, or with a friend, one is the target and one is the assassin," Josh explained.

Frank was right when he said that the murders were realistic. What captured Mali's attention, however, was the accuracy of the locations. An advanced GPS system had to be coded into the program. The streets were real with restaurants, shops, apartments, and other existing landmarks.

They asked the boys to play a game in New York City so they could watch. The streets and venues in the game were actual places. To her knowledge, there was no other application that used real locations instead of computer-generated ones. Alarming.

"Thanks for the lesson, boys." Frank said. "Time to get ready for bed. We'll talk about this some more in the morning."

To a chorus of goodbyes, Frank, Jake, and Mali walked downstairs and into the living room.

"Unbelievable," Jake said.

"So if the murders are based on this game, then we have a serial killer on the loose?" asked Mali.

"It's hard to say if there is one killer or multiple, given that this is occurring across multiple states." Frank paused to take a drink. "This case has just been elevated. I'll set up a task force and move the operation from the conference room to a control center which will be set up by the time you get into the office on Monday. Jake, as senior agent, you will lead this investigation and will have whatever resources you need at your disposal. In addition, I will request one of the specialized Information Technology Analysis Teams from headquarters in Washington, D.C. to assist. We need to work fast to catch whomever is involved."

As they left Frank and Carol's house, in a much more somber mood than when they arrived, Jake insisted on driving Mali home.

"I have no idea what to think about all of this," she said, shifting to face Jake. "I now understand what those tweets and other comments meant. But how can people be so uncaring, so numb to the reality?"

It was a rhetorical question and Mali didn't expect an answer. She didn't get one.

They rode in silence. The only conversation was when Mali gave directions to her apartment. At the entrance, Jake turned off the car. The silence was palpable.

"I'm still trying to process all of this. If players are involved and can select the weapon and location, finding the killer or killers will not be an easy task. And are the players playing at one or multiple locations? Who are the players? How are targets selected?" He shook his head. "I don't want to wait until Monday. Can you meet with me this weekend?"

Mali nodded.

"We won't be able to meet at the office since everything will be in a state of chaos. Let's meet at my house tomorrow morning. Ten o'clock?"

"Sounds good, Jake."

Jake scribbled his address in Weehawken on a piece

of paper and handed it to Mali, who had opened the car door.

"Thanks. Goodnight Jake. I'll see you tomorrow."

Before she stepped inside the building, Mali looked over her shoulder at Jake. He was watching her from his car. The gesture comforted her.

* * *

Weehawken, NJ
Saturday, March 28, approx. 9:30 a.m.

MALI BUTTONED UP her coat and pulled on her gloves as she left her apartment. Her nose burned in the frigid air and her eyes watered. The air was heavy and the clouds were bloated with rain, maybe snow if the temperature dropped any lower. Mali jogged to the station to catch the train before the downpour caught her unprepared.

The weather had not changed when she exited the subway line on Thirty-fourth street. A brisk wind smacked her in the face as she walked down Thirty-fourth making her way to Sterling Avenue where Jake lived. Pulling her wool full-length coat tighter, she yanked her warm pink beanie cap down over her ears.

Mali admired the quaint homes she passed along the street, with small apartments tucked in between. Most were made of brick although there were many with siding. As were many of the streets in the area, this one was one-way. Parking spaces lined each side of the road with a small lane in the middle to drive. Multiple electrical lines crisscrossed the road above her head and the trees were bare of leaves. They seemed to be shivering, like herself. She turned down Park Avenue to Thirty-fifth which led to Sterling Avenue. It was quiet as Mali turned onto Jake's street. There were no moving cars on Sterling, although every parking space was taken. It was too cold for kids to play outside. Mali looked up and down the street, imagining it on a summer day full of children playing, their laughter bouncing off the cars and balls bouncing down the street.

The station was only a half mile to Jake's house so it didn't take her long to arrive. Standing on the sidewalk in front of his home, she found it charming. It had a small grass yard, now yellow in its dormant stage, and was surrounded by a low stone wall with wrought iron fencing on top. The entire enclosure was no more than four feet high. The house was a two-story brick home, windows trimmed in white, framed by two beautiful old oak trees. Smoke rose from the chimney and curled its way up to the sky. Mali walked through the wrought iron gate, up the path and stairs to the front door. She knocked on the wooden door and sighed. *Wow, it's so peaceful here.*

Her thoughts were interrupted when Jake opened the door. Dressed in jeans and a navy blue '#1 Dad' sweatshirt, Mali tried not to stare as she said hello and stepped inside.

Jake led her into the family room. "Excuse the mess. Life with a six-year-old."

Her eyes widened in surprise. "You have a lovely home, Jake."

"You sound shocked."

"I guess I am a little."

The room was full of life, bright and sunny. There was a stuffed bunny on the sofa, children's books on the coffee table, and a doll sitting in a mini crib in front of the fireplace. Other toys were scattered across the room which, in addition to the sofa, had two leather chairs, one on each side of the sofa, a coffee table in front of the sofa, and two side tables. The fireplace was the focal point of the room. Its facade was made of the same brick as the front of the house and the brick climbed all the way to the ceiling. A log fire warmed the room. The mantle was made of wood and there were multiple family pictures plus a small trophy of a ballerina in an arabesque pose sitting on top of it. Above the mantle, a large framed print of Jake, an older man, and presumably his daughter hung on the wall.

Mali walked over to the mantle, slowly perusing the pictures, smiling at a picture of Jake throwing his daughter in the air. She moved on and stopped at a picture of a younger Jake in uniform. Raising her eyebrows, she looked over her shoulder at him.

"That was a long time ago. Let's move into the dining room and get started. Would you like something to drink?"

"I'd love some water, thanks. I've been thinking a lot about the live game. So many questions." She set her bag down and pulled out her laptop, placing it on the table before continuing. "Regarding the players, who are they and do they realize that they're killing real people? If so, do they choose the victims? The victims certainly don't seem to have any connection or similarity between them.

Where are they taken to insert whatever it is behind their ear and what is its purpose? What was that device on the assassin's wrist? And who is driving the game, the players or the assassin?"

Jake excused himself while Mali powered up her computer. He returned with her water and a cup of coffee for himself then sat down next to her. He moved his laptop, which was already open, in front of him. "I've begun to research the game itself. Look what I've found so far."

Mali's eyes were drawn to a picture of a young man, in his twenties she estimated. Anthony Hunter was listed as the Founder and CEO of Hunter Games Inc., a gaming company he created four years ago when he launched The Hunted Ones game. *A self-made millionaire, he looks to be at the top of his game.* She chuckled at her pun.

"What's so funny?"

"Nothing." She shook her head, reading aloud and paraphrasing an article on the screen. "The Hunted Ones was his first game but the company has developed several more as well as a merchandising branch with paraphernalia related to his games, including the cards that Josh and Kevin talked about being able to buy with the gold coins they earned."

Jake and Mali spent the next couple of hours researching the company and the game. The Hunted Ones was successful beyond expectation even as it was widely criticized as being too realistic. The game's success was due, in large part, to the breakthrough use of GPS and satellite technology within the game. A player could select any city in the world and play the game on the actual streets of the city, real time, walking or running down the street as if physically there. The player could even go inside retail businesses and restaurants, however when inside a building the computer graphics seamlessly took over. The company's IPO had been listed on the stock market less than one year after the game launched and it shot up like a rocket. The games Hunter had created after the Hunted Ones used the same technology but were not as successful. And, while still a viable company, stock prices had fallen fifteen percent in the past year due to a lack of new innovation in more than ten months.

"The man is brilliant," commented Jake.

Mali's phone rang. "Yes, although it doesn't appear as if he's doing anything new. His stock has steadily declined this past year."

She answered her phone but before uttering a word, Kirsten interrupted, "You need to download the Periscope app right now."

"Periscope?"

"Yes, it's an app that allows people to live stream videos that anyone can watch. As soon as you download it, click on the live link for Chicago. It's a blue dot. Hurry."

Mali looked at Jake as she put her phone on speaker and set it down so she could work on the computer. "I'm here with Jake, Kirsten. What's going on?" Periscope finished downloading and she opened the app, looking for the blue dot for Chicago.

"The assassin is on the move again and he's live streaming."

"Christ," Jake said.

CHAPTER SEVEN

Little Italy, Chicago
Saturday, March 28, 12:30 p.m.

THE WOMAN TRUDGED along the streets of Little Italy, dead-tired, legs shaking with each step, occasionally swiping her greasy brown hair away from her face. She wore a long sleeve red shirt with black leggings, both wet from the snow that had fallen in the overnight and early morning hours. The gray clouds threatened more inclement weather. She was cold, shivering uncontrollably, and her breasts ached from the lack of ability to express the milk in them.

She shuffled into a fast food restaurant to get warm. It was not crowded, one person at the counter placing an order and two tables filled with diners. No one paid attention to her as she proceeded to the restroom in the back. An older woman was drying her hands and glanced at her with disdain as she threw her paper towel in the trash and stormed out.

The woman walked to the sink and turned on the

faucet, waiting for it to get warm. Splashing her face with the lukewarm water, she sighed, grateful for this small comfort, and let it run over her hands. Finally turning off the water, she wiped her eyes and looked in the mirror. Grabbing the sink with both hands, she tried to will away the pounding in her head. Her eyes were sunken into the sockets, her lips cracked, and cheeks chapped from the wind. Who was the stranger staring back at her? How could this have happened?

They took her two or three days ago, or was it longer? She had lost all concept of time.

She was shopping at the bakery near her home in Evanston buying a little cake for her daughter's sixth month party that afternoon. Her husband, who was fifteen years older and had two children from a previous marriage, found it amusing that she wanted to celebrate every month of Clarissa's first year, but enjoyed participating. His two girls had volunteered to watch Clarissa while she made her run to the shop.

When turning onto the street out of the parking lot, someone threw eggs on her windshield. Her mouth dropped open in surprise. How juvenile! She turned on her windshield wipers, spraying the windshield with water, shaking her head and continuing onto the street. The water mixed with eggs made a smeary mess on her window so she pulled over to wipe it away with a towel that was sitting in the back seat. As soon as she got out of the car, a van pulled up alongside her. Two men jumped out and grabbed her, throwing her inside. Before she could scream, a needle was jabbed into her arm. She remembered hearing screeching tires as the van raced away, before everything went dark.

She awoke in what looked to be an empty warehouse, lying on the floor dressed in the clothes she now wore, her things nowhere to be seen. Her head spun as she sat up, bile rising in her throat. She closed her eyes until the dizziness passed, not noticing the note and picture of her family for a few minutes.

With increasing dread and horror, she read the note while studying the picture of her husband and baby. The note said that, to survive, she had to make it to the 63rd Street Beach in Jackson Park within seventy-two hours. A rough hand-drawn map accompanied the note. She was not familiar with the south side of Chicago, rarely leaving the Evanston area to the north. If she refused to participate in the game or spoke with anyone, they would kill her baby girl. If she did not make it to the beach in the allotted time, they would kill her.

On the run now for twenty-six hours, she questioned how she'd make it another forty-six, doubting her ability to do so. Following the rough map, she wasn't even sure how many more miles she had to travel.

Clarissa came to mind now. She pictured her daughter's sweet smile, her giggles when mommy tickled her belly, her soft snorting noises when breastfeeding. She had married Tim at the age of twenty-one; Tim was thirty-six. They had Clarissa right away because her husband did not want to be forty and still having kids, not to mention the fact that he already had a sixteen-year-old and a thirteen-year-old. She loved her family, and

Clarissa was her heart, one she would protect at all costs. She could not give in to the terror that was threatening to consume her.

With that in mind, she walked into the cubicle to use the restroom.

* * *

Watching from a hidden location, a player controlled the game and the assassin's moves communicating via a console. The only other person in the game room was his host, who plied him with food and whiskey and lots of laughs. This was his first game. He had been playing this one for twenty-six hours, and was having a ball.

A large projection screen on the far wall showed the movements of the assassin when the GoPro camera was turned on. It was currently focused on the restaurant. The assassin texted his location across the street from the restaurant to the player.

"Good job. She's in the john. Wait for further instruction," he murmured aloud, typing the message in the console and then sending it.

Knowing that he could monitor the movements of the target on a smaller picture-in-picture screen and flip back and forth between the two, similar to a smart TV, was an added bonus for him. He had been watching her moves all along.

The player observed her as she looked at herself in the mirror. Since she was not on the large screen, the volume was off and he could only observe. With something akin to sympathy, his features softened, knowing that she wouldn't be alive much longer. Even though she was young, he was somewhat amazed she had lasted this long.

He watched her walk into the cubicle. "Go. Move in for the kill after she finishes taking a piss. No one else is there."

The message was sent and the player's excitement escalated as the scene unfolded from the assassin's GoPro camera. The assassin quickly crossed the street, entered the restaurant, and walked to the back. The door to the restroom slowly opened. It was empty. The target was still in the cubicle. The assassin walked in and stepped into one of the other cubicles, closing the door behind him.

The player grinned when the gleam of the seven and a half inch saw blade caught his eye as the assassin slipped it open. He had selected the Laplander folding saw because it was light and sexy as hell. He had one of his own and enjoyed the feel of it in his hand. He squeezed his right hand imagining that he was the one holding it and not the assassin. His breathing quickened as his emotions intensified and he shifted restlessly in his seat, in part due to the upcoming kill but also because of the inherent risk of someone walking in on the target and assassin.

The only sounds the player heard was the assassin's slow and steady breathing and water draining down the toilet as the target flushed it.

The player flipped the picture-in-picture so the target was magnified on the larger active screen. The assassin's view shrank into the small window. He watched her walk to the sink again. Her mouth opened and closed like a fish out of water, he thought with glee, as she reached for the faucet.

Although resigned to the fact that only twenty-six hours had passed, a far cry from the seventy-two hours of the game, the player was ready to end it. Flipping the picture-in-picture again so he could watch the kill on the big screen, the player leaned forward, sitting on the edge of his seat, eyes glued to the screen. His heart pumped faster, his breathing became erratic, his hands shook. He did not expect it to feel so good.

The player waited and watched in anticipation.

As soon as the faucet was turned on and water poured into the sink, the assassin left the cubicle and rushed behind the target. Startled, the target did not have time to react. Trapping her against the sink, the assassin wrapped his arm across her body grabbing her forehead with his left hand. Using the saw blade in his right hand, he slit the target's throat. Blood spurted onto the mirror and down into the sink, mixing with the water and giving it a pink tinge. The target gurgled and choked on her blood as the assassin laid her on her back. The player watched the blood rhythmically pumping out of the target's neck. As the life drained out of her eyes, the large screen went black.

"Yes! Awesome! God, that was incredible. Shit, it gave me a hard on," he exclaimed, adjusting himself before pumping his fists in the air and grinning at his host.

Looking back at the picture-in-picture screen, the player glimpsed the assassin removing the device that had been implanted behind her ear. When he saw the assassin's hand reach for the go-pro camera that was stitched into the target's sweatshirt, the player flipped the switch on the console. The smaller picture-in-picture screen went black. He was told that as with the implant, the camera would be removed.

The player's console beeped and he looked down at a picture of the target, lifeless eyes staring at nothing, a card lying on her chest. When the console beeped again, the message 'Game Over' displayed.

He stood up, drunk on the excitement of the kill and the whiskey, clapped his host on the back, and thanked him before leaving the room.

CHAPTER EIGHT

"Oh my God," Kirsten whispered.

Mali jerked back from the laptop, swallowing hard.

Jake stood and paced behind the chairs. "Kirsten, what happens to this live stream now? Is it automatically saved?"

"It can only be saved for twenty-four hours since the point of the app is to allow live interaction with audiences while live streaming. After that, the broadcast goes away."

"Play it again," he told Mali and Kirsten, sitting down again. "We need to look at this closely."

"So it's obvious who the target is since the focus of the assassin never changes, even when others walk by," Kirsten stated as they watched the assassin follow the target.

"He's, what, about two hundred feet behind her?" asked Mali.

"Roughly," said Jake. "He must be dressed in a fairly innocuous manner if no one is paying attention to him.

And they either don't notice the camera, perhaps it's hidden, or they don't care."

"Jake, look at the comments that were posted during the live stream," Mali murmured, scrolling down the screen.

"Take the shot."

"What are you waiting for?"

"Patience people, he's got to wait until it's a little less populated."

"I wonder what weapon he'll use. Maybe a machete this time. That would be cool."

"I've been watching for a few minutes now. He could have taken her out anytime. Why didn't he?"

The comments continued. People were eager for the assassin to kill the target. *What is wrong with them? Couldn't they discern that this was real?* Mali shook her head.

"Why didn't she talk to anyone or ask for help?" Jake muttered, thinking out loud. "In the app game, according to Frank's sons, there is a time limit to the game. Is that the case in this real game? If so, where is she going? Somewhere specific?"

No one answered Jake. They had no answers.

More time passed before the target walked into a fast food restaurant and proceeded to the back. It appeared as though the target assumed she was safe because she was not in a hurry as she walked inside.

The assassin paused across the street from the restaurant and looked down. They observed him typing a message into the device on the screen. Less than a minute later, the assassin looked at the device again. Mali shivered as she read, "Good job. She's in the john. Wait for further instruction."

Jake and Mali read additional comments from those who watched the game live.

"What's he waiting for?"

"Come on, do it. It's getting boring."

"Who's the player and how can I play this game?"

"I hope he breaks her neck; the crunch of bones would be awesome to hear."

After thirty-two seconds, the assassin looked down and they read the message, "Go. Move in for the kill after she finishes taking a piss. No one else is there."

Mali commented on the exchange. "The player is controlling every move of the assassin. And the assassin is actually waiting until instructions are received. Interesting."

They watched the assassin walk into the restaurant and to the back. He slowly opened the restroom door . . .

"Daddy!"

Mali and Jake jumped. Mali tried to calm the fluttering in her stomach. Jake stood and turned, holding his arms open for his daughter, who was running toward him. She barreled into him at full speed. Forcing a laugh, Jake picked her up, hugged her, and pretended to bite her ear which sent her into a fit of giggles.

"I contacted the local police and they are on the scene," said Kirsten.

"Gotta go, Kirsten. I'll talk to you later." Mali whispered.

"I'll capture the video and comments and send them to you and Jake. Then I'll contact Periscope to have it all removed."

"Thanks." Mali hung up the phone and closed her laptop as well as Jake's.

Wiggling out of her daddy's arms when she spotted Mali sitting at the table, Jake's daughter walked over to her and rattled off, "I'm Heather Christine Black and I'm six years old. Who are you? Are you Daddy's girl-friend? He needs a girlfriend. Your hair is red! You're so pretty. Papa, I'm hungry." And with that, Heather skipped into the kitchen.

Mali glanced at Jake, a bemused expression on her face. Before he could say anything, there was a noise behind him.

Jake's father approached, his face full of unleashed laughter, and held out his hand. "You must be Mali. I'm Jake's dad, Jerry."

Mali stood and shook Jerry's hand. "It's a pleasure to meet you, Jerry. That's quite a granddaughter you have. She's beautiful." Heather Black had long, curly, ink black hair, currently tied-up in a ponytail with a pink ribbon. Her dark blue eyes mirrored her Daddy's as well as the dimples on both of her cheeks when she smiled. Heather was dressed in pink jeans, that were dirty from her knees to her feet, and a white turtleneck under a pink sweatshirt with 'Daddy's Girl' written in white across the front.

"Thank you. She is quite the precocious one, never stopping for long, and she has an opinion on everything." Jerry said warmly. "I'm going to make some lunch. You're welcome to join us, Mali."

"We're wrapping up here, Dad."

Frowning in confusion, Mali rubbed the back of her neck and turned to the table, packing up her laptop. With a silence that had become a little awkward, she turned back to Jerry, computer bag in hand. "It was nice meeting you, Jerry."

"Likewise. Come back again when you can stay for a while." He turned to walk into the kitchen, giving his son a reproachful look.

As Mali headed toward the door, she said, "I'll contact the local FBI office so they can work the details with Chicago PD."

"I'll update Frank. Let's plan to meet with Anthony Hunter on Monday."

Mali nodded and left.

The return trip home wasn't as enjoyable as the trip to Weehawken had been, the peace of the morning shattered. She was empty inside after witnessing the latest murder. A gentle icy rain fell on her face as she approached the station. The cold weather suited her mood perfectly. As she walked into her apartment, a light snow fell softly outside.

* * *

Office of Hunter Games Inc
Monday, March 30, 9:30 a.m.

"WE'RE HERE FOR Anthony Hunter," Jake said, showing his badge to the receptionist on the top floor of the Hunter building.

"Just one moment," she replied, and picked up the receiver to make a phone call. "His assistant will be right with you."

Mali looked around the outer office area. The contemporary style and impressionist art on the walls, meant to impress visitors, was lost on her. She turned to gaze out the floor-to-ceiling windows, enjoying the view of the financial district and the Statue of Liberty in the distance. Jake stood next to her.

An older woman soon approached them. "Good morning. My name is Rebecca Smith and I'm Mr. Hunter's assistant. How may I help you?"

Jake and Mali shook hands with his assistant.

"My name is Agent Black and this is Agent Hooper from the FBI. We're here to see Anthony Hunter."

She perused his credentials. "Mr. Hunter is in a meeting right now. If you'll follow me, I'll take you to his office where you can wait for him."

"Thank you."

They walked to an office at the end of the hall. It was decorated in the same contemporary, minimalistic manner as the outer office. The left side of the room had two large impressionist pieces of art on the wall. A black, low-backed leather sofa was situated below the art. There were black leather and chrome chairs on either side of the sofa and a glass-top coffee table in the middle. On the right side of the room was a bar and beyond that, at the back of the room, was Hunter's desk with two chairs in front of it and a bank of floor-to-ceiling windows behind it. A small room was located on the right near his desk, presumably the bathroom.

"Can I get you a drink while you wait?"

Jake shook his head.

"No, thank you," Mali replied.

Fifteen minutes after they arrived, the door opened and a man and woman entered the room.

"Good morning. My name is Anthony Hunter and this is my Chief Financial Officer, Janet Simpson," said Anthony as he walked toward Jake and Mali.

Standing less than six feet tall, Anthony Hunter was the epitome of success. He wore a charcoal gray Italian suit, crisp white shirt, and silver tie, and looked every bit the successful businessman. With his short sandy blonde hair thinning on top, wire-frame glasses over pale blue eyes, and manicured hands, the total package was not at all what Mali expected. She assumed jeans and a t-shirt, similar to the genius of Mark Zuckerberg, were the standard fashion for these creative types.

His CFO, on the other hand, while dressed well, was wearing yesterday's outdated fashions. Her thick black glasses overshadowed her brown eyes and long nose and chin, and her dull hair was pulled into a severe bun. A bit mousy looking and a tad overweight, she reeked of stale cigarettes. Her eyes and the look on her face were devoid of emotion even though there was a smile on her lips.

"How can we help you today?" Anthony asked, offering them a seat and walking to his desk to sit down. Janet moved behind Anthony's desk and stood next to his chair, her arm resting on the back.

"There have been a series of murders in recent weeks that appear to be copycatting your Hunted Ones game," Jake said.

"That's horrible," Janet exclaimed, adjusting the glasses on her face then placing her hand on her chest.

Anthony was flustered. "What? I haven't heard about any murders in the city tied to my game!"

Mali said, "The murders are spread across multiple states and we have not made any information public as of yet. We want to ensure that we have our facts straight. Do you have any disgruntled employees or enemies who might want to implicate you in these murders?"

"Well of course I have enemies. That's the nature of this cutthroat business where being the first to deliver new innovation is the key to success."

"And yet, you haven't had any new games or significant updates—including any security updates—on your existing games in more than a year," Jake observed.

"What are you implying, Agent Black?" huffed Anthony, affronted.

"I'm not implying anything, Mr. Hunter, merely stating a fact."

"We need the names and addresses of anyone you

think is capable of creating your game in real life to commit murder," Mali interjected.

"Of course, Agent Hooper. We will help in any way possible. If someone is murdering people under the auspices of my game, I want him or her captured as quickly as possible." Anthony turned to Janet. "Go and work with Rebecca to put this information together."

She nodded and left the room.

"How are they using my game, specifically?"

"The murders have occurred in New York City and San Francisco, the victims were a man and a woman," said Jake. "Different weapons were used. Both victims had a cut behind their ear with a trace of cyanide and—"

Anthony interrupted. "So far, what you've described doesn't in any way tie to my game. How can the murders even be tied together?"

"A calling card was left on each victim with a silhouette of the city in which they were murdered, the weapon used, and a number written on the back," concluded Jake.

"The calling card is the same as my game, except for the number on the back. What does that number mean?"

Mali said, "There is a time limit for each game of The Hunted Ones that the player sets at the beginning. We believe the number on the back might be the length of time that the target was in the game before being killed or possibly the time remaining."

"In addition," Jake said, "the game is being publicized through social media. Twitter and YouTube accounts have been hacked so far and the killer used Periscope to live stream a kill. He used a hashtag on Twitter, #HuntedLives, that is likely in direct reference to your game."

"Shocking, absolutely shocking." Anthony popped up from his seat and paced back and forth behind the desk. "Unbelievable," he muttered before sitting down again. A vein pulsed in his neck as he crossed his arms on the desk and flexed his fingers before his hands slowly formed into fists. "Why would anyone desecrate my game in such a manner?"

Mali's eyes narrowed. "I'm more concerned with the victims than your game, Mr. Hunter."

"Wha— of course, of course," he stammered.

Janet walked in with a sheet of paper and handed it to Anthony. Leaning over his chair, one hand on his shoulder, she pointed to names on the list and they spoke in whispered tones. His fists opened and the tension in his body eased when she squeezed his shoulder.

Taking a pen in his hand, Anthony scribbled something on the paper then handed it to Jake. "Based on what you've described I added two more names to the list, fired employees who would have the knowledge to do something like this."

"Thank you." Jake and Mali stood. "We appreciate your time and assistance."

"If there is anything more we can do, please don't hesitate to contact me personally. Here is my card with my cell number." Anthony ushered them out of his office.

Jake and Mali didn't say anything as they made their way back to the car. Once inside, Mali said, "There is something 'off' about Anthony Hunter and his CFO."

"Is that your professional opinion?" Jake asked with a smirk.

"Come on, you don't think so? They were helpful enough although Hunter appeared a little nervous. He didn't look too surprised of our visit or to hear the news. Perhaps he had seen some of the videos on social media although he acted like that was news to him. And Janet Simpson? Contrived and cold."

"Not everyone is comfortable talking to the FBI."

"That's not it. I can't put my finger on it but something feels off. Maybe they're involved with each other." She shrugged. "Who knows?" Mali proceeded to read the names on the list. "Hopefully, we will get some leads from this list."

"With luck," Jake turned his focus to the road as a taxi abruptly cut him off.

CHAPTER NINE

AFTER THE TWO FBI agents left, Anthony turned to Janet, who was leaning against his desk, her butt on the edge.

"You handled that perfectly, Anthony."

Walking over to her, Anthony nudged her legs open with his knee and stepped into the space he made. He leaned over her to reach for his phone. Punching a number, he spoke into the receiver, "Rebecca, I don't want to be disturbed under any circumstances." He hung up without waiting for a reply and pulled her closer, nuzzling her neck.

"You were brilliant and there is no reason to believe that they suspect anything." Janet placed her hands on his shoulders and squeezed. "Was it just two years ago you began this journey? It's been so exciting to watch your plans come to fruition."

"I couldn't have gone on this adventure without you. You are my muse, Janet. The best journey of my life."

April, two years ago

"You said you were bored, Anthony. This could be an . . . intriguing way to add excitement back into our lives," purred Janet, stroking her hand down Anthony's chest. They were standing in Anthony's living room, near the picture windows in his Carnegie Hill apartment.

"There's a lot of risk in this," he replied, absently grabbing her buttocks and squeezing. Refocusing on her, Anthony pulled her close, close enough for her to feel his growing excitement. A little on the plump side, yet attractive enough in her own way, Anthony always had a thing for Janet. They had known each other since they were kids and he was a little astonished when she agreed to work with him. Bringing her on was the best thing he could have done for Hunted Inc. Janet was a financial wizard. They had a great working relationship.

Anthony wanted more; he had always wanted more. Groaning, he moved against her.

"Darling, anything worth doing has risk." Reaching between them, her hand slid down his stomach to stroke his manhood. "We'll take our time planning this out to the smallest detail in order to mitigate that risk. We'll hire the right people, pay them over and above what they're worth to keep them quiet. Think of the fun we'll have playing the game for real! And you will be directing every aspect of it. Imagine, your baby coming to life!"

Anthony groaned again, turned on by her hand as well as the idea she had planted in his head. Pulling her even closer, if that was possible, he kissed her over and over, moving against her, lost in her scent, her lushness. The onslaught continued, pushing Anthony closer to the precipice. He couldn't get enough of her. He turned her so that her back was against the glass window and slathered her with awkward wet kisses.

To say he was frustrated when Janet pulled away and walked over to the bar was an understatement. Flipping so his back was against the window, he rested his head against the cool glass and continued to stroke himself, trying to control his breathing. He watched her through slitted eyes as she grabbed a Waterford crystal glass from the cabinet and poured herself a whiskey neat, tossing it back in one gulp.

His breathing had returned to normal when the sound of liquid sloshing in a glass jarred him into awareness. He opened his eyes as Janet approached and handed him the glass of whiskey she had just poured.

"You can be a cold bitch, Janet," he groused, the tension in his voice palpable. "Jesus, I've never been so hard. When are you—"

"Now, now Anthony. Don't be mean," she pouted. "Much as I'd like to continue, we'll have to pursue this another time. Right now, it's important to move forward with your new project. I'll make a few discreet inquiries for you. Figure out how you want the real game to work and we'll set the wheels in motion."

He sipped the whiskey, savoring the taste of it in his mouth before swallowing. "I already have some thoughts in mind. I'll map out the consoles tomorrow." Anthony took a deep breath. "You do know I'm going to have to finish this, don't you?"

Janet laughed. "Enjoy and I'll see you at the office in the morning." She leaned in to kiss him then turned and sauntered out of his apartment, closing the door behind her.

Walking into his plush dark bedroom, the sparse furnishings and sixty-five-inch Samsung TV on the wall opposite the bed as well as the black and gray accents throughout, were lost to him. His focus was on the massive king-size bed with the tufted black wall behind it serving as the headboard.

Anthony couldn't get Janet out of his mind. Nor could he stop thinking about bringing his baby to life. Both thoughts had him nearing the edge of release. Rushing to the bed, he unzipped his pants and pushed them, along with his briefs, to the floor, not bothering to remove his socks or shirt. He settled himself in the middle of his king-size bed with pillows plumped behind him and turned on the television, navigating to his favorite porno flick. Stroking himself, absorbed in his show, he imagined Janet in the face of the whore on the screen. He moaned and whispered her name as his focus was on one thing and one thing only.

* * *

New York City
One year later

THE GAMING ROOM, built in a hidden space in the basement of Anthony's office building, was set up for comfort and to maximize the viewing pleasure of the players. On the wall at one end was a large one-hundred-inch projection screen. Facing it were two rows of three black leather recliner chairs. Each recliner was equipped with a pull-out game console. A massive mahogany bar loaded with only the best brands of liquor lined one side of the room. The back housed a restroom, the elevator to his office, and a door leading to a secret exit out of the basement. There were no windows and the room was sound proof due to the thickness of the concrete walls. Black velvet drapes lined each wall, adding to the intimacy. Canned lights were the only lights that softly illuminated the room.

Sitting in one of the recliners next to Janet, Anthony stared at the body on the screen, the game console hanging limply in his hands, and cursed loudly. "Damn it! This first test is a disaster. The hunted one didn't read or understand the note and evidently didn't even feel the implant. Damn fool was probably high. He didn't make any attempts at evasion. I could have ordered the kill in the first two hours. Unbelievably boring! If the cyanide had not released prematurely and with no provocation in the sixth hour, I would have shot myself to end this painfully pathetic game. Who's going to pay for this kind of drudgery?" he whined.

"Don't be melodramatic, Anthony," Janet cooed, placing her hand on top of his. "From your years in gaming development, you better than anyone understand that testing is critical in order to work out the defects. And there are always defects." She paused. "So we have a few problems to work out. Not a big deal! We need to work through the issues."

Standing up from the recliner, Janet walked to the bar, sat down on the plush stool to make notes on the pad she had left there. "Selecting a homeless person to be our hunted one is out. We'll have to figure out who to target and what criteria we need. It should be someone who has something to lose, is intelligent, an upstanding citizen."

"That's good." Anthony set the game console on the recliner he had just vacated and paced the small room. "We can re-write the note easily enough. And I'll contact the lab to figure out what happened with the implant. I'm sure they can discover the design flaw that caused the early release of the cyanide."

"Don't forget about the successes of this test, Anthony. The assassin did as instructed, for the most part, and there were no communication issues with him. In addition, he followed the protocol we established and removed the implant and GoPro camera before indicating that the game was over. And there were only minor problems 'obtaining' the hunted one and outfitting him with the implant."

"You're right. Thanks Janet. I appreciate your objectivity and support. My plan can work. We just need to work the kinks out and try again." Anthony stopped and stared at the body again. "I also have a few ideas of who I want the first player to be. Ted Springs and Bill Markham are good options. They would enjoy this kind of game. They can afford the fee and they have wanted a merger for quite a while. I can dangle that carrot in front of them."

Anthony walked to the bar and reviewed the notes Janet had written. Absently stroking her neck, he said, "I want to be ready to go by my thirtieth birthday."

"Anthony, officially beginning this new chapter of your game on your birthday is a brilliant idea and the perfect way to celebrate turning thirty." She stood and turned to Anthony. Leaning in to kiss him, she whispered, "With a little less than a year, I have no doubt that you can fix the problems. Let's go celebrate your success and a profitable launch."

"What did you have in mind?" He held her loosely in his arms and rubbed his nose against hers.

"Let's go out to dinner, paint the town."

"I was kind of hoping for something else," he whispered against her mouth.

Janet kissed him. "In time, my sweet, in time. Right now, I want some food. I haven't eaten since breakfast and I'm starving." She playfully pushed him away and headed for the elevator.

Anthony smacked her on her rear. "Far be it from me to keep a hungry woman waiting." Anthony turned off the lights and projector as they stepped into the elevator.

The screen with the body slumped on the ground, foam coming out of his mouth, slowly faded to black.

* * *

SHAKING OFF THE memories, Anthony said, "We've come a long way in two years. But damn it! How the hell are we just learning about social media now, and who gave that piece of shit Drake the authority to tweet '#HuntedLives' . . . and with videos of each kill, for Chrissakes. Black even said that there was a live stream on Periscope." Pacing his office as he ranted, Anthony did not notice the view of the city from his floor-to-ceiling windows. His office had its perks, the view of the financial district being one of them.

Janet lit a cigarette and walked over to the sofa to sit on the armrest. She adjusted her glasses and took a drag, blowing the smoke out through her nose. Her eyes followed Anthony as he paced back and forth.

"Aren't you going to say anything, Janet?"

"Yes. You're overreacting. And before you go off on another rant, I agree that Drake overstepped his authority. We can easily correct that. But the tweets and videos can work to our advantage. People are taking an interest in The Hunted Ones again."

"Which is going to point the finger right back at us," Anthony said, cutting her off. He leaned both forearms on the window and gazed down toward the street, eyes unfocused, not seeing anything.

Janet inhaled one more drag from her cigarette then crushed it in the ashtray and stood up. "Not necessarily,

Anthony, as was just demonstrated in our meeting with the FBI."

"I can feel you rolling your eyes at me. Don't."

She ignored his comment. "Anthony, we should allow the tweets and videos to continue. Once they go viral, the FBI won't be able to keep up with the various social media outlets and will not be able to remove all of them. Sales of The Hunted Ones will increase as people realize that the game we're playing on the streets is your baby. They will want more. That only makes this game more intriguing and exciting, don't you think? We'll make sure that Drake takes every precaution to avoid any connection with us. Nothing will be tied to us."

Janet walked over and wrapped her arms around him from behind. Rubbing her breasts against his back, her hands slid down, toying with his belt buckle. "Darling, you worry needlessly," she cooed in a soft voice. "You are the master and, with a little creativity, you can come up with a plan to deal with the authorities as this progresses. Now, don't let this spoil your birthday celebration. We've delayed it too long as it is. We're not going to let anything spoil the night. We need to leave shortly for our dinner reservation but, first, I have something for you."

"For me?" He danced a little jig, his excitement paralleling a child at Christmas. "You already gave me my birthday present and I wear it all the time. I love that you gave me a watch made specifically so I can enjoy the game from anywhere," he said, admiring the watch.

Janet smiled.

She took Anthony's hand and led him to his sofa, sitting down on his lap, straddling him. "I'm glad you like it, Anthony. But I have something that is sure to ease your stress better than any watch. And it's a long time overdue," she purred, kissing his neck.

"Show me," he said, his voice deep and thick. His head fell back on the sofa as Janet rubbed herself against him.

Anthony was panting as he ground out between clenched teeth, "Damn right it's overdue. I've been waiting for this for a long time, Janet." He hissed as she continued to move slowly against him. "God, you're killing me . . ."

"Mr. Hunter?" Rebecca's voice was on the phone speaker. "I'm sorry to bother you. Mr. Hunter?"

"Damn it. I said I didn't want to be disturbed." Anthony moaned, still moving against Janet. "Can't that bitch follow simple instructions? Don't go," he whimpered as Janet shimmied off his lap and stood.

"She'll come in if you don't answer her, Anthony. We don't want to give her a show now, do we?" Janet walked over to the phone and picked it up, punching in Rebecca's extension.

"No need to apologize, Rebecca. We were just going over the quarterly figures. What's up?" Her gaze stayed on Anthony as she concentrated on the call. "Get Jones on the phone and patch him through. Anthony will take care of it. Hmmm? Yes. And thanks for the alert, Rebecca."

Janet ended the call, put the phone on the receiver,

and stepped over to the bar, pouring herself a stiff drink. Anthony's eyes followed her every move. Sipping at first then swallowing the rest in one gulp, she grabbed a cigarette from the pack sitting on the bar, lit up, and took a deep drag, smiling at Anthony.

"Get up, Anthony. There's a production problem with the new game. Rebecca is getting Jones on the phone. He needs to talk to you ASAP. We'll head to the restaurant after your call."

Grumbling, Anthony stood up, adjusted himself, then walked over to the desk just as the phone rang.

Janet remained by the bar, sipping another whiskey and blowing 'O's with the smoke she exhaled.

Twenty minutes later, they headed out of the office. "Now, tell me about our next game, Anthony. It's in San Antonio, right?"

CHAPTER TEN

BACK AT HEADQUARTERS, Jake and Mali walked into the control center that had been set up for the task force. The room was twice as large as the conference room with three screens mounted and covering the top half of the front wall. There were six computer stations, each station with three monitors that seated two people. The entire right-side wall was a white board and Mali's information about each murder had been transferred to the left section of this wall. The other section was currently blank. The side wall on the left had two standard issue prints on it, different angles of New York and the field office. The back of the room had double doors leading inside and there was an access pad at the entrance to the room. The room was dark so that the screens on the front wall could easily be seen and there were track lights on each side of the room focused on the prints and white board.

On the left screen was a map of the United States with the murder locations pinpointed. The center screen was currently black. The right screen was split with the

YouTube website on one side and the Periscope app on the other.

Jake headed over to one of the computer stations to speak with two agents working there. Mali walked to Kirsten, handed her the list and said, "Hi Kirsten! Please scan this in and put the information on center screen."

"Sure thing."

Kirsten scanned the list and it appeared on the screen. Jake walked to the front of the room, starting with "Good morning everyone. I'd like to thank Amy Jackson, Brad Perkins, and Joe Alters for joining the team and flying in from D.C. so quickly. Thank you for joining this task force. Now, let me bring you up to speed."

Jake spent the next hour discussing the case, outlining the sequence of events, discoveries made, and finishing with the meeting they had with Anthony Hunter and Janet Simpson. The list on the screen was divided among six agents and they were tasked with researching each individual. "Hoop and I are not convinced that any of these names will provide a solid lead but we're hopeful." Mali smiled when she heard her nickname fall from his lips so easily. "You know the drill," he continued. "We have to check all of them to eliminate every possibility. And, maybe we'll get lucky. Amy and Brad will continue to search and monitor all social media, focusing on YouTube, Twitter, Periscope, Facebook, and Instagram while Kirsten and Joe will track down all IP addresses and related technical leads. Hoop and I will run down Anthony Hunter and Janet Simpson. We have put all state offices on alert and will share anything we find with them. Let's go people. We need to move quickly before he or she strikes again."

There was the buzz of conversation, phones ringing, and the tapping of keyboards, as everyone buckled down to work.

"I'll open a file on Anthony Hunter. Mali, take Simpson," Jake said as he walked back to her.

By the end of the week, progress had been made on the list, with all names eliminated as suspects except for the two handwritten names Anthony had added to the list. The two fired employees had motive, opportunity, and the skill set to pull off something like this, but they were also both family men with good jobs, albeit in different states. And they didn't have the financial means. So if one or both of them were behind this, then someone was financing them. The team had plans to bring each in for questioning as soon as they were located. The New Mexico and Maryland FBI offices were working on that and would conduct the initial interviews.

Files had been opened on Hunter and Simpson with basic background information.

Anthony Hunter grew up in New Jersey, had three brothers and one sister and, by all appearances, had enjoyed a happy childhood. He never got in trouble nor did he participate in sports. He was a classic computer geek growing up, nerdy and unassuming, focused on his school work. His dad was an auto mechanic and his mother an elementary school teacher. They had lived in a modest home in suburbia, where his parents still resided.

Today, Hunter was a self-made millionaire, many times over, due to the success of the Hunted Ones, never married, no children, and lived alone.

On the other hand, there were many gaps in Janet Simpson's life that Mali was still trying to fill. No official documents, like a birth certificate, could be located so there was no information on her childhood. Her bio on the website indicated that she was born to a crack-addicted sixteen-year-old and her father was unknown. She had worked her way through school, successfully beating adversity down with a stick. She had one prior accounting job before joining Hunter Inc. Where Hunter was brilliant in gaming development, Janet Simpson was unequaled in finances and was Hunter's second in command. The company had increased its holdings and wealth ten-fold since she joined the company and Hunter had her to thank for making him the multi-millionaire he was today.

Before everyone was released for the day, Jake called the team together to assess their findings.

"There is still no connection between the victims. They come from different backgrounds. There is a broad range of ages. Male and female victims. Varying locations." Jake ticked off each finding on his fingers.

Mali walked over to the white board where all of the victim information and timeline were outlined. Studying it, she stated, "Margie Thornburg, Ken Miller, and Sara Epstein (our last victim) were married with children. Even though Ken was working undercover, in that role he had a wife and teenager in college. The first two are the oddball cases. Our John Doe was homeless, died by cyanide and there was no card on his chest. The murder of our second vic, Glenn Marker, was closer to the other three. There were only traces of cyanide found and he was killed with a gun, but no card was left behind. Marker was also married but had no children. There was no video of either vics and the murders occurred quite awhile ago compared to the last three."

Jake leaned against the front computer station and studied the board. "Where are you going with this Hoop?"

She paced in front of the board. "I'm not entirely sure yet. Thinking out loud. Correct me if I'm wrong, Kirsten, but all computer programs are thoroughly tested before being released to the public, right?"

Kirsten perked up. "Yes. All new applications and games are tested to remove any defects and to ensure a sound product. Do you think the first two were tests?"

"Yes, I do," Mali answered, looking first at Kirsten then Jake.

Jake nodded. "That makes sense. Whoever planned this would want to make sure the process was sound before implementing it full scale. Operating under that premise, what can we surmise?" he asked the team at large.

Mali picked up a marker and walked to the center of the white board. She drew a line down the middle and on the left side wrote 'Process' with 'Unknowns' on the right side.

The team worked for an hour brainstorming ideas on the process as well as remaining unknowns.

Their list under 'Process' included:
* Target who has family is identified
* Assassin communicates via wrist console
* Assassin only kills when instructed to do so
* Some type of implant is removed from victim after murder
* Video posted on social media by hacking into account
* Card placed on chest with city skyline and weapon used
* Cyanide inside implant

For 'Unknowns,' the list was lengthy:
* How is city selected?
* How is target selected?
* Do they threaten family of target to get compliance?
* Where is target taken to install implant?
* Who installs the implant?
* Who are the players? Where are they during the game? How are they selected?
* What does the number written on the back of the card represent?
* Who are the assassins and how many?
* Purpose of the game?

* How long does the game last?
* Can target ever win? If so, how?
* Why doesn't target seek help?
* How does implant work?
* How does the assassin find the target?
* Who is running the game?

When ideas dwindled, Jake straightened and said, "This is progress. We still have many questions and as we answer one, more will surface. We'll have to work through each one. Good job everyone. Amy, Brad, and Joe, plan to work on Saturday to continue research. Be prepared to discuss what you discover first thing on Monday morning."

They nodded as the meeting ended and everyone prepared to leave for the day.

* * *

Mali's apartment
Saturday, April 4, 9:05 a.m.

"Jasmine, is that you?"

Much as she didn't feel like talking to her mother, having just returned home from a long run, Mali couldn't avoid her. "Yes, Mother. How are you and how are the plans coming along for your anniversary?"

"That's why I'm calling, darling. Everything is as ready as it can be for the party in one short week. Don't forget it's next Saturday. We expect you to be there. Our colors are pale yellow and teal. Your sisters have dresses in teal and I want you to wear the same. It will go nicely with your hair and coloring and I want all of you to match."

"Yes Mother."

"David Anderson is coming with his parents. We're good friends with his parents and David recently divorced that dreadful woman he married four years ago so he's available."

Her mother must be getting desperate if she's willing to look at a divorced cheater like David. "Used goods, Mother."

"Don't take that sarcastic tone with me, young lady. You have had your fun, now it's time to come home and start a family."

Mali's nostrils flared as she inhaled and the grip on her phone tightened. "Mother, I'm not interested in David Anderson, I have never been interested in him. And Tammy divorced HIM after she caught him cheating on her."

"That should be familiar territory for you, Jasmine Suzanne. Not that David would cheat on you. His mother says he's changed and he IS from a good family."

And that's what mattered most. Mali clapped a hand over her mouth to stop the words from spilling out. Her mother never missed an opportunity to bring up her failed marriage, something Mali would rather forget. She inhaled deeply, trying to remember that her mother was only doing what was familiar and would never accept any of her children deviating from the chosen path. Her mother wouldn't change, even if Mali wished things were different. She learned this long ago.

"Mother, pursuing a relationship with David is moot anyway. I'm bringing a date," she blurted out. *Oh, I'm in for it now.* Mali squirmed in her seat. *Good thing this is a phone call or her mother would recognize the lie for what it was.*

"Do we know him? What does he do? Is he from a prominent family in New York?" The questions were rapidly deployed, her voice rising several notches in her excitement.

"You haven't met him, Mother. I work with him." Another cringe for the lie.

Silence on the other end of the line.

Mali sighed. "We'll be there on Friday night, Mother. We can stay in a hotel if you'd prefer."

"Don't be ridiculous. Of course you and your . . . guest . . . will stay here at the house. I look forward to meeting him." A delicate sniff followed.

They said their goodbyes. Mali shook her head, hanging up the phone. What the heck was she going to do?

* * *

FBI Control Center
Wednesday, April 8, 12:20 p.m.

Research had continued with few results in the last week. The two additional persons-of-interest on the list

Anthony Hunter had provided were located—the first one, Tom Whiteman, in Taos, New Mexico.

Jake had personally wanted to question each lead and had flown to New Mexico on Monday afternoon, spending all morning on Tuesday questioning him. The lead was a dead-end. Whiteman had reason to hate Anthony Hunter, and spared no time listing all the reasons why, but he did not have the financial means nor the desire to do something like this just to frame Hunter. All of his alibis had checked out.

Jake had returned late Tuesday night and now updated the team.

"Are you sure he isn't involved in some capacity, Jake?" asked Amy. "He improved the Hunted Ones console initially created by Hunter, creating a more realistic experience for the user. He could have been a part of this scheme . . ."

"No, Amy," interrupted Jake. "There is no doubt that he has the skill set needed, and he believes Hunter is a 'vile, reprehensible snake who only looks out for himself.' His words not mine," Jake paused. "But there is no deep-seated motive and he readily turned over his financial records which showed a good salary but a modest lifestyle. We need to look elsewhere."

A woman walked into the room pulling a cart loaded with sandwiches and other lunch items.

"Let's break for lunch and reconvene in thirty minutes."

Mali and Kirsten grabbed their food and sat down at Mali's computer station.

"You don't look too good. Are you worried about this weekend? Couldn't find a dress?" Kirsten asked between bites of her ham and cheese sandwich.

Mali finished chewing her slice of apple. "I wish it was simply a matter of not finding a teal dress. That's not the problem. I'm worried because of the white lie I told my mother."

"Honey, that wasn't a little white lie. That was a whopper. You told her you were bringing a date?" Her voice had escalated.

"Shhhh." Mali glanced to her left and right. "I did it without thinking, to get her off my back. And because I was irritated at how she's trying to set up a match between that jerk, David Anderson, and me. Now I'm paying the price." She sighed, wishing she wasn't so impulsive where her mother was concerned. Shaking her head, she took another bite of apple.

"There still might be time to find someone."

"I doubt that," Mali interjected. "I'll come up with an excuse why my date couldn't come. Oh well, que sera, sera." She glanced up from their conversation to find Jake standing a lot closer to them than she realized, and he was watching her with an inexplicable look on his face. She blinked twice then turned back to Kirsten, trying to ignore the flutters in her stomach.

Conversation moved on to other topics and the next time Mali glanced up, Jake was talking with two agents holding a can of Dr. Pepper in his hand.

Clearing his throat, Jake turned to the team. "Let's keep going while we finish lunch. The second person-of-interest is located near Baltimore, Maryland. He will be brought to the local field office for questioning. Hoop and I will fly to Baltimore late tomorrow afternoon and will meet with him on Friday morning. Hopefully, we'll get some answers."

That was news to Mali. She opened her mouth to say something but remained silent. Kirsten leaned over to her and whispered, "Close your mouth, honey, before you catch some flies."

Mali snapped her mouth shut and glared at Kirsten, who grinned back at her, before returning her attention to Jake who continued with tasks that needed to be completed in the next few days.

When he finished, Mali walked over to him. "Can I speak with you, Agent Black?" They walked to the back of the room. As soon as they were out of earshot of the others, she said, "I told you a week ago that I had an approved absence this weekend for an event at my parent's home."

"I remember. Your parents live in Philadelphia, right?"

"Yes." Her voice rose in pitch as she drew out the affirmative. Her forehead wrinkled as her eyes narrowed.

"The interview in Baltimore shouldn't take more than a day. Your parents live in Philadelphia, a mere hour and a half away. You can continue on to your parent's home when we're done."

Mali didn't say anything.

"Is there a problem?"

"No, I suppose not."

He leaned toward her and whispered, "I didn't mean to eavesdrop on your conversation with Kirsten, but if you need a date for your event, I can play the part."

Mali pulled back, eyebrows arched, and gaped at Jake. That's the second time in five minutes he had surprised her. How did he do that? And dare she take him up on his offer?

"Why would you offer to do that?" Suspicion dripped from her tongue. She cocked her head to one side to study him.

"We're both going to be in the area, and why not?" Jake answered with a sly smile. This side of Jake was disconcerting. She inwardly cringed. "Think about it and give me your decision by two. I need to finalize our flight arrangements and I need to know when I'm returning to New York. If it's yes, you'll have to tell me what to bring."

"So, are you going?" Kirsten asked when Mali returned.

"Yes, and Jake offered to play the part of my date at my parents' anniversary."

"You're kidding! That's perfect, Mali, the answer to your prayers."

"Jake Black is NOT the answer to my prayers," Mali whispered, getting flustered.

Kirsten looked closely at Mali, then grinned.

"What are you grinning at?"

"Nothing. Nothing at all. It's up to you, of course, whether or not Jake goes to the party but I wouldn't look a gift horse in the mouth if I were you," Kirsten said, before returning to her computer and her assigned tasks.

For the next hour, Mali could not focus on work. She kept fluctuating back and forth between having Jake go with her and going alone. Having him there would certainly get her mother off her back about moving back to marry, but two nights at her parents' home with him? She wasn't sure that was a wise idea.

"Well?"

Startled, Mali's eyes jumped up to Jake, his silent approach lost on her. "I . . ." she cleared her throat. "I accept your offer and I appreciate it." *More than you know.*

"Good. What do I need to bring?"

"It's my parents' fortieth wedding anniversary. We'll be staying at the house on Friday and Saturday night, returning Sunday morning. Dressy casual wear during the day on Saturday, dark suit with tie on Saturday night."

"Should I bring a gift?"

"No. Gifts are not expected. I can fill you in on what to expect as we drive there on Friday."

"Okay. I'll send you the travel information as soon as I have it. It's going to be an interesting few days."

Ya think!?!

CHAPTER ELEVEN

Baltimore
Friday, April 10, 10:00 a.m.

DEFINITELY A NERDY computer geek was Mali's first impression upon meeting Jim Wells when he walked into the conference room of the Baltimore field office. Forty-four years old and slight in build, Wells wore baggy tan pants and a pale yellow short sleeve shirt with some sort of stain on the front. His black-rimmed glasses were propped up on his head and there was a mechanical pencil tucked behind his ear. He had a distracted demeanor, as if he had some place important to be, *and it's not with us.*

"As senior developer of The Hunted Ones during my time at the company, I was responsible for making regular improvements to the game after the initial creation and release by Hunter himself," he explained. "The game was originally developed for Xbox 360 and I was also tasked with making the game compatible on other devices: smart phones, all tablets, and on smart TVs. My proudest achievement was developing the link between

GPS and satellite that allowed the game to be played on actual city streets." According to Wells, Hunter fired him because he was jealous of his work on the GPS and satellite link. He said Hunter claimed it was his work and Wells just improved it. *Something to ask Hunter about when they returned to New York.*

"Have you seen any of the pictures and/or videos that have been posted on social media?" Mali asked.

"My wife is the social media nut. I stay away from it."

Mali opened her laptop, logged into the secure server, and navigated to the folder where the information was stored. She turned the laptop toward him. "We want to show you videos of two of the murders." She played the first video of the Margie Thornburg murder in New York and followed it with Ken's murder in San Francisco.

The blood drained from Wells' face and he looked like he was going to be sick.

"Are you all right?" Jake asked.

He swallowed a few times then nodded. "I'm just shocked. Can you play back the part that shows the console on the assassin's wrist? I want to take a closer look at it."

Mali returned to the part of the video that showed the console and pressed 'Play.' Wells watched it again. "It seems to be a simple text messaging system between the assassin and whoever is playing the game, although it could have a GPS system as well. Hard to say. Regardless, it would require some sort of signal tower, a Wi-Fi or cell tower for example, to pass the information back and forth."

"That's what Tom Whitman said when I spoke with him earlier this week," said Jake.

"Tom Whitman? We worked together for a couple of years. He's a good man. Surely he's not involved in this."

Neither Mali or Jake replied.

"You said that there was an implant of some sort?" Wells asked.

"Yes, with a cyanide payload," replied Jake. "Behind the right ear."

"In order to create an implant capable of holding cyanide and releasing it at some pre-determined time or on demand, the person or persons behind these killings needed a specific type of lab to create it, one that contained both medical and technical elements. Such a lab could be anywhere."

After making a few notes, Mali said, "We have learned that, in the game, the assassin will only take action if the player directs him to do so."

"That's correct. He can't move or shoot or do anything unless instructed by the player. If the live game is being played with the same rules, then the assassin isn't tracking the target, the player is."

"How can that happen?" asked Jake.

"I'm not sure but the player is somehow watching the game from a remote location."

They took a lunch break so Mali and Jake could talk and make some calls. They asked Wells to return at two o'clock.

"Thoughts?" asked Mali as they left the building and made the quick drive to Jae's Grill.

"Hard to say. Wells appears to be helping us with details of the program but most of what he told us only confirmed what we already suspected. We need more information."

The conversation stopped as they arrived at the restaurant and were seated in a booth. After receiving their drinks and ordering their food, they picked up where they had left off.

"I'm curious about the lab," Mali said between bites. "It seems like the skill set of the people involved in creating the device, producing them, and implanting them in each target would be unique, specialized. And how many medical personnel could create a device that releases cyanide on demand or at a predetermined time?"

"Good point. We can have the team research this but we may be searching for a needle in a haystack. Our time might be better spent looking for a lab with those specifications."

They wasted no time eating their meal and returned to the office just after one o'clock. Jake placed calls to the New York office and to his dad while Mali called Kirsten for an update before they resumed talks with Wells.

An hour more of discussions revealed minimal new information.

As the meeting wound down, Mali asked, "Can you tell us anything more about the game, Mr. Wells?"

"Not without getting more technical. I can have a video conference with your technical team to discuss the code in more detail, if you'd like."

"Excellent. We'll have our team contact you to

schedule it." Jake said. "Is there anything else you'd like to tell us?"

"Two things. First, the person with the most capability of doing this, and who has plenty of funds, is Hunter himself. Why he would do something like this is beyond me. Second, with respect to being fired two years ago, I was furious at first but I'm now grateful. I never would have found my current job or met my wife of three months otherwise."

Jake smiled. "Thank you for your time, Mr. Wells. We'll contact you if we have any additional questions from our meeting today."

As they left Baltimore in the rental car and headed to Philadelphia, Mali reviewed her notes.

"We have to assume that, as much as is possible, the live game is being played the same way as the app game."

"I agree." Jake nodded.

"So how is the player able to watch the game and where is he or she located? Is Wells involved?"

Jake rubbed his chin. "I'm skeptical. His insight today and his offer to meet with our technical team could be a ruse to throw us off. He knows the game inside and out and could pull this off if he has the green backs to do so. Let's check his financials when we get back to the office."

"Good idea."

"What do you think about his assessment of Hunter?"

"That he's behind it? Unlikely. He's got the money to pull something like this off but why jeopardize his entire gaming empire? More than likely, Wells is just pointing the finger at Hunter to get back at him for being fired."

"Possibly. But we need to dig deeper into Hunter's past, perhaps his CFO's, as well."

Facing forward, Mali turned inward, thinking about the weekend ahead. The changing landscape, from heavy congestion on the highway and many businesses passing by to lush trees along the road with little traffic and few businesses, went unnoticed.

To get her mind off what apparently was going to be an ordeal for her, Jake said, "I haven't spent much time in Philadelphia. I've passed through Philly but I've never explored it. I'd like to bring Heather here when she's a little older to show her the Liberty Bell and take her to Independence Hall where the Declaration of Independence and Constitution were signed."

No comment from Mali, who was staring out the window.

"She'd like it. I also plan to take her to Washington D.C. so she can learn more about our history through the Smithsonian museums, the White House, and all the monuments."

Still no response.

"Maybe if I click my heels three times, . . ."

Mali sighed and looked over at Jake. "Dorothy you are not."

Jake smiled. "How long have you known Kirsten?" he asked, changing the subject.

"We met through the FBI, joined and went through basic at the same time. I introduced her to my college roommate, Jennifer. They've been together three years now."

"They live in the City?"

"Yes, in Greenwich, not too far from me. Jennifer is an event planner, very good at her job, extremely busy. We're like three peas in a pod, well, four when you count Sara."

"Sara?"

Mali reminisced. "Yes. Sara is my oldest friend. We met at summer camp when we were ten years old and have been best friends ever since. She's salt of the earth. I love her perspective on life." Then she added, "I'm god-mother to her three children. The four of us gals try to get together every four to six weeks."

"I can only imagine what it's like when you hook up with them," Jake said dryly, smiling at her.

"We do have a good time together. We laugh a lot." Mali turned back to the front and gazed out the passenger window. Philadelphia was looming ahead and Mali was getting more and more tense the closer they got to the city.

After some time, Jake cleared his throat. "Tell me about this weekend, Mali. You said it was your parents' fortieth anniversary?"

Mali bent her left leg, shifting in her seat so she could face Jake. "Yes. Forty blissful years together," she said with a sardonic smile. "Don't get me wrong. They are content, I believe, but my parents were married at a time when families arranged the best matches. They met at my mother's debutante ball, had three or four supervised meetings after that, followed by the announcement of their engagement."

"They expected to arrange a marriage for you as well?"

"Yes. You have no idea how accurate your statement was the day we met. Although my mother would be thrilled if I had two kids, not necessarily a dozen."

Jake reached out to touch her hand then pulled it back. "I was talking out of my ear that day. I'm sorry."

"No need to apologize. You were right. I have two sisters, both older than me, both in arranged marriages, both unhappy. I swore I would not take the same path. Take the 476 exit. We're not too far."

"When was the last time you were home?"

"I go home for the requisite holidays, Thanksgiving and Christmas, plus any other special occasions like this anniversary. My last visit was Christmas. My parents have never visited me in New York."

Mali continued directing Jake to her parents' house. After they entered into an elite neighborhood, she said, "Turn right into the next drive."

They pulled into a majestic tree-lined drive winding up to Mali's family home. The drive was lined with white, pink, and blue hydrangea bushes. Red hibiscus plants in ornate planters welcomed guests at the top of the drive.

Built with gray brick, the design of the house was typical of the Victorian era, with a pointed, projecting porch, bay windows, and five tall chimneys. Multiple spires rose up toward the sky and were capped by a red tiled roof. Dark red shutters framed the sides of the upper floor windows and the look was pulled together by impressive front double doors painted to match the color of the shutters and roof.

"This is beautiful, Mali." Jake said, admiration in his voice. "I wish I could keep my flower beds as impeccable as these, and the lawn looks like a lush carpet."

"Thanks, Jake. It's a Victorian built in 1866. Mother painstakingly renovated the entire interior of the house about eight years ago."

Jake stopped and turned off the motor. Mali looked at him and took a deep breath. "It's not too late to change your mind."

"Not a chance."

"Okay. Well, stiffen your spine and gird your loins. This will be a weekend for the record books." And with a humorless smile, she stepped out of the car.

"Thank you, Roger," she said to the butler, who had helped her exit the vehicle.

* * *

They walked through the massive front doors to a large entry hall, twenty feet high. Wood floors were partially covered by a dark blue and white Persian rug that ran the length of the hall. The lower four feet of the walls in the foyer were lined with wood paneling while the rest of the walls were covered in a pale blue wallpaper. Double wooden doors, leading to other rooms, were on both sides of the hall and there was a grand wooden staircase on the right side leading to the second level.

"Jasmine, darling, I'm glad you are finally here." Entering the foyer from the back of the hallway, Mali's mother was a striking woman. Petite with long, blonde hair, always worn in an elegant chignon, she looked to be half the age of her fifty-seven years (thanks to two trips to her favorite plastic surgeon). Her skin was flawless, not a wrinkle in sight. She gave her daughter an air hug with an air kiss on each of her cheeks before stepping back to study her. "You've been in the sun too much, Jasmine. You have freckles on your nose."

Mali was about to respond when Jake put his arm on her shoulder, pulling her to his side. He looked down at her with a smile and said, "I find her freckles charming, if you don't mind my saying so." Mali tried not to stare at him with her mouth open. *He's getting into this role.*

"Mother, this is Jacob Black. Jake, this is my mother, Willow Hooper."

Taking her right hand in both of his, he smiled down at Willow and said, "It's a pleasure to meet you, Mrs. Hooper. I can certainly see where Mali gets her beauty."

Willow looked disparagingly at Jake from head to toe, delicately sniffed, and retrieved her hand from both of his. "Thank you." She turned to Mali. "Your sisters and their families are here already. We have a full house this weekend so you and Jacob will have to share a room. It goes against the grain but your father says I'm being parochial. I have you in the green room. Get settled and come downstairs in one hour for dinner. Be sure to change your clothing to proper dinner attire." And with that, she turned toward the interior of the house and sauntered out of sight.

Mali mouthed "I'm sorry" to Jake. Out loud, she said,

"Follow me." They climbed up the wide staircase saying nothing as they walked down the hallway to the bedroom. Mali opened the door to a lovely room with pale green walls, a king size bed at the far end of the room, and a large fireplace to their left. Mali's two-inch FBI heels (as she called them) clicked on the wooden floor as she entered.

"Jasmine?"

"My mother named all of her girls after flowers: Rose, Lilly, Jasmine. I grew up with a Siamese cat and changed my name to Mali when I left for college. 'Mali' means Jasmine in Siamese. I thought Mother would find it humorous. She did not." Feeling a little awkward, Mali turned and walked to one of the bay windows, sat in the cushioned window seat, and looked outside to the grounds below. "This was my room growing up."

"It is?" Jake studied the impersonal but delicate room.

"You expected something else?"

He shook his head. "I guess it's not surprising that she changed the room after you left."

"Nothing has changed," Mali murmured, still looking out the window.

"Hmmm."

"I always enjoyed sitting in this window seat with a good book." Mali turned her head and gazed at Jake, who was standing by the fireplace. "I'm sorry we were both put in here. Had I known that was the plan, I would have booked hotel rooms for us. I can sleep here in the window seat. I've done it before many times. The bathroom is through that door over there," she added, pointing to a door to the left of the fireplace. "And our things should arrive momentarily."

As if on cue, there was a discreet knock at the partially open door. Both turned as a man in uniform entered holding their bags. He smiled at Mali and set the bags inside the door. With a half bow, he exited the room. No words were exchanged.

Jake closed the door and watched Mali walk over to her bag. She placed it on the bed, unzipped it and shook out the dresses one by one. She pointed to a dresser and the closet and both spent the next few minutes unpacking their things. They took turns freshening up and changing in the bathroom and it wasn't long before they headed downstairs for the evening meal.

"You look lovely, Mali," Jake said, placing his hand on the small of her back as they left the room. Dressed in an Oscar de la Renta black and white floral jacquard knit cardigan dress with matching bolero jacket and four-inch black patent leather stiletto pumps with red soles (Louboutins were her favorite shoes), Mali was the epitome of a high society miss. Her auburn locks were pinned up in a loose bun with a few escaping tendrils.

Mali thanked him and added, "You don't look so bad yourself." *Boy, is that an understatement.* She admired his dark gray pinstriped suit, black silk shirt, and gray and black tie.

The scene as they walked into the formal living room was one of studied elegance and manners. Mali's mother was sitting on the sofa with her oldest sister, Rose, who was smoking her favored vanilla clove cigarettes, the sweet scent permeating the air. Her other sister, Lilly, was sitting on the chair across from the sofa and coffee table. She sat up straighter and her smile widened when she spotted Jake. The men were standing at the fireplace mantle with drinks in their hands, bourbon for her father and whiskey for her brothers-in-law, if their tastes had not changed since the last time Mali was home.

The chatter in the room slowly stopped at the arrival of Mali and Jake. With a tight smile, Mali ushered Jake into the room and made the introductions. She did not hug her sisters or touch her sisters' husbands and briefly leaned in to kiss her father on the cheek.

After Mali and Jake were seated in the love seat next to the sofa, Rose took a drag from her cigarette, blowing the smoke out through her nose. Her eyes narrowed. Inspecting Jake, she said somewhat disdainfully, "Mother says you are an employee of the FBI like our dear sister." Rose had never worked a day in her life and would never consider working. She was the carbon copy of their mother in her delicate looks, her mannerisms, always dressing right, knowing her duty.

"That's right. Mali and I are working together on a case right now."

"How dreadfully boring," Rose responded with a sniff.

"Rose, don't be rude, at least not so early into the weekend," Mali said, which earned her a glare from Rose. "And you're three months pregnant, you shouldn't be smoking."

Rose looked at her sister and deliberately took a deep drag of her cigarette blowing the sweet-smelling smoke toward her. "They are clove cigarettes and I've cut way back."

Darren, Rose's husband, walked over to her and leaned down to whisper something in her ear, after which Rose snuffed out the cigarette in the ashtray on the coffee table and excused herself to go check on their five-year-old son.

Lilly had not spoken a word since they entered the room. Nicknamed Minney because of her quiet demeanor, a phrase often used when referring to her was 'Quiet as a mouse.' Moving to the side of the sofa closest to the love seat, Lily leaned toward Jake. "Don't mind Rose. She can be a bitch when she sets her mind to it. The bitchiness come out strongest when she's pregnant. You should have seen her when she was pregnant with Scott. Whew!" Placing her hand on his arm, her voice got softer as she leaned in closer. "I bet your life is so exciting. Mali is lucky to be working with you."

Extracting his arm from her hand, Jake said, "There's not a lot of glamour in what we do, just hard work."

"Oh, you're being modest I'm sure. You obviously work out."

"Lilly, come here please." Robert, Lilly's husband, requested although it was more of an order. Lilly immediately stood up and walked over to him. He pulled her close and kissed her on her brow, murmuring softly in her ear.

Mali's father ambled toward them. Charles Hooper was a big man in his late fifties. His slight paunch was managed by his belt and his effort to hold in his stomach. Exercising was not something Charles Hooper deigned to do. He kept his red hair cropped close, and the graying at his temples made him appear distinguished. Her auburn tresses came from her father's side of the family. He wore a trimmed goatee, mostly gray now with a trace of red in it, and he was all business, wearing suits all the time. Charles Hooper was very good at making money and was happiest when he was doing just that.

Jake stood and stepped toward him. Her father had run a background check on him, as he did on anyone who was in his daughters' lives.

"How long have you been in the FBI, Jake?" Charles asked.

"Three years."

"And before the FBI?"

"I served in the military for fifteen years."

"I've always appreciated the work of our military. What branch, Jake?"

"The Army, sir."

Willow had been silently listening to the exchange between her husband and Jake. "Do you have any children, Jacob?"

Jake looked at her, his face softening. "Yes, I have one daughter, Heather. She's six years old and lives with my dad and me."

"Where's her mother? Why isn't she living with you?"

"Mother!" Mali exclaimed.

"It's a natural question darling." Her eyes never left Jake.

Jake's demeanor changed. His facial muscles tightened, all softness gone. "My wife passed away a little more than three years ago."

Mali opened her mouth to intercede when the butler entered and announced dinner. The conversation ended as the group followed Willow and Charles into the dining room.

Three hours later, Jake and an exhausted Mali returned to the bedroom. Jake closed the door, leaned against it, and watched Mali, who stepped out of her stilettos and sat down wearily on the bed.

"Boy, I bet you're glad you came." She laughed and pulled the pins out of her hair, running her fingers through it. Glancing over at Jake, she shook her head. "I'm so sorry, Jake. My family is my family and I love them, well, most of the time. They love me in their own way despite the fact that I did not follow the path they chose for me." She took a deep breath and let it out slowly.

"I'm glad you didn't follow in their footsteps, Mali."

Sighing, Mali stood and pointed to the bathroom, raising her eyebrows in a silent question.

"Go ahead. I need to call Heather before it gets any later. She'll want all the news of the day." Walking over to the bay window, Jake pulled out his phone.

Pausing at the door of the bathroom, she looked back at Jake. "Jake?"

He glanced up from the phone.

"Thanks for being here."

CHAPTER TWELVE

The Alamo, San Antonio
Saturday, April 11, 5:45 p.m.

THE STREETS SURROUNDING the Alamo were bustling. The Alamo, where Davy Crockett and others died in the Battle of the Alamo, was in downtown San Antonio, Texas. Surrounded by tall buildings, hotels, and a vertical shopping mall that was five stories high, it was hard to imagine the Alamo in 1836, with nothing but plains and rolling hills as far as the eye could see.

Birds were chirping their pleasure of the sunny and mild evening. Spring was in the air. Cars drove by, some folks were heading home after a day of work while others were coming into the city for an evening on the Riverwalk. Three young men were jogging on the sidewalk across the street from the Alamo. A few twenty-somethings whizzed by on electric scooters.

An older woman in her late sixties with short, silver, frizzy hair, clearly not in the best of shape, was sitting on the ground with her back against the Alamo's wall.

She was resting and trying to calm herself. No passersby looked at her. No one noticed her. She wore a faded oversized floral print dress. Her bare feet were bruised and scraped, and one heel bled from a piece of glass she had stepped on awhile back. Her head hurt and a thin trail of dried blood dribbled from just behind her ear, down her neck and beneath her dress.

She was not sure how this had happened to her. A few days ago, she was a retired accountant who volunteered her services at the missionary downtown. She and her husband of fifty-one years had lived in San Antonio for the past twenty-five. Meeting at a museum—she loved history and he was an artist—theirs was a whirlwind courtship. While they never had children and the romance had long since faded, it was a solid union and she was where she expected to be. If she felt lonely at times, so be it. Life was good overall.

Until it wasn't anymore.

On her early morning walk with Coco, her miniature schnauzer, she was on Babcock Road following the same two mile route that she walked every day. A dark, windowless van had pulled up alongside her. Two men jumped out of the back and pulled her and Coco inside. It had happened so fast. Coco yelped when they grabbed him and continued to bark furiously, wiggling and trying to bite the man holding him. The woman watched in horror as the man in the front passenger seat turned and snatched Coco, rolled down his window, and tossed him out. She screamed just before feeling the sting of a needle in her arm.

When she awoke, God knows how many hours later, she was lying on the floor of a grungy, dark room. The room was small and a wooden chair and fold-out card table were the sole pieces of furniture. A tiny dirt-encrusted window next to the door offered minimal light. Everything was covered in dust, including the floor. Her nostrils flared and her eyes teared with the strong musty odor permeating the room, not to mention the stench from an unidentifiable smell.

Dressed only in her underwear, she sat up and rested her back against the wall. She wrapped her arms around her bent knees and laid her head on her arms. She sobbed for the loss of her fur-baby and for what was happening to her, before finally realizing that her ear hurt like the devil. She stopped crying and moved her hand to her ear to inspect. When she brought her hand down there was blood on her fingers.

She looked over at the table and noticed a dress, note, and picture lying on top. She cautiously stood and hobbled to it, still feeling woozy. After reading the note and staring at the picture, she had slipped the dress over her head being careful not to touch her ear. She picked up the picture one more time, raising her hand to her mouth and kissing her fingers before tenderly placing her fingers on the face of her husband in the photo, his smiling face burned into her memory. Without further hesitation, she turned and shuffled out of the room, the picture floating to the ground behind her.

She had been on the run now for a few hours. It had taken her awhile to get her bearings and recognize her surroundings. Once she did, she had made her way to the Alamo and downtown. She felt safer near people. She barked out a laugh that approached hysteria, realizing that it didn't matter how many people were close to her. No one would help her. No one could help her. The note said she couldn't talk to anyone or ask anybody for help, or they would kill her. She considered trying to find some way to communicate without saying anything but shrugged the idea away.

Knowing she couldn't sit for long, she slowly inched her way up to a standing position, using the wall of the Alamo for balance. When she was confident that her legs could hold her, she pushed herself away from the wall and staggered toward the Riverwalk.

She was halfway across the street when a police car approached the intersection. She put her head down and kept walking, trying to be invisible.

"Ma'am, are you all right?"

She began to shake uncontrollably. Wiping her clammy hands on her dress, she looked toward the car and the police officer, who was leaning out his window to ask her the question.

"Ma'am, are you all right?" the officer asked again, concern in his voice.

She licked her lips, her trembling mouth drier than cotton. "I . . . I . . ." Without another word, she turned and bolted down the street in the opposite direction. Her movements were jerky as she raced for the stairs leading down to the Riverwalk, the pain in her feet forgotten as she focused on escape. The tires of the cruiser crunched on gravel by the side of the road. They were stopping. Pushing people out of her way, panic took hold and she stumbled down the stairs. She couldn't let the police question her.

When she reached the bottom and rushed down the path alongside the river, a wave of dizziness engulfed her. She lurched around the corner then fell to her knees as nausea slammed into her. A few tourists glanced at her, some in disgust, others in curiosity, but no one stopped to help. Leaning over, she puked repeatedly, the force of it racking her body. Her heart was pounding in her chest as she gasped for air. Sinking further down, her body convulsed and she slumped over into her vomit. She was dead in minutes.

The assassin moved in quickly, a protective mask covering his face. Ignoring the onlookers' gasps, he turned the woman onto her side and wasted no time removing the implant and placing a card on her unmoving chest. The number five was scribbled on the back of the card. No time to retrieve the Go-Pro camera. No time for a video. He raced down the riverwalk as the police rounded the corner and located the woman.

A short time later, a picture was posted on YouTube with the caption, '#anotheronebitesthedust #HuntedLives.' In the picture, the woman was lying on her side, white foam sliding down from her mouth, her wrinkled hands gripping her waist, curled in the fetal position. And in the distance, a man dressed in black ran away from the scene.

* * *

Hunter's Gaming Room, New York
Saturday, April 11, 9:00 p.m. EST

"I HAD NO choice, Tony. The broad was going to talk."

CEO of Lakeway Technologies, Ted Springs, had been trying to convince Anthony to sell the patent and rights to his GPS and satellite technology for two years. His company, a Fortune 500 technology company specializing in products for everything from automobiles to the movie industry, could capitalize on that technology beyond gaming, and Anthony enjoyed playing on Ted's greed and desperation. He knew that Ted had big plans for his company and needed Hunter's technology for those plans to come to fruition.

He was Anthony's first player and had been thrilled beyond expectation when the bolt slammed into the target in New York. Ted had been looking forward to playing a second game ever since. The $500,000 fee was inconsequential to him the first time and especially this time. However, the game did not go well. They were only a few hours into it when Ted released the cyanide. The woman would have talked to the police, that was a given. Releasing it was the only viable option.

Anthony watched Ted wring his hands repeatedly and wipe them on his pants. Sweat was dripping down the side of his face, past his jowls, and down his neck beneath his shirt even though the room was a cool seventy degrees. It gave Anthony great satisfaction knowing that Ted was worried that the truncated game might affect their business negotiations.

"Ted, you're right. She was not the right selection for the game, did not have the stamina. My bad. The next target is yours at half price if you want. You can pick the location and the weapon, of course." Ted's shoulders slumped in relief. Anthony finished his drink and set it on the bar, smiling inwardly.

"I appreciate that. I'd prefer a male target. And can the game take place in D.C.? I've always loved our Capital."

"Of course, Ted. Whatever you want."

"And I want to continue our discussions on the sale of your GPS/satellite patent when we meet for the next round."

"The perfect time. I look forward to it." Anthony patted Ted on the back and escorted him to the elevator. "We'll need to wait awhile before the next game. I'll be in touch when we're ready to go."

"Sure, Tony, sure."

They shook hands and Ted stepped into the elevator with Janet, who had entered the room as soon as Anthony texted her that the game was over.

Anthony had been playing that conversation in his mind ever since the game ended, getting more and more irritated as the evening progressed. By unspoken agreement, after escorting Ted out of the office, Janet would order their favorite Chinese take-out to bring to the game room.

While he waited for her, Anthony went to the wet bar and tossed down a few doubles. He was working on his fourth when Janet came in with the food.

They both sat at the bar and ate, not talking about the game.

After finishing, Anthony poured himself another double and sipped it as he stared at the blank screen.

Janet reached for his glass and finished his drink before pouring him another. She lit a cigarette and leaned back on the bar stool, inhaling deeply and making O's as she exhaled the smoke through her mouth.

"What a mess!" she said, tapping her lacquered nails on the bar. Click-click-click-click.

"I've never liked being called Tony."

That's your take-away, Anthony?"

Frustrated, Anthony sighed, stood up and paced back and forth. "Of course not. What else can I say though? Ted was right. She would have talked had the police caught up to her. It never occurred to me that we'd have to actually release the cyanide as a means to end the game though." He slumped into one of the recliners, his face crestfallen.

Crushing her cigarette in the ashtray, Janet stood up and walked over to him. She sat sideways on his lap and nuzzled his neck. "Darling, we knew that was a risk. That's why we put the cyanide in the implant. And she didn't suffer long. How is that any different than the assassin killing her?" She shifted against him and smiled. "You're right that we'll have to wait awhile before the next game. The FBI will no doubt jump all over this."

Forgetting about the game, Anthony held her close and moved against her with increasing ardor. He pulled her head down to kiss her hard, grinding his teeth against her mouth and shoving his tongue down her throat.

"You need to see something," she said once her mouth was released.

"Sounds good to me." His voice was rough with passion.

"Anthony," this said with some exasperation. Pushing away, she moved to the recliner next to Anthony and picked up the remote. "When I was upstairs waiting on the food, I checked a few social media sites." She opened the browser on the big screen and navigated on the internet to Twitter and '#HuntedLives'.

She scrolled through the comments.

"I was right there when it happened. Awesome!"

"I wish the assassin wasn't wearing the mask. He's in awesome shape. I'd love to see his face."

"The Riverwalk looks like a pretty place."

"She was too old to play the game. What were they thinking?"

"I haven't played The Hunted Ones in a long time. I need to pull my Xbox out and play a few rounds."

"I'm going to buy the game tonight and learn how to play. It looks like fun!"

"There's no live stream from the assassin. What's up with that?"

"Yeah, and there's no video either. What's going on?"

The comments went on and on. A picture of the

dead woman was also posted, not from the assassin but from a by-stander.

"This was also posted on Facebook. The game is growing, Anthony. People are clamoring for more. And they want your baby to play at home. Your vision is becoming a reality. But we need to be careful and we need to plan how we're going to respond to the FBI when they visit us again."

Elated, he jumped up and pulled her up to stand with him, wrapping her in a bear hug and swinging her in a circle. He laughed out loud. "What would I do without you, Janet? You've always been there for me. No one understands me the way you do. You're my rock." Setting her down, he nuzzled her neck and nipped her earlobe, pulling her close. She tasted like a combination of whiskey and cigarettes when he kissed her, an aphrodisiac to him because it was her. He rocked against her with growing passion.

"We don't have to be anywhere for a while," he gritted out, walking her backward until she bumped into the back of the recliner. Spinning her around so she faced away from him, he folded her over the recliner chair in front of them. "I've waited all my life for this. Don't deny me now, Janie." He reached for the remote and turned on the recording of the Chicago game, his favorite thus far. He hit play and tossed the remote onto the chair. Throwing up her skirt and yanking her underwear down, his left hand molested her breast while his right unzipped his pants, all while slobbering kisses on her neck. He slammed into her from the rear and watched the game, grunting and pumping with more urgency as the assassin moved in for the kill. The blood spurting on the mirror pushed him over the edge.

Her reluctant submission, fury, and calculating eyes as she watched the game were lost on him.

When he finished, Anthony sank to the chair behind him, eyes closed, pants still circling his ankles, and breathing heavily. "I finally know," he mumbled.

Hearing a noise, he opened his eyes and frowned as he observed Janet pulling her underwear up and yanking down her skirt as she rushed to the elevator, the doors swooshing closed behind her.

CHAPTER THIRTEEN

Mali's Family Home, Philadelphia
Saturday, April 11, 7:30 p.m.

THE PARTY WAS in full swing. Most of the guests were in the massive living room enjoying the classical music being played by a string quartet on loan from the Philharmonic Symphony. The Hoopers were major donors of the symphony, borrowing a string quartet was one of the perks.

The living room was old school with dark wood flooring, wood paneling surrounding the windows, and an ornate coffered wood ceiling. The wall facing the expansive backyard was lined with picture windows that offered unfettered views of the gardens and pool, and allowed plenty of light in during the day. In the evenings, the wrought iron lamps placed strategically around the room inspired intimacy and coziness. The main focal point of the room was the fireplace, one of five in the house, which had a unique wood mantle exquisitely highlighting a hand-carved scene of the Philadelphia harbor in the late eighteen hundreds with multiple schooners as well as people walking on the docks.

Charles Hooper was standing next to the mantle, holding court with his cronies. Impeccably dressed with whiskey in one hand and a cigar in the other, Mali's father was the epitome of a wealthy and respected businessman. His booming laughter bounced off the walls and he occasionally shook the hand of a colleague or friend who passed by to say hello.

As the living room filled with the two hundred plus who's who of guests, many flowed naturally into the adjoining state dining room, which was similar in look and decor to the living room. The table's chairs had been removed and mountains of food covered the table. From shrimp cocktail to various cheeses and fruits, and a huge array of meats like duck, pheasant, pork, and beef, there was something for every discerning palate. At the far end of the dining room, a bar had been set up with only the finest liquors and French wines and there were waiters in black suits walking through the house with trays of hors d'oeuvres and glasses of champagne.

Some hearty souls were braving the cool evening and enjoying the patio in back, enticed by the fresh air and clear sky. There were multiple pub tables, each with its own patio heater, and guests were clustered by them, talking and laughing. The patio was favored by many because of the beautiful view of their pool and Willow's award-winning gardens beyond strategically lit with yellow and green lights to beckon the garden lover in for a walk. A second bar was set up outside, equally stocked with only the best libations, and a piano was situated in the middle of the patio, soft jazz whispering from the black and white keys.

Inside, Willow Hooper was stunning in an off-the-shoulder pale yellow gown that shimmered with every step she took. She glided from guest to guest, briefly stopping to chat with each one, ensuring that everyone had exactly what they needed. All smiles, she was in her element, the perfect hostess, the perfect wife.

The Hoopers always threw the best parties.

* * *

"You look beautiful," Jake said, turning from the window as Mali walked out of the bathroom. She wore a Chanel vintage sleeveless cocktail dress, teal green as her mother had requested, with a black lace overlay on the full skirt.

"Thank you." Mali walked to the bed, sat down, and stepped into her Valentino black glittery pumps, topped with a svelte, grommet-detailed wraparound ankle strap. Standing up, she moved to the dresser and added a double strand pearl necklace around her neck with pearl drop earrings in her ears. Her auburn hair was pulled back into a loose ponytail tied with a teal green ribbon, simple yet elegant.

Picking up something from the dresser, she walked over to Jake, who still stood by the window, hands in his pockets.

"You look great yourself. Would you be insulted if I

gave you this tie to wear?" She held up a teal green silk tie that matched her dress. "You don't have to say yes."

His cheeks dimpled. He untied his black tie, removed it, and traded it for hers. Moving to the mirror, he knotted the tie then stared at her through the mirror.

The sound of Tchaikovsky's Symphony Number Six floated up the stairs as they stared at each other.

"Do I pass muster?"

Do you ever. "You'll do." Mali turned to leave the room, releasing the breath she was holding.

Heat rose on her cheeks and she tried to control her breathing as Jake placed his hand on her lower back and escorted her out of the room. They proceeded downstairs, the noise of the crowd increasing with each step they took.

Over the next thirty minutes, Mali and Jake weaved throughout the room, Mali greeting the guests as if they were old friends and introducing Jake to everyone. She had transformed into the daughter she was expected to be.

Jake grabbed two glasses of champagne from a passing waiter and handed one to Mali. As they stepped out onto the patio, her mother called out, "Jasmine darling! Come here and say hello to David."

Cringing, Mali glanced at Jake and rolled her eyes as they turned and walked over to her mother.

"Jaz, it's good to see you," David said, leaning in to kiss her cheek. Impeccably dressed, David stood over six feet tall and, with his sandy brown hair and blue eyes, had always been in high demand with the ladies. 'Charming' is how they described him. 'Snake' was Mali's preferred description. And she did not care for the abbreviation of her name, especially by him.

"Hello David. I'd like to introduce you to Jacob Black. Jake, David Anderson." They shook hands as Willow stepped between Mali and Jake, effectively moving Mali closer to David.

"Jasmine, I'm going to steal Jake to introduce him to the Mayor. We won't be long." With that, Willow whisked Jake away.

Can you be more obvious, Mother? Mali sighed and took a sip of her champagne.

"Your mother tells me you're still in New York. Not tired of it yet?"

"No, David. I love the city and I love my work with the FBI." She changed the subject. "How is Tammy?"

She detected a momentary flash of irritation in his eyes. His lips pressed tight in a grimace. "Alas, Tammy and I divorced six months ago. We just sadly grew apart." He took her hand in his. "Perhaps we can get together for a drink while you're in town and catch up."

Mali shook her head and pulled her hand out of his. "Would you excuse me please? I need to find Jake and ask him a question." Without waiting for a reply, she turned and walked over to Jake, who was engrossed in a conversation about the military with the Mayor.

They were interrupted when Charles called all of the guests into the living room. It was time for a toast.

Willow joined her husband at the fireplace and Mali

and her sisters moved to stand beside their mother, in birth order. Champagne was handed to all of the guests.

When everyone quieted down, Charles boomed, "I want to thank all of you, our closest friends and family, for joining my wife and I in celebrating our fortieth anniversary." He picked up Willow's hand and kissed the back of it before placing it in the crook of his arm. "We have been blessed over the years, blessed to have three beautiful daughters, a thriving business, and great friends and business associates. For me, personally, I am grateful for this beautiful woman standing next to me. She has been my rock, my staunchest supporter and partner, and I am a lucky man. To Willow." Charles raised his glass.

"To Willow!" "Happy Anniversary" and other accolades were touted as glasses clinked together and the chatter resumed.

Willow and Charles toasted each other and drank to their anniversary then Charles excused himself. He weaved among some guests, chatting with a few here and there before stopping by a young brunette in a svelte black dress. He leaned down and whispered something in her ear then, after she nodded, he left the room.

Willow and her daughters watched the encounter.

"Why do you allow his whore into this house, Mother?" Rose hissed.

"Now is not the time, Rose," Willow said, as she observed the brunette eventually stand up and follow Charles out of the room. "If you'll excuse me, I have to check on our guests on the patio." She walked away leaving Rose, Lilly, and Mali standing at the fireplace.

"How can our father behave that way, and on his anniversary!?!" Lilly asked no one in particular.

"He's a man. What do you expect?" Rose retorted.

"You can't lump all men in with our father. Some are honorable," Mali said.

"Really?" scoffed Rose. "After Daniel and his best friends' wife? Even after all the e-mails you found, you still didn't believe he was cheating on you until you found him in your shower going at it with her."

"Quit being so crass, Rose," this from Lilly.

""It's true. Despite the scandal you caused when you divorced him and the effort it took Father to make it go away, Mother and Father were actually relieved that your marriage ended just after a few months. You're looking for Prince Charming among a sea of barbarians, Jasmine, and they just don't exist."

Mali ignored her as she perused the room. Spotting Jake, she excused herself and walked over to him. Through unspoken agreement, they made their way to the patio and some fresh air.

Mali inhaled deeply. "I needed this." She leaned on the rail and looked out toward the pool and beyond. "Would you like to walk through the gardens?"

Without saying a word, Jake took her hand. They ambled down the stairs, past the pool, and into the gardens. Jake offered his arm as Mali slipped off her heels at the entrance and continued barefoot on the grassy path. The soft crunch of ice beginning to form on the grass tickled Mali's bare feet. Meandering through the maze of hedges and jasmine, rosemary, roses, and gardenias, Mali took another deep breath to relax. The garden had that effect on her. She was at peace here.

They didn't speak for a while, both enjoying the quiet as the cacophony of noise from the party faded.

"I've always loved these gardens. While I was growing up, if things got crazy, I could always disappear in here." Mali sat down on a bench. "I would bring a book or my journal to write in and sit on this bench for hours. No one would bother me."

"It's serene, peaceful." Jake looked around, lowering himself next to her. "Were you lonely growing up?"

She shook her head. "Not really. I had my sisters but we didn't view the world in the same way. Out here, I could dream and plan my future without thinking of my parents' expectations. Lilly and Rose were content going along with their plans. It was important to them to get along."

"Do I detect a bit of defiance?" Jake teased.

Mali laughed. "Maybe a little. I'm sure my parents wondered how they ended up with me."

"You found your own destiny. I'm sure they're proud of that on some level."

They sat in companionable silence. No guests had traveled this far into the gardens. They were in their own world and the silence enveloped them.

Mali shivered, the cold from her icy feet having traveled up her body. There were goosebumps on her arms and she absently rubbed them. Standing up, Jake removed his jacket as Mali said, "We should probably head back."

He wrapped his jacket around her shoulders as she stood and closed it in front, cocooning her in its warmth. He held on to the jacket with both hands, effectively trapping her.

Her breath caught and she froze, gazing up at him. "T-t-thank you."

Jake was studying her. He reached out with one hand and ran his finger down the side of her face, moving his thumb over her mouth before cupping her cheek in his hand. There was a warmth inside her that had nothing to do with the jacket around her shoulders. Looking directly into her eyes, he lowered his head. His lips brushed hers then pulled back, and he waited, still searching the depths of her eyes.

Mali's heart was racing, her breathing rapid and shallow. She swallowed hard before stepping into his arms. Placing her hand on his neck, she pulled his head back down for another kiss. Mali savored his mouth on hers, and trembled at the gentleness of the kiss.

Still holding the jacket with one hand, he placed his other hand on her lower back and pulled her in close as he moved his mouth across her cheek to her ear then down to her throat. Mali tipped her head back and gazed at the stars, half-expecting vibrant color and lightning to explode across the sky. Beneath her hand, now on Jake's chest, his heart beat to the same tune as hers. Mali lowered her head and gazed at Jake as he cupped her head in both hands.

They were lost in each other's eyes when Jakes' phone vibrated. He opened the jacket and reached inside to pull out the phone. Mali turned to gather herself and give him some privacy.

"Where?" A pause then, "When? Are you sure it's the same M.O.?"

Mali looked over her shoulder at Jake.

"Fifteen minutes. Book us on the next flight from Philadelphia to San Antonio. We'll leave as soon as possible after the conference call."

"There's been another murder?"

"An older woman. Cyanide. We're video conferencing with Frank, Kirsten, and Joe in fifteen minutes."

As they left the garden, Mali paused to don her shoes and return Jake's jacket to him. Inside, Mali observed her sisters talking with their husbands and other guests but there was no sign of her mother or her father. It was after nine and the party would continue for hours. Willow would not be pleased that Mali and Jake left the party so early but there was nothing she could do about it.

They were entering the foyer when the brunette her father had spoken with walked out of the library, smiling as she sauntered past Mali and Jake. They were halfway up the stairs when the library door opened and her father appeared.

"You're not leaving the party, are you? Your mother will not be pleased."

"Yes, and I'm sorry about that. There's been an emergency. Jake and I have a conference call in a few minutes and we're leaving as soon as possible to fly to Texas. Good night, Father. Happy Anniversary."

CHAPTER FOURTEEN

FBI Field Office, San Antonio, Texas
Sunday, April 12, 6:30 a.m.

MALI AND JAKE left her parent's home at six in the morning to catch their flight to San Antonio. No one arose to say goodbye.

From their conference call last night, they learned that the victims' name was Maria Lupita Stone, age sixty-nine, married to her husband, Robert Stone, for fifty-one years. She died by apparent cyanide. There was a jagged cut above her ear. No other injuries were found. Her body was sent to the local medical examiner for an autopsy, with a request to rush the official results.

They were met at the airport by local agents who drove them straight to the police precinct to meet with the officers who found her.

The officers explained what happened and indicated that when they came upon her, she was already dead, and there was a strong scent of almonds, leading them to suspect that chemicals were involved. They secured the area on the Riverwalk and waited for the medical examiner to arrive. Once onsite, the medical examiner discovered a cut above her ear, same as the other victims, although the cut was not made with any kind of precision. It was jagged and rough, made in a great hurry. The odor was coming from the cut and the M.E. suspected cyanide but would have to confirm it. No other visible injury.

'Two other things," Officer Hamm said. "We found this card on her chest." The card featured the silhouette of San Antonio and the Alamo in the background with a rifle in the forefront. Turning it over, the number five was scribbled on the back. "The second item we found was a small camera sewn into the top of her dress."

After a late lunch, Mali and Jake were sitting in a conference room at the FBI Headquarters on University Heights Boulevard, discussing their findings with Frank, Kirsten, and Joe back in New York via a video call.

"The medical examiner's preliminary results confirm that Mrs. Stone died of cyanide." Jake said.

"And this is the same M.O., it's the game?" Frank asked.

"Yes. The victim had the same cut behind the ear and a calling card was left on her chest," Jake confirmed.

Mali interjected with, "The difference is that she died by cyanide."

"The first victim, our John Doe, died by cyanide too," Kirsten offered.

"That's true," Frank agreed. "However, if your hypothesis is correct that the first two victims were tests for the real-life game, how does Mrs. Stone's death correlate?"

"Exactly my point, Frank." Mali said. "Something went wrong."

"Why do you say that, Hoop?"

"All other victims with the calling cards died by the weapon on the card. The weapon on this card was a rifle. I believe Mrs. Stone was supposed to die by a shot from a rifle. And consider the cut above her ear, even the number scribbled on the back. Both were obviously done in haste. The assassin was in a hurry to extract that device and get away from the scene."

Jake nodded his head. "I agree with Hoop. Looking at the other victims, all had a hole in the clothing they were wearing near the top. It stands to reason that all victims had a camera sewn into their clothing that the killer extracted. He obviously did not have time in this case."

"So someone watches the target's moves?" Kirsten asked.

"Have videos from any of the target's perspective ever surfaced on any social media sites?" Jake asked. At everyone's negative response, he continued, "Joe, after the meeting, have Amy and Brad work on this. If any exist, they might shed additional light on how the game is being played."

Joe, who was sitting off camera, said, "Will do."

"Has a video from this latest murder shown up anywhere yet?" asked Jake.

Kirsten shook her head.

Mali responded. "If the killer was supposed to take her out by a rifle shot and something went wrong, he may not have had his camera on."

Joe, who had been quietly working on his computer during the conversation, popped into view and said, "I haven't found a video by the killer on YouTube or Twitter. I'm running a quick program to check other social media outlets. I have run across a series of tweets, however, by bystanders." He stopped to look at Frank. "And there's a picture." Joe sat back down. Frank and Kirsten moved to stand behind him so they could look at the comments and image on his computer as he told Mali that she'd find it on #HuntedLives on Twitter.

They read the comments in growing disbelief.

"How can people be so callous? A woman is killed in front of them and they're upset because there's no video?" exclaimed Kirsten.

"Joe, take a copy of the picture for analysis. We won't be able to get a facial recognition on the assassin because he's running away and wearing a mask, from what the bystanders have said. Kirsten, make sure all of this is saved then contact Twitter and have them take it down." After giving those instructions while sifting through the comments, Jake added, "There's a reference to #anotheronebitesthedust. Can we look at that?"

Mali and Joe each navigated to that location on Twitter and there was a collective gasp from everyone.

Two more pictures of the victim were on the feed, each from different angles. One was a close up of her face. The look of pure agony was heartbreaking. The second picture was from across the water just before her death. She was on her hands and knees vomiting. There were a handful of people standing nearby but no one was helping her.

And the comments.

"Hey, another one bites the dust. Cool!"

"She's a frumpy old hag. Where did they get her?"

"I can't believe my good fortune to be here when it happened!! It's like the front seat at a rock concert!"

"Why is foam coming out of her mouth?"

"How did she die?"

"Who cares how she died, if she's even dead at all. For all we know, this is live theater at its best. This is entertainment!"

"I need to bring my friends here and show them where it happened."

"Did anyone get a look at the assassin?"

"No, but a few people blocked the cop who tried to chase after him."

"When's the next game? I'll go play at home but it won't be the same."

There were hundreds of comments. Mali was stunned. *How can they be so uncaring about this murder? They were more interested in posting what they were seeing than helping her.*

"Just found a video. It's not from the assassin," said Joe. The video began by panning the Riverwalk. The tourist was commenting on how thrilled he was to finally be in San Antonio. It stopped moving when it reached the victim puking on the ground. Initially assuming that she must be drunk, he questioned out loud what was going on until she fell on her side and foam dripped from her mouth. There was a noticeable change of tone in his voice when the assassin ran to the victim. He guessed what was going on and his excitement about being there was unmistakable. The video ended with the tourist saying that if his vacation ended right now, he would go home a happy camper because of the game he just witnessed.

Silence from everyone after the video ended.

Finally, Kirsten stated, "I've captured all this information and will contact Twitter to remove both series of tweets."

"Thank you, Kirsten." Jake replied. "Joe, track down the owner of this video."

With a heavy sigh, Frank said, "I've set up a press conference for two o'clock tomorrow afternoon so I need you both back here by noon. I've kept the Assistant Director informed throughout this case but I want you to brief him at one o'clock, Jake, to bring him up to speed. Hoop, prepare a statement for him to make. The AD will open the press conference then hand it over to me for questions and answers. With this latest, and very public death, it's time to inform the public of the serial killer and the game."

* * *

Press Room, FBI Field Office, New York City
Monday, April 13, 2:05 p.m.

FORTY REPORTERS WERE gathered in the press room of the FBI Field Office on a mild spring day and all eyes were trained on the two men who walked into the room and proceeded to the front. The mood was somber.

A tall, stately man stepped up to the podium. "Thank you all for coming here today. My name is Ben Casey and I am the Assistant Director in Charge of the FBI New York office. I will make a brief statement then our team will take some questions." He looked around the room before continuing. "The FBI is investigating a series of murders that have taken place across multiple states over the past six weeks. Two additional murders occurred two years ago that we surmise are related. These serial killings are unusual in that different weapons were used for each murder. In addition, the victims have no connection to each other. Most disturbing, the murders appear to copy a computer app game called The Hunted Ones. Social Media is exploding with videos and comments about each murder which are being removed as we find them. We ask the public to consider the families of those lost and refrain from commenting on the various social media outlets. While we continue to investigate and follow up on all leads, we are far from solving this case. We ask the public to contact the FBI at huntedlivestips.fbi.gov or 1-800-fed-9999 with any information you may have on this case, no matter how insignificant it might seem. I want to thank the local FBI offices and police agencies in the affected states for their continued assistance. We will work diligently to find the killer or killers and bring them to justice. Thank you."

Hands were quickly raised and there was a chorus of "Director Casey" from the reporters.

"Gentlemen, Ladies, we will get to your questions momentarily. I have asked Frank Grant, Special Agent in Charge, to answer your questions. Frank?" Ben Casey turned toward Frank and gestured him forward to the podium.

Frank pointed to a reporter in the first row.

"Special Agent Grant, my name is Kim White, WABC. Can you tell us what weapons have been used and, if the weapons were different for each murder, how can they be related, especially since they occurred in multiple states?"

"Kim, the weapons used were a crossbow, a Glock 43, a Laplander folding saw, and cyanide. Even though different weapons were used, there are commonalities between the murders that irrefutably tie them together. Since the investigation is on-going, I am unable to discuss the details at this time." He glanced at the reporters and pointed to a young man a few rows back.

"John Spencer with the Associated Press. Where did the murders take place and why do you think the murders are copying The Hunted Ones?"

"The murders occurred here in New York City as well as San Francisco, Chicago, and San Antonio. There are certain elements of the game that are being used in these murders. Again, I cannot go into much detail." He nodded to an older journalist in the front.

"Grayson Shepherd, *New York Times*. Who are the victims? And did you say cyanide was used on one?"

"We'll release the names of the victims after we talk to the families about these developments, which is ongoing as we speak. And, yes, to your question about cyanide. I have time for one more question. Liz?" He pointed to a young woman sitting in a wheelchair to the side of the room.

"Liz Specter, *New York Daily News*. I watched a live stream video on an app called Periscope. The victim was in Chicago, if I recall correctly. Why didn't anyone help her? Who was doing the live stream? And why did it take so long to go public with these serial killings?"

"We are baffled as to why the victims are not seeking help. It's a mystery to us. As far as local police, there was no way they could have known that this was happening. Keep in mind that the Periscope live stream, and subsequent video in Chicago, was only about twelve minutes long. By the time we were made aware of it, eight or nine minutes had already passed. We contacted local police and gave them the location of the intended victim. Unfortunately, the victim was already dead when they arrived."

Frank paused to take a sip of water. All was quiet in the room. "The killer was running the live stream for reasons unknown at this time. And to answer your last question, Liz, this is a difficult case to investigate. There are a lot of moving parts and we needed to make sure of our facts before informing the public. Rest assured, the FBI is doing everything we can to track down this killer or killers and we appreciate the help of the agencies assisting in this investigation. Thank you."

Frank and the Assistant Director left the room to a barrage of questions.

* * *

Task Force Control Center
FBI Field Office, New York City

FOLLOWING THE PRESS conference, Jake gathered everyone for a meeting. Mali walked up to the white board and wrote down Maria Stone's information underneath that of the other victims and revised two process questions that now had answers.

Jake cleared his throat. "As you can see from Hoops' update to the white board, we have learned a little bit more about the killer's M.O. Jim Wells, ex-employee of Hunter Inc, told us that in the app game, the assassin or target, depending on who the player chooses to be, does not move unless instructed by the player. All games work this way, obviously. If the real game is being played like the app game, and considering the messages on the assassin's console that we've seen, then we can assume with a high degree of confidence that the assassin does not move or kill unless instructed by a player. In addition, we discovered that there is a Go-Pro camera sewn into the clothing of the targets, presumably to allow the player to watch the game from the target's point of view. It is our belief that the most recent victim did something to induce someone, the player or assassin perhaps, to release the cyanide early. In his or her haste to leave the scene, the assassin removed the device but forgot the camera."

Mali, standing at the white board, said, "Can I add something, Jake?" After his nod, she pointed to the question 'Why doesn't target seek help?' and read it out loud. "The police officers in San Antonio told us that they saw the victim on the street above the Riverwalk. They described her as being in pain, obviously scared of something or someone, and when they asked if she was all right, she bolted for the Riverwalk. She died minutes later. She had an opportunity to accept their help and didn't take it. Why? I assume that our victims are told that if they ask for help, the cyanide in the device implanted behind their ear will be released."

Jake nodded. "I agree with that assessment. Amy, Brad, continue checking social media outlets for any video from the perspective of the targets. If the player is watching for his own enjoyment and to ensure the target does as told, it stands to reason that you will not find any such videos online. Let's confirm that." Mali drew a line through that question and added 'Cyanide released if victim asks for help' in the Process section.

Turning to Kirsten and Joe, Jake asked, "Have you spoken with Jim Wells yet? And have you found the owner of that video of the San Antonio victim?"

"We were supposed to have our conference call this

morning at eleven but Wells was a no-show," Joe said. "We've tried contacting him on his cell with no luck yet."

Mali's eyes flew to Jake. "I'll contact Fred Smith at our Baltimore office and have him call Wells' employer and his wife."

Joe said, "With respect to the video, we tracked down the IP address to Bill Johnstone. He lives in Pittsburg and is in San Antonio on vacation. There is a Bill Johnstone currently staying at the Hyatt San Antonio."

"Good. We'll send local authorities to the hotel to have a conversation with him."

Kirsten raised her hand. "Jake? I have been playing the game non-stop since last Thursday and Joe has been analyzing the code. We have a few observations."

"Continue."

"In the game, the player selects a length of time to play, regardless of whether the player chooses to be the target or the assassin. If the player is the target, he wins if he stays alive for the duration of the game. If the player is the assassin, he wins if he kills the target before the game clock winds down. In the real game, the target is told he has a certain amount of time to 'play' and if he can make it that length of time, he'll live. It's impossible to determine if the intent is to ever let the target live but the target may believe he has a chance. Related to this, our assessment is that the number on the back of the card is how long it takes the assassin to kill each target."

"Great observations, you two, and I agree with your assessment. Continue to analyze the code, Joe, and send it to the lab in D.C. so they can assist and help expedite."

Mali drew a line through the question 'What does the number written on the back of the card represent?' as well as 'Can target ever win? If so, how?' and added two more process bullets '# on back of card = length of time to kill target' and 'Target wins if stays alive x # of hours.'

"Kirsten, research facilities that have both medical and technical branches capable of creating a device with cyanide and a remote-controlled release." Jake took a breath and looked at each team member, his eyes finally resting on Mali. He rubbed the back of his neck. "We've made good progress but there are still many questions that need answers and, more importantly, we have no solid leads on either the assassin or the players. There's no reason to suspect that the murders will stop and we have no way of identifying where the next one will occur. Let's get back to work."

Just after six o'clock, Mali hung up the phone and walked over to Jake. The rest of the team had left for the night.

"I just got off the phone with Fred Smith. Jim Wells did not report back to work last Friday afternoon after our meeting with him and they have not seen him since. No one is at home. It looks like they cleared out of there fast. Only the essentials were taken."

Jake stood, shaking his head. "Christ. He's either running because he's guilty or because he's afraid of someone. Or both. We need to find him."

CHAPTER FIFTEEN

FBI Field Office, New York City
Wednesday, April 15, 5:20 p.m.

"Good afternoon, Mali Hooper speaking."

"I didn't call you at a bad time, did I?"

"I'm headed to a meeting in a few minutes but I always have time for you, Sara. How are you all?"

"Everyone is doing well. Hey, I know you're busy so I'll keep this short. The kids have been asking when Auntie M is going to visit again. It's been a long time. How about coming over Friday after work? Spend the night, relax a bit, and we'll catch up."

"That sounds lovely, Sara. I would love to come over. Tell those munchkins I'll see them Friday evening and that they'd better be ready for a serious take-down in Twister."

"Oh, they'll love that, Mali! How are you doing? And how was your parents' anniversary?"

"I'm doing all right. Tired is all. I'll give you the

complete run down on the party this weekend. I've got to run for now."

"I understand. Just come over whenever on Friday. We'll see you when you get here."

"Perfect. Don't hold dinner for me." Mali paused. "I'm looking forward to seeing you, Sara."

Mali walked into Frank's office where he and Jake were already talking about the case. Mali sat down in the second chair in front of Frank's desk.

"Jake and I have been talking about the news media. Reports on the killings have been non-stop. Local stations as well as national media outlets are reporting that the FBI is moving too slowly and not doing enough to protect the public. It's turning into a firestorm and headquarters is not pleased. Where are we on the investigation?"

Jake leaned forward. "We have more insights into features of the app game that are being used in the real one."

"Go on."

"There is a time limit on the game. The player wins if the target is assassinated before the clock runs out. In addition, the number on the back of the card represents the time it takes to kill the target." Jake looked at Mali.

She continued, "The person of interest we spoke with in Baltimore, Jim Wells, was helpful and willing to hold a video conference with our team but they never connected. He has not been seen since last Friday."

"So he's either a suspect or in trouble."

Jake nodded. "That's correct. He's not using his credit

cards and left his phone at his house so we haven't been able to track him. Wells ditched their car at a bus station in Frederick, Maryland, but there's no evidence that he and his wife boarded any bus. We reviewed security footage. The car was parked in a location that the cameras did not cover and Wells did not go into the station. All bus and train stations, area ports, as well as the Baltimore and D.C. airports are on alert. Smaller airstrips are also being checked. We've covered all bases. If they try to leave the area via public transportation, we'll catch them."

"Do they own any other vehicles that they could be using?"

"His wife owns a red Toyota Corolla but it was still in their garage. We're checking car rental agencies but without using a credit card, it will take time."

Frank nodded. "Thank you for the information. Keep me posted."

Mali and Jake headed out of his office as Frank's phone rang. He picked it up, listened to the caller, then waved Mali and Jake back in.

"Anthony Hunter is giving an exclusive interview on ABC," he said as he picked up the remote and turned on the TV in his office.

Anthony Hunter was in his office with a reporter. ". . . and I am horrified that this serial killer is, in any way, being tied to my groundbreaking game, The Hunted Ones." Hunter was sitting on the sofa, the reporter on the chair next to it.

"And yet these killings are helping your stock."

Anthony stiffened, looked directly into the camera,

and snapped, "I don't appreciate the inference that my company is profiting from the tragedy of these deaths." He paused then looked back at the reporter. "The Hunted Ones is the most life-like game on the market, still the leading hunting game four years after its release. But it's just a game. What's happening across multiple states is real and tragic. It's horrific! Any short-term increase in my stock is purely coincidental."

"Were you aware of the buzz on the various social media outlets after each murder?"

"Yes. We found out after the Chicago murder."

"Have you spoken with the FBI at all?"

"Yes. They came to my office a couple of weeks ago. Actually, it was the FBI agents who told me about those awful comments being made. It's confusing and disheartening, I must say," Anthony muttered, looking visibly shaken. "Hunter Inc is fully cooperating with the FBI and will continue to do so until those responsible are caught. The agents appear to be competent and I am confident they will find whoever is responsible for this. I just hope they can find the killer or killers before any more innocent people are murdered."

The reporter thanked Hunter for his time so Frank turned off the television. There was silence in the room.

Finally, Mali said, "Why do I feel like someone just tried to sell me a used car?"

Jake agreed. "It didn't ring true."

Frank picked up his cell phone when it rang. "Damn, I'm sorry honey. I'm walking out the door right now." Pressing the button to end the call, Frank stood up to put on his coat. "I forgot that Kevin has his first baseball game tonight. It starts at six forty-five. We'll continue this tomorrow."

Mali and Jake followed Frank out of his office, and then walked back to the control center where Kirsten and Joe were working.

"We need to talk to Anthony Hunter again," Jake said.

"I agree. I'll set up a meeting for tomorrow morning."

"Are we getting together this weekend, Mali?" Kirsten asked, as she reached for her purse, getting ready to leave.

Mali shook her head. "I'm going to Sara's on Friday after work and plan to spend the night. Maybe next weekend?"

"Sure thing. Have a good night, Mali, Jake."

Joe shut down his computer as Jake walked over to speak with him.

Mali went to her desk and placed a call to Hunted Inc. While the phone rang, she closed her laptop and prepared to leave. Hanging up the phone when no one answered, she said goodbye to Joe who was walking out the door, then picked up her bag, turned, and bumped into Jake.

"You've been avoiding me."

"I've been here all week, Jake, hardly avoiding you." Mali tried to pass him but he moved to stand in front of her. She looked up in exasperation.

"So we're not going to talk about last weekend at all?"

Mali sighed. "What is there to say? That's my crazy, dysfunctional family."

"I wasn't talking about your family."

Mali bit her lip, not saying anything. Jake narrowed his eyes, arriving at some sort of decision. Reaching into his pocket, he pulled out an envelope and handed it to her. "This is an invitation for lunch from Heather."

Setting down her bag, she took the envelope from Jake and unsealed it. She pulled out a folded white piece of paper and opened it. Inside, there was a drawing of a red house with green grass and black sticks at the edge of the grass representing the wrought iron fence. Standing next to the house were two large stick figures and a small one in between them. There was an arrow pointing to each stick figure labeling them 'Daddy,' 'Me,' and 'Papa.' Below the drawing written in sky blue crayon were the words 'Can you come to lunch? Heather.'

Mali swallowed as she studied the picture and read the note, trying not to tear up. She glanced at Jake and smiled. "This is a very sweet invitation."

"You made an impression on her. I think it was your red hair, her words not mine," he said, chuckling.

Mali laughed softly. "I would love to come over for lunch."

"How about Sunday morning at eleven thirty? But instead of coming to my home, I want to go to Central Park. It would be fun for Heather. She hasn't been there in a long time and she loves the carousel. We can pick you up."

"That sounds wonderful." Mali folded the invitation,

returned it to the envelope, and tucked the envelope in her purse.

"Thank you for the invite, Jake. See you tomorrow." She picked up her bag, edged past him, then stopped and turned back. "No one answered the phone at Hunter Inc. I'll call first thing in the morning to set up an appointment."

* * *

Hunter Inc Office, New York City
Friday, April 17, 9:00 a.m.

"AGENTS BLACK AND Hooper." Anthony Hunter walked over to them and shook their hands. "May we get you some coffee, water, anything?"

"No thank you," said Jake. Mali shook her head.

Hunter waved Rebecca out of the office and offered them a seat on his sofa, making himself comfortable in the chair across from them.

"I apologize that I couldn't meet with you yesterday. I was out of town. What can I do for the FBI?"

"Your interview on Wednesday . . ." Jake began.

"Ah yes," interrupted Anthony. "My lawyers said I needed to get out in front of this. We don't want to scare our investors."

"Scare your investors!" Mali exclaimed. "Mr. Hunter, this is an on-going serial murder investigation—"

Again, Anthony interrupted, "that affects MY business because the FBI says these murders are tied to my game." Holding up his hands in a placating gesture, he continued. "I don't dispute that, given all you've told me. But I have a fiduciary responsibility to my stockholders and employees."

Janet Simpson came into the room, said hello, then sat in the chair next to Anthony.

"Were the names I gave you any help?"

"Only one," Jake said. "Jim Wells."

"Fired for insubordination. I'm not surprised he's a suspect."

"Just a person of interest at this point." Mali said. "He claims he was fired because he created the link between GPS and satellite that made your game such a huge success. He says you were jealous."

Anthony bolted forward in his chair. "That's bullshit. Everything about that game was designed by ME. He was only tasked with improvements and leading the development team that made the game compatible across multiple devices."

Janet placed her hand on Anthony's forearm. Glancing at her, he inhaled and relaxed back into his chair.

Janet shook her head and adjusted her glasses. "Jim was the contemptuous one, envious of Anthony's programming skills, and he was bitter when he left. Of course he would say that. The poor man just didn't measure up and was quite verbally abusive toward Anthony. That's why he was fired."

Changing the subject, Jake asked, "Are there any stockholders who don't like the direction your company has taken this past year and have threatened you?"

"No. And no one has sold their stock. Quite the contrary. This company is on solid ground and is at the forefront of gaming technology. A few months of a downward turn in our stock price is natural. We are close to releasing our newest game that also uses the GPS-Satellite technology but with a twist. While it's not a hunting game, we are confident our customers will love it."

The phone rang. Janet walked over to Anthony's desk and picked up the phone. "Give us a few minutes, Rebecca, and we'll go straight to the lab."

"Problem?" Anthony asked, looking over his shoulder at Janet.

"One that only you can fix, apparently. They're having problems in the final conversion testing for the iPhone and Samsung Galaxy."

Anthony turned his attention back to Jake and Mali. "If there's nothing else, I am needed in my computer lab."

"No. Thank you for your time, Mr. Hunter," Jake said.

Shaking their hands, Anthony escorted them out of his office then shut the door.

After leaving Hunter Inc, Mali and Jake walked down the crowded sidewalk to the parked car. As they drove back to the office, Jake asked, "What do you think?"

"Jim Wells is not the only person of interest."

"I agree. I want all of the financials and holdings of Hunter Inc from the time they opened until now. So far, my research into the private Anthony Hunter has not raised any red flags. He grew up in New Jersey, both parents worked, three older brothers and one younger sister, worked his way through college. Nothing out of the ordinary."

"I haven't found much on Janet Simpson. Her past is sketchy. I'll focus on her the rest of the morning and then compile the company financial information this afternoon."

* * *

ANTHONY WAS SITTING at his desk working on his computer when Janet came in and handed him some papers.

"Thanks Janet. I'm sorry I haven't gotten back with you sooner on the quarterly financials. The problems at the lab took longer to resolve than I expected."

"Not a problem." Janet lit a cigarette and settled into the chair across from him. "You had just the right amount of justified anger when you spoke with Black and Hooper, by the way. Good job." Grabbing an ash tray, she inhaled the smoke deep into her lungs, held it briefly then blew the smoke out through her nose. Flicking the ashes into the tray, she stared out at the city behind Anthony.

Anthony walked over to the bar, held up the bottle of whiskey in silent question.

She nodded and joined him. "I still feel we need to wait a few more weeks before the next game."

"I'm willing to wait two more weeks, that's it." He gulped his shot then poured himself a coke, adding a hefty amount of whiskey. "Ted Springs is chomping at the bit for the next game. We've selected a target and the team is doing the research on him right now. The game will be played in Washington, D.C., as Springs requested."

"Who is the target?"

"The good Senator from Wyoming."

"Senator Hamilton?" Janet's eyebrows drew together and her lips thinned in disapproval. "Not a good idea to pick someone so well known, Anthony." She finished her cigarette and crushed it in the ash tray on the bar.

"Lighten up, Janet. It's an excellent idea. And Springs thinks so too. He has hated the Senator ever since he voted against the bill that would have helped take his company to the next level financially. Springs needs our technology now more than ever. The excitement of this game should placate his hunger for our patent for a while. I want him off my back."

"Think Anthony. Killing a Senator who has voted against one of our stockholders will eventually lead the FBI and the SEC directly to us."

"I disagree. There's no way they can tie the game to us much less a particular target." His eyes bored into hers. "It's a done deal, the wheels are already in motion."

Janet lit another cigarette and smoked in silence, rapidly tapping her foot on the floor. Anthony's eyes narrowed as he observed her. He knew she was pissed.

Her face cleared and with a nod, whether in agreement or coming to some sort of decision, Janet extinguished the cigarette and acquiesced. "Perhaps you're right. It will be trickier than the other games since word is out now. We need to talk to Drake about changes in our process so that he doesn't get caught. We also need to shorten the length of the game. But if we play this right, it could work to our advantage, in more ways than one."

"Now you're talking." Anthony grabbed her and turned her to face him. "I'm having so much fun with this game and I have YOU to thank." He gave her a hug and would have pulled her in closer but she wiggled out of his arms and walked to the desk.

Janet reached for some paperwork. "I have to run some final numbers for your report to the board next week. Review the info I've left for you and call if you have any changes. Thanks for this additional information." She jostled the papers in her hand.

"See you later tonight?"

"No. I have a lot of work to do."

Frowning, he walked over to her and leaned close to her ear. "We haven't been together since the San Antonio game."

"Stop pouting, Anthony." She kissed him lightly on the lips then moved away. "We have much to do between the Board's report next week and the upcoming game in D.C." Janet smiled at Anthony and walked out the door. "Later."

After she left, Anthony reached over his desk to grab his cell phone and dialed a familiar number.

"I want to meet." A pause and then, "One hour from now, my place." Another pause. "Cost doesn't matter. Just be there. And bring your whip." He hung up then left his office. On his way out, Anthony told Rebecca that he'd return later.

CHAPTER SIXTEEN

Sara West's home, Newark, NJ
Friday, April 17, 9:30 p.m.

"HI SARA! I'M sorry I'm so late." Mali hugged Sara and set down her overnight bag in the foyer.

"You don't have to apologize, Mali. You're family. I'm grateful for any time we have together. The kids tried to stay up but they konked out about thirty minutes ago."

"Rats. I tried to leave earlier but it just didn't happen. Hey Tom, it's been awhile."

Sara's husband, Tom, was a short, balding man with the kindest light blue eyes Mali had ever seen. They hugged and then all three stepped into the living room.

"I always love walking into your home," Mali said. "It's full of love and peace." She slipped off her shoes and sat down on the large, overstuffed chair, tucking her legs beneath her.

Sara and Tom cozied up on the sofa. "Wait until tomorrow morning. It won't be so peaceful at seven." Sara laughed.

Mali admired the homey living room with toys scattered everywhere and magazines and children's books covering the coffee table. The all-stone fireplace dominated the living room. No fake fireplaces for Tom and Sara. Theirs was a chop your wood, build your own fire variety. And it was huge. They even had a cast iron pot on the side that Sara used to pop corn for the kids, much to their delight. Their L-shaped sofa was big enough for the entire family. Mali grinned, picturing the family snuggling there.

"It's even more peaceful when the kids are up, noise and all."

Tom leaned down and kissed Sara then hefted himself up, saying, "Speaking of tomorrow morning, I'm going to let you two catch up and take this opportunity to get some shut-eye before those little terrors wake us. Can I get you gals anything before I go upstairs?"

"How about some Chardonnay, Mali?" At Mali's nod, "It's in the fridge, honey. Thanks."

Tom went into the kitchen and returned a short time later with two glasses of wine. Handing one first to Mali, he leaned over to kiss his wife again and placed the second glass in her hand. "Anything else?"

"Could you take the laundry basket upstairs in addition to Mali's bag, please? The basket is on the first step."

"Sure thing. Good night you two." He picked up the basket and bag, and trotted up the stairs, disappearing around the corner.

"Has it already been a month since our brunch in the City?" asked Sara. "Come over here and tell me everything that's been going on since then. How was the party? Kirsten told me that your gorgeous co-worker went as your date." She patted the sofa next to her.

Mali plopped down on the sofa next to her friend. "Yes, Jake offered and since I had boxed myself into a corner, I accepted. You know my family. Mother looked down at Jake the entire weekend, my father grilled him at every opportunity, Rose put him down constantly, and Lilly looked like she wanted to gobble him up."

Sara nodded, chuckling. "He's gorgeous from what little you've said."

"Mother put us in the same bedroom." Mali rolled her eyes. "Had I known, I would have booked two hotel rooms."

Sara doubled over in laughter at the look of horror on Mali's face. "Oh my gosh," she snorted, sucking in air. "I can just picture it." Sara's giggles continued as Mali described her discomfort and the awkwardness of sharing the bathroom among other things. Seeing the humor of the situation from her friend's reaction, Mali laughed so hard she had to grip her sides before wiping the tears that ran down her cheeks.

Gasping and trying to breathe, Mali patted her face, trying to cool down. "This is why I am so glad to be here. My side hurts from laughing so much."

Sara reached over and squeezed her hand. "You just needed a good laugh. So did I. There's no better release. How was the anniversary party?"

"Aside from my father shtooping his secretary in his

library after the anniversary toast and Jake kissing me, it was pretty ho-hum!"

"What?"

"I know, right? He could have waited until the party was over."

"I wasn't talking about that. Jake kissed you? Where were you? How was it? Did it lead to something more? I want the details . . . now!"

A flush crept up Mali's cheeks. "We were in the garden by my bench. It was just a kiss, Sara." She paused to reflect on it. "Although I have to admit, it was a tender kiss. Unexpected coming from him. It didn't lead to anything more, nor will it."

"Why not? I understand you might be hesitant considering what happened with Daniel. I could just shoot your ex for what he did to you."

"That's history, Sara."

"It might be history but you were devastated."

"It was pride more than anything else. And embarrassment to have to go to my parents for help. Facing them and their I-told-you-so's was worse than finding David with Kara."

"And yet your father took care of things for you." Sara paused. "Not all men are jerks like Daniel."

"I know. Jake's a widower, Sara."

"Sounds like he's available."

"Okay. Well, I work with him."

"So?"

"He's leading the task force on this case."

"So?"

"So, the FBI has strict rules about relationships within the force, especially in the same chain of command."

"But he doesn't normally work with you, right?"

Mali nodded.

"Mali, you can toss out any excuse that you want. And, yes, they're all excuses. But if something is there between you two, you should see where it goes. You owe that to yourself and you deserve it."

Mali sighed, wringing her hands.

Sara glanced at the clock. "Oh my gosh. It's after midnight. You're off the hook for now, my friend. But this talk isn't over."

They stood up and Sara turned off the lights. They walked over to the stairs and climbed up to the second level.

"Your bag should be in your usual room."

"Thanks for everything Sara. You're a good friend."

After a day full of chase, hide-and-seek, Twister, jumping in the inflatable bouncy house, reading stories, and so much laughter that her sides ached, Mali headed home. There was no chance to talk further about Jake, for which she was grateful. She wasn't ready to delve into that topic with herself, much less with Sara.

After arriving home, Mali hopped in the shower and then sat on the balcony with her laptop. If she had to get some work done, what better place than to relax to the sounds of the Hudson?

* * *

Mali's Apartment, New York City
Sunday, April 19, 11:30 a.m.

THE DAY WAS sunny and clear with blue skies, the temperature a comfortable sixty-eight degrees. Wearing a pleated mid-skirt with a black long-sleeved crop top, Mali was in the kitchen putting their lunch in a cooler when the doorbell chimed. Smoothing her skirt, she walked over to the door and opened it.

Jake and his daughter were standing there, Jake with hydrangeas and Heather cradling a box of chocolates.

"Hi Miss Mali. I told Daddy that we needed to bring flowers and chocolates to you. That's what every girl likes, right? These flowers are from our garden and we bought the chocolates on the way here. You look pretty. I love your hair. WOW! Look at the river from up here, Daddy!" Shoving the chocolates into Mali's hands, Heather ran to the windows.

Mali ushered Jake inside, laughing, "Whew. I couldn't even get a 'hello' in. The hydrangeas are beautiful, Jake. Are they really from your garden?"

"Like I said before, Heather is a pistol, from the time she wakes up until she falls asleep." The affection in his voice was unmistakable. "And, yes, they're in our backyard."

"I love the different colors." Smiling, Mali walked to the kitchen, set the box of chocolates down and located a vase. Reaching for the flowers, she put them in the vase, adding water. She walked over to the table and placed them in the center. "Heather, is this a good place to put the flowers?"

Heather turned from the windows, skipped over to the table, looked them over carefully before pronouncing it perfect.

"Can I look at the rest of your house?"

"Of course, Heather. Go ahead and explore."

"Don't go out on the balcony alone, Heather." Jake added. She nodded and walked into Mali's bedroom.

Jake watched her go then turned to look at the open living room and kitchen. "Not what I expected."

Mali gazed around the room with pride. "What did you expect?"

"Maybe something more contemporary." He looked around then walked over to the window. "This view of the Hudson is stunning."

Mali joined Jake. "Every day, I sit on the balcony and stare at the river. It's mesmerizing to me. When I'm out there at night, there may be one or two boats passing by but the reflection of the moon on the water is what captures my attention most. It speaks to me. I find it calming."

"I understand. I . . ."

Heather raced into the room and over to Jake, jumping up and down in her excitement. "Can we go on the balcony now?" She looked at Mali, her eyes wide and an impish smile on her face. "Please?"

Who could resist those dimples? "Let's go!" Mali walked to the sliding door on the far side of the room and opened it. All three stepped onto the balcony and stood by the rail. Heather ooh'ed and aah'ed, pointing at the boats chugging down the river and the birds flying overhead, bouncing up and down the entire time.

"It's time to head to the park," Mali finally said, gesturing everyone inside. "Our lunch is ready. I also have a blanket to take with us."

Jake picked up the cooler. "I have one in the car."

They left her apartment and headed down the hallway to the elevator, the non-stop chatter of a lively six-year-old echoing around them.

It was a quick drive to the park. They parked the car near the entrance closest to the carousel. By mutual agreement, the carousel would be first before finding a place to enjoy their picnic. Mali carried the blanket while Jake handled the cooler and Heather, who was riding piggyback. Heather's excitement was barely contained as they drew nearer to the carousel. Hearing the music, she bounced up and down on Jake's back and urged him to hurry.

Jake handed the cooler to Mali as they approached the carousel, which was crowded on this sunny Sunday afternoon. He lifted Heather off his back and set her down.

Housed in a six-sided brick building with openings on each side and with a cupola-style roof, the carousel was one of the largest in the nation and housed fifty-seven hand-carved horses and two decorative chariots. In each opening of the building was a wrought iron fence. Those not riding could stand outside the building and take pictures through the fence.

The trio stood in line. As they waited, Heather studied

each horse, trying to decide which one to ride. When it was Heather's turn, she pranced to the horse she had chosen, a spirited black beauty. She waited for her dad to catch up and lift her onto the horse.

Mali moved to one of the fences to wait for Jake. Once Heather was settled and buckled in, Jake joined Mali. Both waved to Heather as they waited for the music to play and the ride to begin.

"When was the last time you were here with Heather?"

"Three years ago, a couple of months before her mother died."

"I'm sorry, Jake. If this is too painful . . ."

"I'm glad we brought Heather here, Mali. She has seen pictures of herself riding in one of the chariots with her mother and I believe this makes her feel closer to Christa."

A bell rang and Heather giggled as the music played and the carousel lurched forward.

Jake snapped photos and took videos from his iPhone. No one could mistake Heather's delight given her squeals and laughter. When the ride was over, Jake went to get Heather and Mali met them at the building exit.

They walked to Laughing Rock and veered off the path to find a shady place under one of the massive oak trees. Many others had the same idea. As they spread the blanket on the grass, Mali observed two colorful kites flying in the blue sky, one a huge cat and the other a mean looking snake. An impromptu mini-game of football between six college-aged kids, and two young children playing with a frisbee, were interspersed between the various blankets, chairs, and beach towels spread out on the grass. Most people sitting down were either talking or texting on their phones, snapping selfies, or comparing whatever was on his or her screen with the person sitting next to them.

"It's so beautiful here. How can anyone be staring at a phone when all of this beauty surrounds us?" Mali asked. "I never tire of being in Central Park." She opened the cooler and pulled out chicken sandwiches for herself and Jake, a cheese sandwich for Heather, as per Jake's suggestion, apples, grapes, Cheetos, chocolate chip cookies, Pinot Noir for the two of them, and chocolate milk for Heather. All three ate their lunches with gusto, not talking much until the last cookie was finished.

"Daddy, can I go play with those girls over there?" Heather asked, pointing to three girls playing with a ball.

"Of course, Heather. Stay close. What do you say to Mali?"

"Thank you for lunch, Miss Mali." And, with that, Heather skipped over to the girls to play with them.

Jake stretched his legs out in front of him and leaned back on his hands. "That was delicious. Thank you."

"You're welcome. Would you like a little more wine?" At his nod, she poured another glass for him. There was a companionable silence as they watched all of the activity in the park.

"How did your wife die, Jake?"

He didn't answer right away. "An aggressive form of pancreatic cancer. I took an early retirement from the Army when Christa was diagnosed. She was gone within three months. The carousel ride was Christa's last outing before she passed."

"Does Heather remember her?"

Jake shook his head. "Not consciously. She was three. There are certain scents that trigger some memories which is why I keep a diffuser with lilac in her room. Christa loved lilacs. I joined the FBI a few months after we moved in with my dad. He's been a tremendous help."

"It's obvious that he loves his granddaughter very much."

"Yes." Jake smiled. "Enough about me. Tell me something about you."

"You read my bio."

"You and I both know how little is in those bios."

"All right." She hesitated. "I was married once."

His eyebrows shot straight up and his mouth dropped open.

Mali grinned. "I surprised you, didn't I?"

"What happened?"

"He was a football player." At his raised eyebrows, she laughed. "Typical, right? I was a junior in college, Daniel was a senior. We married on a whim. I convinced myself at the time that I loved him, but I think I loved the idea of shocking my parents more than anything. Daniel was not a suitable match from their perspective and I did not want to be told who I was going to marry." She shook her head at her foolishness. "I was rebellious." He chuckled. "Our marriage was annulled after a few months when I caught him with a cheerleader after a game. Also typical, right?" This said with a self-deprecating laugh. "My father worked hard to keep all of that out of the papers and off the record."

"Is that why you joined the force? To rebel against your parents?"

"At first. But then I found that I liked the work and I was good at my job. Mother hopes I'll come to my senses so she keeps trying to set me up with suitable matches. She was trying to do that prior to their anniversary. When we spoke of it on the phone, it just popped out of my mouth that I was bringing someone."

"And an unsuitable someone at that."

"Please don't take it personally, Jake. That's just who they are. And I haven't wanted to talk about what happened during their anniversary weekend because I wasn't ready. I'm still not."

"I'm not Daniel, Mali. Not all men are untrustworthy. And you can't deny that there's something between us."

"I don't deny it. But that doesn't mean I want to act on it."

Before their conversation could continue, Heather screamed. Jake was up in an instant running to her. He looked at her face, then picked her up and returned to the blanket where Mali was now standing up.

"The ball hit her in the face. You're all right, peanut. No blood, maybe a bruise."

Heather sniffled as a big tear ran down her cheek. "Maybe if I had some ice cream?"

Mali covered her mouth with her hand and looked down, stifling a laugh.

"You little trickster. All right. We will pack up our picnic, with your help young lady, and then we'll get an ice cream on our way out of the park. Deal?"

"Deal!" Heather wiggled out of his arms to pick up the trash on the blanket.

The ice cream was a sloppy hit as they walked back to the car. Jake picked up a sleepy Heather and carried her the last half of the way. It was quiet on the ride back to Mali's apartment. A sleeping Heather softly snored in the back seat. Jake pulled up to the entrance of her apartment, put the car in park, and turned to Mali.

"I understand your caution, Mali. I have to be careful too because it's not just me. I have to consider my daughter and what is good for her as well." He glanced back at Heather before turning his eyes on Mali. "I never thought I'd feel anything for anyone again after Christa died. I don't know what this is." He pointed between them. "And I won't do anything that could hurt Heather. But what if this turns out to be something extraordinary?" Jake reached over and ran his finger down Mali's cheek. "Think about it. Thank you for today. It was fun for both Heather and me."

With a cautious smile, Mali opened the door and stepped out. Opening the rear door, she quietly removed her cooler. She leaned into the window that Jake had opened on the passenger side. "I enjoyed the time with you and Heather, Jake. Thank you."

CHAPTER SEVENTEEN

FBI Field Office, New York City
Monday, April 20, 7:45 a.m.

"Looks like someone had a good weekend." Kirsten said as she stopped at Mali's desk in the control center.

"I had a great weekend. How about you?"

"Busy. We went hiking in Connecticut on Saturday. Jen had to work on her big event on Sunday so I read. Invigorating and relaxing as well. Did you enjoy your time with Sara?"

"We had a great time. The kids are getting so big. We had such fun playing Twister and other games . . . non-stop action. I haven't laughed that much in a long time. And Sara and I had good 'us' time and caught up on everything."

"Sounds wonderful. What did you do on Sunday?"

Mali hesitated. "I went to Central Park for a picnic lunch with Jake and his daughter."

Kirsten's eyes got as round as saucers.

"Before you say anything, Heather, Jake's daughter,

invited me. I met her that day I went to Jake's house to work."

"Yesterday was a beautiful day, Mali. I'm glad you were able to go out and enjoy it."

Changing the subject, Mali said, "Hey, can you help me with research on Janet Simpson? I haven't found much information on her before 1996 and I question the validity of the birth certificate I obtained. There is no other information for a Janet Simpson in New Jersey where she was supposedly born and raised. So far, I've looked at a ten-year period, 25–35 years ago. It's like she didn't exist before 1996. There has to be information somewhere. I need to work on the Hunter Inc financials. I didn't have a chance to work on them on Friday."

"Sure thing. What are you looking for?"

"A past. Something that might help us in the present."

As Kirsten walked to her desk, Mali pulled up the Hunter Inc. website and perused the posted financials. She spent the rest of the day comparing financials from when Hunter Inc. became public to present day.

The remainder of the week was spent on research. In addition to reviewing the financials on the company website, Mali searched all of the company filings on the Securities and Exchange Commission to compare with those on Hunter's website. Nothing out of the ordinary so, by Friday, Mali had requested access to bank records and had compiled a list of the biggest shareholders in order to research them.

Before everyone was released for the weekend, Jake called the team together for a status report. Each team member spoke of their progress.

Amy and Brad reported that no new videos had been posted on the most popular social media outlets. Putting Twitter on the right screen that was mounted on the front wall, Brad navigated to #HuntedLives and they showed the team that, other than users wondering when and where the next game would take place, there was no activity. They were expanding their search to other apps, like Instagram. Nothing so far.

Joe reported that all of the IP addresses that showed the videos to date had been tied to hacked accounts or had been shared by users. He was currently trying to capture the location of Jim Wells via his IP address. The working assumption was that Wells took his laptop with him. That being the case, Joe confirmed that he could catch Wells if he went online. So far, no luck.

"Any word from the lab on the The Hunted Ones program, Joe?" Jake asked.

"Nothing new. There's still a lot of code left to review. They're working on it."

"Has anyone looked into Jim Wells's bank and financial records?"

"I have," Kirsten said. "There has been no unusual activity. The only large withdrawals can be tied to his wedding. No withdrawals from his known accounts in the past week either."

"Thanks for taking the initiative on that, Kirsten. Keep looking."

Kirsten also reported that Janet Simpson did not exist prior to 1996. With the exception of when she started working with the company, all of the information about Simpson on the Hunted Inc. website was false. Kirsten ran Simpson's press photo that was on their website through facial recognition programs but there was no hit.

". . . and I'm currently researching adoption agencies and Child Protective Services in New Jersey, assuming that's where Janet is from. If no luck there, I'll expand the search."

"Check Interpol and other agency databases, maybe she has a record outside the U.S."

"Will do."

Mali reported that Hunters' financial records were sound thus far and she hoped to have his bank records by Monday. She put the list of the six biggest shareholders on the middle screen for all to view.

"I have started preliminary research on the shareholders and hope to have more information Monday."

"Great, thanks Hoop," said Jake.

Jake then talked about Anthony Hunter and his past. Both of his parents were deceased, two of his brothers lived in Boston, and the third brother was in California. No known whereabouts of his sister. "I want to obtain a little more information on his family before I contact his brothers. Hunters' college years are where he discovered his true calling. He developed his signature game, The Hunted Ones, his senior year. He currently lives in the Upper East Side, Carnegie Hill."

That caught Mali's attention. "Wait a minute, Jake." She shuffled through some notes, searching. "Here we are. Janet Simpson lives in Carnegie Hill as well, 1110 Park Avenue, penthouse apartment 6C."

Jake stared at Mali in disbelief. "Hunter lives in 6B."

"They live next to each other?" Kirsten asked. "That's kind of weird."

"Jake, do you have a picture of Hunter with his family?" Mali asked.

"Working on it. What are you thinking Hoop?"

"If we can find one picture, maybe there are more, and with friends. Perhaps their families were friends? Perhaps his sister and Janet were BFFs growing up? Do you remember when we first met them? I was sure something was going on between them. Perhaps they ARE involved in some way. It could be relevant if one or both of them are responsible for these murders."

"Maybe they are romantically involved and just want to keep it private," Kirsten offered.

"That's also a possibility."

Jake nodded. "On that note, let's wrap it up for the week. A skeleton crew will be here over the weekend and will contact us, if needed. Plan to hit it hard on Monday. We still have too many questions. We also have no idea when the next game is or where it will take place. We can all agree that it's just a matter of time before there is another game, so time is of the essence. I'd like to prevent it, if possible." With that, Jake thanked everyone and ended the meeting.

Mali walked over to Kirsten. "Send me what you

found on Janet Simpson and where you left off. I plan to do a little work this weekend."

"Sure thing. Are we getting together? Jen and I would love to have you over for dinner?"

"Can I take a raincheck, Kirsten? I need to work this weekend."

"Of course. Don't work too hard, Mali. You know what they say about all work and no play."

Mali laughed and walked back to her desk to collect her things.

Jake was on the phone. As Kirsten walked past her with a wave, Mali said, "Wait up, Kirsten. I'll walk out with you." She grabbed her things and escaped.

* * *

Mali's apartment
Sunday, April 26, 3:40 a.m.

FAST ASLEEP, IT didn't register initially that the ringing phone was not part of her dream. The ringing stopped just as she reached over to pick it up. She rolled over, groaning when it rang again. Mali answered it on the second ring.

"Jim Wells is dead."

Mali sat up, instantly awake. A chill ran down her spine. "What? How?"

"Wells and his wife were killed in a car accident in West Virginia. They had been holed up in a cabin at Summersville Lake. Their car went off the road and into the lake. They couldn't get out and drowned. I've been in touch with the field office in Beckley, about an hour away. Agents were dispatched to the site of the accident as well as their cabin."

"Wow. That's a little too convenient for me."

"I agree. I just crossed the bridge into the City. There is a video conference call at four thirty with an update."

"I'd like to be there."

"I thought as much. That's why I'm headed to your place. Pick you up in ten." The line went dead.

Mali jumped up, dashed into her closet and dressed, then stepped into the bathroom to brush her teeth. No time for makeup. Putting her hair in a loose bun, she walked into the living room, picked up her laptop, and grabbed the relevant paperwork sitting on the dining table where she had worked last night. Shoving it all into her bag, she walked out of the apartment complex as Jake pulled up.

"Thanks for picking me up, Jake. I appreciate it." She closed the door and buckled the seat belt. Turning to him, she asked, "So Wells and his wife have been in West Virginia these past two weeks?"

"It would appear so." Jake put the car in gear and pulled out into the street.

At this hour and on a Sunday, the West Village was quiet as was most of the City. Few cars were on the streets although numerous trucks carrying food and other products were speeding to their destinations. It was all a blur to Mali as they made their way to the office.

Arriving at the Federal building, Jake parked the car in the garage and they hustled up to the control center.

While setting up her laptop, Mali said, "I spent time this weekend continuing my research into the top share-holders of Hunter, Inc."

"Anything interesting?" Jake asked as the internet came on the center screen and he navigated to the secure website for the conference call.

"Three of the six shareholders have a particular obsession with Hunter's company."

"What do you mean?"

"Collectively, they own thirty percent of the com-pany stock. One shareholder, Ted Springs, CEO of Lakeway Technologies, owns fourteen percent of the stock and has made no secret of the fact that he wants the patent to the GPS/Satellite technology. His com-pany is not doing well based on the financials I read and his stock has been slipping for months now. I plan to review his bank records and should have them later this morning. The other two shareholders, Jane Bellows, CFO of Enterprise Trading Firm, and Hernando Guti-errez, President of Bank of Mexico in New York, own ten and six percent of the stock, respectively. I'll look into their financials as well. The four of them play golf regularly."

"Interesting. How often—" Jake was interrupted by the video conference call.

After introductions, Agent Anderson spoke.

"We arrived in Summersville approximately two hours ago, three hours after the car was found with the bodies inside. Two agents were dispatched to the cabin and Agent Woods and I went directly to the site of the accident." He reviewed his notes then continued. "The bodies were recovered from the car first and sent to the medical examiners' office earlier. They were pulling the car out of the water as we arrived. Forensics was still on site as was the Police Chief. We discussed the Chief's preliminary findings. According to him, the car was speeding and took the turn too fast. There were skid marks on the road but no evidence of braking. The car went through the side rail and plunged into the water. He said that the two bodies had no visible signs of trauma. The air bags deployed and the windows were rolled up. The PC believes that the two panicked and were unable to get out of the car. No witnesses."

"How did the car look when it was pulled out of the water?" Jake asked.

"Damage on the right front side of the car, probably from hitting the rail. And there's a substantial dent on the driver side door."

Mali spoke for the first time since the introductions. "So the right front is damaged because it hit the side rail then went into the water. Did the car roll at all?"

"No."

"So if it didn't roll, how did the car get damaged on the driver side of the vehicle?"

"Perhaps the dent was already there?" Agent Anderson offered.

"Possibly, but we need to make sure. Have a team inspect the car thoroughly. Check for paint chips in the dent on the door. Also check if it's consistent with getting hit by a car. Did that dent occur from the accident or from something else?"

"Yes Ma'am," the young agent replied.

Boy does that make me feel old. "Call me Hoop, everyone else does."

"Yes Ma'am, er, I mean Hoop. We'll make sure the car is inspected first thing this morning."

"What about the bodies?" Jake asked.

"The medical examiner said there were no visible signs of trauma other than bumps and bruises consistent with hitting a deployed air bag at high speed. They were wearing seat belts and had belt marks and bruises consistent with that as well. The bodies were under water nine hours putting time of death at approximately seven thirty last night."

"And you said there were no witnesses?" Jake asked.

"That's what we were told. We plan to canvas the area ourselves to verify."

"Good," Jake said, as he absorbed everything they were being told. "What led the police chief to conclude that the two panicked? How did he know they were conscious after they hit the water? Is that assumption or fact?"

"I'm not sure," Agent Anderson replied. "I'll check with him. The medical examiner knows that time is of the essence and said we would have some preliminary findings by end of day and the full results in forty-eight hours."

Mali asked, "Was anything found in the cabin?"

Tami Weathering, sitting next to Anderson, spoke up. "A few items of clothing, food, five hundred dollars and change, a laptop case."

"Was his laptop there?"

"No. Nor was his wallet or his wife's purse. The items weren't in the car or on their bodies either. In addition, it was obvious that the place had been tossed."

"Someone went through the cabin?" Jake asked.

"That's what we believe. We're dusting for prints."

The conversation continued for another thirty minutes with tasks assigned and an agreement to have another conversation when they received the report from the medical examiner's office.

After they hung up, Jake turned to Mali in frustration. "How did someone get to them before we found them?"

"I'm not sure, although I think we can both agree that Anthony Hunter has just moved to the top of our suspect list."

Jake agreed. "I'm going to have Ron and John tail Hunter 24-7 beginning this morning. Where does he go? What does he do? Who does he see? And I'll work on a warrant so we can tap his office and personal cell phone." He slammed his palm down on the table. "Damn it!"

CHAPTER EIGHTEEN

Anthony's apartment
Monday, April 27, 6:30 a.m.

USING HER KEY, Janet entered Anthony's apartment, furious by what she had just learned. She marched through the living room and threw open the door to his bedroom.

"Anthony . . ." She trailed off when she observed Anthony kneeling on his bed, facing his television and watching a porn film, his hands on the head of a naked blonde who was servicing him.

He looked at her with lust-filled eyes and invited her to join them.

"We need to talk. NOW!" She turned on her heel and stormed back into the living room.

Ten minutes later, Anthony sauntered out of the bedroom wearing a black robe. Smiling at Janet, who was standing by the kitchen counter smoking a cigarette, he strode to the bar and poured himself a shot, downing it in one gulp.

Before he could say anything, a giggling blonde came

into the room and snuggled next to Anthony. She kissed him deeply, one hand on his shoulder, the other holding the whip she had brought. "Thanks for the ride, Tony. When will I see you again?"

Without taking his eyes off Janet, Anthony reached into his robe pocket and pulled out a few hundred dollar bills, tucking the money in her blouse. "I'm not sure, doll. I'll be in touch. Now get out of here."

She glanced at Janet, blew her a kiss, and sashayed out of the apartment.

"I hate being called Tony." Anthony watched her leave, a bored look on his face.

Janet took a final deep drag from her cigarette then crushed it in the ash tray.

"I've been informed that Jim Wells is dead."

Anthony smirked. "Pity that he was on such a treacherous road. Poor fool drowned from what I understand."

Janet looked at him incredulously. "Have you lost your fucking mind, Anthony?"

His smile faded. "I did what had to be done, Janet. The FBI would have caught up to him sooner or later. I couldn't let that happen."

"Jesus! I'm gone one day." She drew in slow, steady breaths and, in a more controlled tone, spit out, "You fool! Jim Wells became the prime suspect when he ran. You just took that suspect away. Who do you think they're going to look at next?"

Anthony reached behind him for the whiskey, poured another shot, and tossed it back. "It was made to look like an accident, Janet."

"It doesn't matter, Anthony. If there is another game now, they'll know that Wells wasn't involved. The games have to stop." Pacing, she lit up another cigarette. "We can spin this to our advantage and lay the blame on Wells, disgruntled employee seeks to destroy creator of The Hunted Ones. I'll contact Drake, pay him a final fee, and tell him to disappear."

Before she could continue with her to-do list for dismantling the game, Anthony said, "No, Janet. We've already moved forward with the next game. The Senator was taken yesterday morning as he was buying flowers. He is being fitted with the device now. The game is set for tonight at ten. And get this, not only did Ted pay the reduced fee of two hundred and fifty big ones that I promised, but Jane and Hernando paid full price just to watch. They're intrigued. I'm expecting them at nine tonight."

Janet looked at him with narrowed eyes, as though considering her options. She lit a new cigarette with the one in her hand, snuffed the partially smoked one, and took a calming drag, inhaling deeply, holding the smoke briefly in her lungs before releasing it. She walked over to Anthony, leaned in and kissed him on the mouth.

"Anthony, you're obviously set on doing this. You just have to be careful how the game plays out. I will help you, naturally. Why don't I bring dinner to the gaming room for your guests, say nine thirty?"

"Thank you, Janet." Anthony pulled her into his body, his arms wrapping her in a hug. "Ted and I already discussed how this game will have to be conducted mostly at night since the Senator is such a high-profile target. And we're changing his appearance a bit so he's not as recognizable." Changing the subject, he nuzzled her neck moving his hands to her butt and squeezing. "You should have joined us, Janie. It could have been fun."

Extricating herself from Anthony, Janet forced a smile, "Another time perhaps, although I don't like the idea of sharing you." She turned to leave, extinguishing her cigarette in the ashtray on the bar. "I'm headed to the office."

* * *

Washington, D.C.
Wednesday, April 29, 12:10 a.m.

It was quiet at the Jefferson Memorial. The moonlight reflected off the calm water in the Tidal Basin and the Washington Monument stood sentinel across the water in the distance. The beauty of this part of D.C. was not lost on him.

Bone tired and smelling of stale beer and sweat, the Senator hid in the shadows of the man who inspired him to be the man he was today. 'We hold these truths to be self-evident: that all men are created equal; that they are endowed by their Creator with certain unalienable rights; that among these are life, liberty, and the pursuit of happiness.' Those words by Thomas Jefferson meant something to him, they always had. He had worked toward that end for others his entire public life.

The irony of his situation was not missed. In two never-ending days, he had experienced how all men were not created equal. Dressed in ill-fitting jeans and a long-sleeved flannel shirt that was soaked with beer when he had donned it, he sported a fishing hat that covered his bald head from the buzz cut they gave him and now wore a straggly beard. He was invisible. The letter said he couldn't talk to anyone, not a problem because no one would even look at him much less talk to him. He was less than equal and that saddened him because of the cavalier way he had unknowingly treated home-less people over the years. Liberty? No more, as of five days ago when he was taken. Life? Doubtful. Surviving another twenty-four hours seemed impossible. Pursuit of happiness? He wasn't sure he understood what that state was before being taken, much less now. His humorless laugh did nothing to dispel his melancholy mood.

He sat on the steps of the memorial with his back against a marble column. The wind slapping him in the face and the waving branches of a nearby tree both seemed to mock him. He watched the branches bend and listened to the leaves rustle. Other than that, and the sounds of an occasional car driving along Maine Ave toward the Mall, it was quiet. Under normal circum-stances, he would have reveled in the silence and serenity.

Sighing and knowing it was time to move, he stood up and grimaced in pain as his knees complained. He stumbled down the stairs and made his way toward the Capital building. The Capital wasn't the destination given to him, but it had been home for him for the past twenty years and he headed there without conscious thought. The blisters on his feet prevented him from jogging but he walked as quickly and stealthily as he could. There was no real plan other than to keep moving and to stay on well-lit streets, albeit in the shadows.

Turning right on Independence Avenue, he continued down the road, passing the Freer Gallery and other museums. Turning left on Fourth Street, he crept between the Air and Space and American Indian museums before walking a few steps down Jefferson Drive toward the Capital. He stopped. His eyes shifted left then right. The darkness closed in on him. The street was too dark. Limping now because of the pain in his feet, he lurched forward through the trees, a veritable bear crashing through a forest. The Mall was his destination, where the lights shone brighter. Like a moth drawn to a flame, his focus was solely on the Capital which was lit up like a star guiding him home. The Senator paused by a tree to catch his breath and look at the Capital. His only focus was to get home. He didn't want to disappoint Thomas Jefferson.

* * *

TED SPRINGS, JANE Bellows, and Hernando Gutierrez were lounging in the game room with Anthony and Janet. The three had been there since a little after nine o'clock Monday night. After a feast of sushi, shrimp tempura, and crab legs followed by chocolate molten cake for dessert, the game had begun just after ten that first night. The booze had been flowing and the laughter was nonstop. The energy level had increased by the hour.

Given the night hunting rule, they had only been able to observe the Senator's actions and whereabouts during the day while the assassin waited in the wings until dark. Ted enjoyed having Jane and Hernando with him. They had been intrigued by the game, how it was played, and how they could follow the Senator's every move. The placement of the GoPro camera made it impossible to view him directly but that didn't lessen the experience. They repeatedly remarked on the various expressions of those who passed him. The disgust, caution, and even fear fascinated all three. Ted had laughed at the look of surprise on Jane's face when a woman pulled her daughter close to her side and gave the Senator a wide berth as they passed him.

The only other rule employed in this particular hunt was for the assassin. No videos, no live streaming during the hunt.

In between the action, the three had used the time to go and take care of business as needed, to nap, and to have some fun. Anthony had been participating in their brand of fun, as he did most days following their golf outings, but Janet left each time, ostensibly to get some work done.

By dusk, the target was only four miles from the assassin. Ted sent the first set of instructions to the assassin at precisely eight in the evening, just after sunset. Since then, the instructions from Ted had been continuous. Jane and Hernando had freely offered suggestions on which streets the assassin should take to get to the target faster but Ted was having too much fun, taking the assassin down alleys and smaller streets to draw it out. Even with the assassin walking, albeit at a fast pace, and Ted taking him on a round-about route, the assassin reached the target in fewer than six hours.

When Ted watched the Senator turn on Fourth Street and head to the Mall, he sent a message to the assassin.

"Hustle past the American Indian museum and wait on the northeast corner."

As soon as the target crossed Jefferson Drive and tottered toward the Mall, the player received a message from the assassin. "He's headed to the Capital."

"This is it, friends," Ted told Jane and Hernando, instructing the assassin to kill the target.

"I never realized how thrilling this could be," Jane cooed, sitting on Ted's lap and nibbling on his ear.

"I haven't had this much fun since . . . never," Hernando hooted as he poured another shot and raised a toast to Anthony. "Well worth the money, mi amigo, and so much more enjoyable with friends."

Laughing, Ted tickled Jane, who squealed in delight.

"Stop, Ted. I don't want to miss anything." She slapped his hands away and moved to the recliner next to him.

Hernando poured four shots, handing one each to the others. "To an excellent hunt, amigos. Salud!"

They downed their shots as the large screen flickered to life. The assassin had turned on his camera. They were glued to their chairs in anticipation as they watched the Senator unknowingly walk toward the assassin.

After the Senator passed a large tree right next to the

path on the Mall, the assassin rushed over to him. The gravel crunched beneath the feet of the assassin and the players watched as the Senator turned toward the sound. There was no chance to react. The assassin easily overpowered him, wrapping his hands around the Senator's neck. The Senator tried to fight him off but the man was too strong, all muscle. He was pulled to the ground and the assassin straddled him, all while continuing to apply pressure to his neck. The Senator tried to throw him off, bucking his body up and down, to no avail. His struggles grew weaker as his eyes bulged. He gasped for air and his face turned beet red.

They watched in fascination until the Senator took his last breath. The only sound heard was the heavy breathing of the assassin.

The three players were silent for a heartbeat before they jumped out of their chairs, cheering. There were pats on the back as they celebrated a successful game.

"Mierda! I've never seen anything like that," enthused Hernando.

"It was beyond my expectations," exclaimed Jane.

"Fuckin' awesome, right!?!" said Ted.

Anthony poured them each one more shot as they looked at the screen for the last time. The lifeless eyes of the Senator stared at them, his neck wearing a red finger mark necklace, with the calling card resting on his chest. The screen went black.

Ted's console beeped and the three ogled the picture, not noticing 'Game Over' written beneath it.

CHAPTER NINETEEN

The Federal building, New York City
Wednesday, April 29, 5:40 a.m.

"THANKS FOR MEETING me here at this hour," Frank said as Jake and Mali walked into his office.

"You said on the phone that there was another murder?" Jake asked.

"Yes. In Washington, D.C., on the Mall, close to the Capital. The body was found by a janitor heading to the American Indian Museum at three twenty-five."

"And we're sure it's another victim of the game?" asked Mali.

"Yes, Hoop. As soon as the card was found on the body, the police chief called me himself. I spoke with him about thirty minutes ago." Frank sat forward in his chair and turned his computer monitor so Jake and Mali could view the body and crime scene. "Senator Hamilton from Wyoming."

"Christ," said Jake. "It looks like the device and camera were removed. Weapon of choice this time?"

"I've asked the Medical Examiner for a video conference at . . . ah, here we go." Frank opened the video conference tab on his secure browser and answered the call. Frank introduced himself and the others to the woman seen on the screen.

With all eyes on her, she said, "Good morning. My name is Samantha Smith, Deputy Chief Medical Examiner here in D.C."

"Thank you for agreeing to this conference call, Samantha, especially at such an early hour," Frank said.

"You said that you believe this murder is part of a series of murders based on an app game?" She shook her head. "I thought I'd heard it all." She took a breath and exhaled. "I can't give you any concrete information until the autopsy is completed."

"We understand that. I'm hoping you can give us your impressions and early findings."

Jake added, "Can you tell us how the Senator died and what weapon was used?"

"The only sign of trauma is on his neck. Given the markings, I would say he was strangled. There are no other signs of injury or trauma. Time of death is roughly three to four hours ago."

Mali stared at the picture of the Senator. "What about the cut behind his ear?"

"Looks to be a clean cut. I was told to check for cyanide so we're doing that now."

"How soon can we have final results?" asked Frank.

"Given the victim and your investigation, we'll put

a rush on the autopsy and should have results before the end of today."

They spoke for a few more minutes, then the call ended.

Frank put two more images on the screen, the front and back side of the calling card.

"Strangulation is consistent with what is on the card," Jake noted. "And according to the number on the back of the card, the game lasted twenty-seven hours. Why weren't we notified about the abduction of a Senator? He had to have been taken a couple of days early to insert the device."

"The Senator's wife is being taken to the Medical Examiner's office to confirm identity. Local agents are questioning her."

Mali said, "Why pick a high-profile politician? That seems risky." Mali's brow furrowed as she considered the implications. "If you'll excuse me, I want to get to the control center to search for any pictures or videos." At Frank's nod, she left.

As soon as Mali entered the control room, she powered up the computer then called Kirsten, who was already coming in for the day, to give her a brief rundown on what was happening and thank her for her consistency in coming to the office early.

"I can always count on you, Kirsten. Thanks."

Mali accessed Twitter and, using the center screen at the front of the room, entered '#HuntedLives.' The latest comment, listed at 2:15am, was simply a link. Clicking it, a new browser window opened, which she moved to the right screen. The Periscope app appeared with a video labeled, 'Latest Hunted One.' She pressed the Play button as Jake walked into the room.

Both watched the video, just under two minutes long, as the assassin moved from the corner of a building and across a street to stand behind a large tree. It was difficult to identify everything on the screen but the Mall was well lit and they easily watched the Senator limping toward the Capital.

"He looks tired and disheveled," Mali observed. "If I recall, the Senator was always clean-shaven and wore his black hair down to his collar."

"It looks like it was shaved off. Probably tried to change his appearance given his position."

As soon as the Senator passed the tree, behind which the assassin was hiding, Jake and Mali watched the assassin spring into action. As the Senator turned toward the sound, the assassin reached for his neck. They could tell that the Senator was struggling by the jerkiness of the assassin's camera, which was mounted on his forehead. He was nose to nose with the Senator so they witnessed the last seconds of his life. Mali grimaced, watching the panic and terror run across the Senator's face before the life ebbed out of him.

Not a word was spoken after the video ended. They turned toward the door when they heard a gasp. Kirsten stood at the back of the room, trembling fingers resting on her mouth, swallowing repeatedly.

"How can anyone do that?" she asked after composing herself.

Mali shook her head. "We're going to catch the SOB who is doing this and put him or her away for a very long time."

"Good." Kirsten looked up at the screen. "I'll save that video then contact Periscope and Twitter and have it removed immediately." She walked to her desk to make some calls.

Jake and Mali looked up at the Twitter feed on the center screen. Messages had been posted since the link was initially added to #HuntedLives and they were still flying in at a dizzying pace.

"OMG! Did you see that?"

"Man, his eyes almost popped out of his head."

"This is the best one yet. I wish I could have seen it live."

"Who's the guy?"

"Who cares? I got a hard-on just watching the assassin at work."

"I live in D.C. and that was on the Mall close to the Capital. I'm going by there this morning to check it out."

"Who's playing the game and how can I get in on it?"

The morning news exploded with the story, and reports continued throughout the day. There were stories about his life and his work in the Senate but the focus was on his death. The White House issued a statement condemning the killing and expressing condolences to the Hamilton family. The FBI was silent.

"The Senator was last seen on Sunday morning," Jake said. "According to our sources, his wife, Angela Hamilton, told friends that he left for the office mid-morning and evidently never arrived. She told our agents the same thing." It was late and pizza had been brought in. No one was leaving anytime soon. "She also said that his absence was not reported because he was working on a bill that was near completion and often spent the night at the office when finishing important legislation. What else have we learned?"

"The Senator reportedly goes into the office most Sundays for a few hours," said Mali. "Rumor has it that he and the wife of one of the junior senators were having an affair. It's possible that he never arrived at the Senate offices because he was meeting with her. Also, it's possible that Hamilton stays with her when he tells his wife that he's staying at the office. We're working that angle quietly. On a side note, we're also checking his voting record from the time he was elected three years ago to identify which bills he supported, or not."

"I don't understand why we're taking the time to check his voting record," Joe interjected. "Wouldn't it be more constructive to bring Hunter in for questioning and play hard ball with him?"

"Joe, Hunter is just a suspect at this point," said Jake. "It's a short list, granted. But if he is involved, we certainly don't want to alert him to the fact that we believe he's the mastermind behind the killings. We need proof. It's a long shot that the way the Senator voted on any given bill contributed to his death but we have to check every angle." Jake drank some water before continuing. "I spoke with Ron Hastings and John Harper. They have been leading the team that is tailing Hunter. On many occasions, Hunter appears to spend the night at the office during the week. He drives into the basement garage, which has one entry and two exits, but doesn't leave. Team members are monitoring every door leading into the building as well as the garage entry and exits. We now have the warrant for tapping his phones as well as Janet Simpson's phones, which will be set up today. My hope is that they will provide valuable information to us."

After the meeting, Mali and Jake reported to Frank's office for an update. Jake repeated what was discussed in the meeting with the team.

"Whoever is behind this is making us look like fools," Frank stated angrily. "We have a press conference at eleven without anything of substance to report. Frustration levels are high and now the President is involved."

Jake said, "It may not look like much is being accomplished, but we have made progress and we are getting closer. Our suspect list is down to two, Anthony Hunter and Janet Simpson, and we are now focusing all of our efforts on them and those in their inner circle."

The discussion ended and Mali and Jake returned to the control center. It was going to be a long day.

* * *

The Federal building, New York City
Friday, May 1, 9:00 a.m.

"SETTLE DOWN PEOPLE. We have a lot of things to discuss and I want to get to it," Jake said. They had been working non-stop ever since the discovery of the Senator's body. News reports were critical of the FBI for not solving this case and everyone was feeling the stress of that. Ron and John had come into the office to report on their surveillance efforts.

"Any news?"

Ron, a portly man who had been on the force for fourteen years, stood up. "As we told you a couple of days ago, Hunter sleeps at the office sometimes, arriving at nine a.m. on the days that he sleeps elsewhere. Despite living in the same building, Hunter and his CFO do not drive to the office together. Simpson arrives early. After Hoop gave us the pictures of the three stockholders she has been investigating, we documented how Hunter is with them constantly. Late Monday night, for example, the three went to the Hunter offices, arriving separately a few minutes apart." Glancing at his notes, he added, "With the exception of Hernando Gutierrez leaving for about two hours on Tuesday morning to go to his bank, they all remained with Hunter until Wednesday. We witnessed Jane Bellows leave from the front entrance at eight forty-five a.m., with Springs and Gutierrez leaving from the parking garage shortly thereafter. All four played golf together yesterday afternoon."

"That's within the timeframe of the game played

against the Senator," Mali noted, pursing her lips in alarm.

Jake nodded. "Anything useful from the phone taps?"

"I'll take that one," John said, standing up. "There is nothing unusual from the office phones. Hunter calls a known prostitute regularly from his cell phone, last time was Sunday night. She evidently spent the night. Left early Monday morning shortly after Janet Simpson went into his apartment."

"Wait a minute. How do you know that Simpson went into his apartment?" Jake asked.

"Um, well, um, we felt it would be a good idea to put eyes inside his apartment building and we didn't have the manpower or authorization to put someone in the apartment across from his, so we installed a camera in the hallway leading to his door. It was hidden inside a picture hanging on the wall," Ron said.

Jake inhaled sharply, his nostrils flaring. "The camera needs to be removed, Ron."

"Yes sir."

"How did Hunter appear when he let her in?"

"Hunter didn't answer the door. Simpson let herself in with a key. But she looked pissed when she approached the door."

"Hmmmm . . . the plot thickens," Mali said.

"Jealous lover?" Kirsten asked.

"Possibly. Kirsten, what else have you learned through the financials?"

"A substantial sum of money was moved from the

accounts of Springs, Gutierrez, and Bellows to an off-shore account last week. I also checked their accounts for other large transfers. Springs had a similar withdrawal in February and also in late March, both to off-shore accounts although they're all different. I'm running them down now."

"While they don't correspond exactly to the Thornburg and Stone murders, they're close enough to raise red flags," Mali added.

"Good work, Kirsten and Hoop. The owner of those off-shore accounts may well be the mastermind behind this."

"I agree," said Mali. "We also discovered that Janet Simpson currently owns ten percent of the Hunted Inc stock, down from the twenty seven percent she had a short time ago."

"Why is she selling her stock?" Jake asked.

"I'm not sure why. It's hard to say if both are involved in this game, or just one or the other."

Kirsten added, "If they're romantically involved and she's the jealous type, maybe she's setting him up."

"That's possible. Do we have any more information on her past? And what about Hunter's stock?"

Mali said, "No more info yet on Simpson. We're still researching her background. We've checked CPS and adoption agencies for all twenty-one counties in New Jersey with no results. We've expanded the search to the surrounding states. As for Hunter, his holdings have decreased as well, although in small increments over the past few months. We're tracking the funds for them both now and hope to have some answers by day's end. On another topic, Kirsten tracked down a Hunter family picture." Displaying the picture on the center screen, she continued. "The picture is probably from twenty years ago or so. Hunter is the youngest of the boys, looks to be nine or ten."

"Another angle to consider is that one or more of his siblings are envious of Hunter and want to bring him down," Joe suggested.

"That's a possibility. While we haven't yet tracked down his sister or one of the brothers, the other two are living modest lives and none of them went to college. Unlikely that they would have the financial means or technical knowledge to do this." Everyone studied the picture. Jake continued, "The picture is blurry but run their faces through the aging program. If we're lucky, we might be able to see what they look like today. We need to find the other two siblings. Any luck on labs with medical and technical capability, Kirsten?"

"Still working on it. I have found five facilities, two in New York, one each in Washington, D.C., New Jersey, and in Dallas that appear to have the capability. I'm checking them out now including who owns them."

"Good. Any news from our D.C. lab on the game itself?"

Joe responded in the negative. "They did indicate that the assassin gets points if the kill is in the heart or the head. That doesn't really help though."

"Jake, back to the stockholders." Mali walked over to the white board. Pointing to the process questions, she said, "I'm thinking aloud here but if we assume that Hunter is behind this, and/or Simpson, and given all of these money transfers, I believe the stockholders could be the players and the money, the fee to play. It stands to reason. Hunter would have to bring trusted people in, people who had the funds to participate. Perhaps he even holds something over them to keep them quiet."

"All supposition, Hoop. But worth pursuing."

"I'd like to set up another meeting with Hunter to try to get more answers. Perhaps they watch the game from his office although I don't recall seeing a television or video system of any kind."

"Good idea. I want to go with you and will make myself available for whatever time you set up. If there's nothing else . . ." Everyone shook their heads. "Ok. Thanks for the update. Let's get back to work."

Just before lunch, Mali informed Jake that a meeting was set up for three o'clock in the afternoon. They agreed to get together after lunch to discuss strategy for the meeting. But during lunch, which was brought in to the control center once again, Jake received a call from his daughter's school indicating that there was a problem and they needed his presence.

"I'm sorry, Mali," Jake said as he explained what was going on. "Dad is fishing with his buddies today so he's out of pocket."

"Go, Jake, go. Heather is much more important than a meeting. Don't worry about Hunter."

"Thanks for understanding. Have Joe go with you.

I'll have my cell and will call you once on the road so we can discuss strategy for a few minutes."

"Sounds good. I hope Heather is all right."

* * *

PACKING UP HER computer, Mali found Kirsten and said, "Hey, do you have a nail file or clippers? I just broke one nail and chipped another. It's going to drive me crazy, especially since I'm headed to Hunter's office for a meeting with him and Simpson." She held up her left hand for Kirsten's inspection.

"No. Since I have no nails, I don't bother with one." She laughed, holding up both hands to show her short, frayed nails.

Mali laughed too. "I brought the wrong clutch today." She shrugged. "Oh well. I'll live. Thanks anyway."

"You're not rescheduling the meeting until Jake can go with you?"

"No. Joe is taking his place. He's meeting me in front with the car. Text me if you discover anything that could change the nature of our questions."

"Will do, Mali. Do you have plans for the weekend?" she asked, changing the subject.

"No. More work. We're finally making progress and I'd like to keep moving forward. But I might have time for a movie on Sunday. Are you and Jen available?"

"Yes! I'll check what's playing at the theaters this weekend and call you."

"Great. Talk to Jen and call me tomorrow. Maybe a quick bite beforehand?"

"Perfect."

"See you on Sunday."

With that, Mali headed out of the office. Walking through the lobby, she exited the building. The sky opened up as she stepped outside, big fat drops fell in increasing intensity. Mali opened her umbrella as she walked toward the curb. Her mind was focused on the upcoming meeting so it didn't register right away that someone was calling her name. Looking through the rain, Mali noticed Janet Simpson was waving to her from the open window of a limousine. She walked over to her.

"I'm glad I caught you, Agent Hooper. I was running late from a meeting and decided to try and catch you. Hop in and we can talk on the way to the office."

"I'm glad you're here, Ms. Simpson. Why don't you come up to our offices and we can have that chat here?"

"Actually, we should continue on to the office so you can speak directly with Anthony. There are a few disturbing developments we'd like to share with you including some information that he has with him. Where is Agent Black, by the way?"

The door opened and Mali responded, looking down the street for Joe. "He had a family emergency and won't be joining us. Although I am waiting for another agent, Joe Alters, to pick me up. He should be here by now."

"I'm sorry to hear about Agent Black. I hope everything is all right. Why don't you get in and wait for Agent Alters inside? It's beginning to pour. We can talk while we wait."

Mali hesitated, looking for Joe one more time, then stepped into the car. Simpson offered her a bottle of water. She accepted it, untwisting the cap and taking a sip.

"Now tell me what we can do for you today?" Simpson asked.

"We have a few questions about three of Hunter's biggest stockholders, Ted Springs, Jane Bellows, and Hernando Gutierrez."

"Stockholders and good friends," Simpson added. "Anthony has known them for years, ever since his college days. They believed in him and The Hunted Ones from the start."

"Do you have any reason to believe that they would want to harm Mr. Hunter?" she asked, drinking more water.

With an astonished laugh, Simpson said, "Do you mean would they set up this elaborate and deadly game in some sort of effort to destroy him? No." She laughed again. "They love his work. Ted even wants to purchase Anthony's patent. Why would the FBI waste their time on such a thing?"

"Our investigation has uncovered some questionable and sizable withdrawals.

Simpson's phone rang. "Excuse me. I need to take this."

"Of course." Mali took the time to look for Joe but he had not pulled up to the curb and she couldn't see the car on the street. Turning her attention to the inside of the car, she acknowledged that it had been a long time since her last ride in a limousine. She didn't miss it. She never rode in a limo as luxurious as this one, however. Soft leather fabric with wooden accents lined the doors and included a bank of USB ports on each one, plush matching leather covered the seats, a fully stocked bar with crystal glasses was nestled next to a tiny refrigerator, a DVD player was tucked in the corner behind the front passenger seat, headphones rested in pockets on the doors, even a small television sat in the corner behind the passenger seat. *No expense was spared here.* She fussed with her nails as she stared out the window.

Movement startled her into awareness. The limo had pulled away from the curb. When she turned her head to ask Simpson about it, she swooned, feeling dizzy, and grabbed hold of the arm rest on the door, closing her eyes.

When the typewriting tone on her phone chimed, Mali lethargically pulled her phone from her purse and punched in the password. Kirsten had sent her a text message. Opening it, she read, 'Jane Hunter is Janet Simpson! Just confirmed that she changed her name when she turned eighteen. Adopted at age of six from a Delaware adoption agency. The agency had a better picture of her. Face aging program confirms an eighty-nine percent match for the young girl to Simpson. Weird, right? Off-shore accounts are tied to ghost companies traced back to her. You and Joe be careful when you meet up with them.'

Blinking, Mali looked at Simpson, who was no

longer on the phone. Simpson was still, eyes pitch black in their intensity, as she stared at Mali.

"Are you all right, Agent Hooper?" Her voice sounded far away, as if from a distance. Mali licked her dry mouth and glanced down at the water. *Damn!*

"What did you drug me with?" She licked her lips again. Her mouth felt like it was filled with cotton.

"A harmless little drug that will let you sleep for a while." She grabbed the phone from Mali's hand, read the text, and shook her head. "Ah, you've discovered our little secret, two secrets actually. And as I'm sure you have figured out, Ted, Jane, and Hernando have not betrayed Anthony. They are, in fact, players in the game. They pay us a lot of money for the privilege and they get as much pleasure from the game as we do. They are going to be so excited to find out that there's another game, and in just a day or two. They'll be even more thrilled to learn that the target is none other than Agent Hooper of the FBI."

"How did you . . ." Her head swam.

"How did I know that you were closing in on us and starting to figure things out? It's called a drop out app. Have you heard of it? Quite the thing, actually, similar to the FBI's roving bug. The last time you visited our offices, Anthony remotely installed a piece of software that activates your mic on command. We turned your phone into a hot microphone and have been listening to your conversations off and on ever since. The beauty of this app is that you don't have to be on the phone for us to hear what's being said, brilliant actually. Too bad Anthony didn't create this technology himself, although he did tweak it so it had a longer range. He could have made a fortune on it. The meeting you had this morning in your control center was very enlightening. It was time to move forward with our plan, a little sooner than we were thinking. Ah well, that's the way the ball bounces sometimes."

"They'll catch you both."

Janet shook her head. "No, they won't. You have no idea where we plan to play the game. Besides, your friends are going to be so busy trying to save you that we'll just slip away before anyone realizes it."

Mali lifted her right hand to take a swing at her but the move was in slow motion and it only made her dizziness intensify. The world was spinning.

Simpson laughed.

Resting her head against the back seat, Mali looked at her and whispered, "Why?"

"Why not? What better way to highlight this great game! Anthony hasn't been this excited since The Hunted Ones first broke on the market. Besides, I have my own plans . . ."

CHAPTER TWENTY

Hunter's Lab, somewhere in New Jersey
Friday, May 1, 6:45 p.m.

AWARENESS CAME SLOWLY to Mali. She was lying on a cold metal table and her hands and feet were tied with straps. There were voices murmuring in the distance although she could not understand what was being said. A whiff of antiseptic permeated the air. Wrinkling her nose at the odor, Mali slowly opened her eyes, cautiously moving her head from side to side. No dizziness. The effects of the drug had dissipated. She initially assumed that she was in a hospital emergency room, considering her surroundings. There was a light over her head, turned on but pointing away from her. Medical instruments were lying on a table next to her and there was an IV bag hanging above her head with a line going to her arm. A clear liquid dripped into her right arm. She noticed medical supplies haphazardly placed in a cabinet with an open door as well as a laptop on a small table with wheels. The room was surrounded by plastic walls and everything beyond was blurry because of the plastic. She was not in a hospital. A warehouse or storage room of some sort? She could not tell the time of day, for there were no windows visible in the room beyond the sterile area so she had no idea if she'd been there for a few minutes or a few hours. And she had no clue where she was.

She must have made a noise or moved because the voices stopped talking. The plastic door flipped open and the sound of footsteps approaching reached her ears. The light above her was flipped to shine down on her. Mali squinted against the brightness. After her eyes adjusted, she observed a person with a delicate build staring down at her. Given the build and petite hands, Mali assumed the person was a woman. She was wearing surgical garb and her face was covered by a mask. Not the mask of a surgeon, however. The woman was wearing a gas mask.

"Where am I? And what are you doing?" Mali asked in growing alarm. She feared the answer.

"Ma petite. You should not be awake." Even though her voice was muffled because of the mask, Mali confirmed that the speaker was a woman and she was French.

"My name is Mali Hooper and I'm an agent for the FBI. Let me go now and I can assure you that I'll help you."

With a throaty laugh, Dr. Simone Dubois picked up a bottle and syringe and filled the syringe with a clear liquid. As she administered the drug to Mali, she shook her head, saying, "Rest, Agent Mali Hooper. You will need it."

Seconds later, Mali was asleep once again.

* * *

"You received the instructions from Hunter, right?"

"Oui," the French woman confirmed. "We will disassemble everything and destroy the data and equipment as soon as you leave with the girl."

"Make sure there is no trace of anything. Mr. Hunter wants this warehouse empty within two hours. Your flight to Paris leaves in six hours." The man handed her some documents. He stepped into the passenger side of the car, an unrecognizable Mali was lying down in the back seat.

After they drove off, Dr. Dubois turned to her partner, Richard, who said, "The team is taking apart the room. A truck should be here within the hour so we can load everything."

"Bien. Give me the laptop and the last implant. Janet, mon amour, does not want everything destroyed. I meet her in one hour. We fly to Geneva on the red-eye before continuing on to Zurich. Paris is not our destination."

Richard nodded and walked into the warehouse, returning a few minutes later with the laptop and a small metal box.

Taking them from him, Dr. Dubois opened her briefcase and set them inside. Pulling out two large envelopes, she handed them to him. "Here is your ticket to Zurich and the remaining payment for those inside as well as a hefty bonus for you." She closed her briefcase and leaned in to kiss him. "Burn the building before you leave. Meet us in Zurich in four days. Au revoir, Richard." She settled herself in the car before quickly speeding away.

Richard turned and walked back into the warehouse and stopped. It was too quiet. Nothing more had been done since he picked up the laptop and implant. The plastic surgical room was still intact. "What the hell?" His hands curled into fists. So much had to be done in a short period of time. Mumbling to himself that it was hard to find good workers, even those who were paid well, Richard stomped over to the plastic room. He was almost upon it when he noticed his three workers on the floor, in various stages of dying. One was violently retching in the corner, another was lying on his side on the floor with foam coming out of his mouth and gasping for air, and the third was already dead. The sweet aroma of almonds was strong.

Richard backed up, wanting nothing more than to get the hell out of there, when he was grabbed from behind. The two envelopes were ripped from his hand as he was unceremoniously shoved toward the plastic room. Turning his head, he caught a glimpse of the person attacking him and only saw a large body in full hazmat gear.

"No, no!" Richard struggled in earnest, putting his feet in front of him and locking his knees in an effort to stop the forward momentum. It didn't work. His feet just slid on the cement floor. "Please, no!" Still struggling to no avail, the attacker opened the Velcro plastic door and pushed Richard inside with such force that he tumbled to the ground. Jumping up, Richard dashed to the door only to be kicked in the stomach. Falling back to the metal table, Richard heard a hissing sound and his eyes darted around the room before spotting the stream of smoke coming in from a small hose on the floor. His face paled as understanding dawned. Now gasping for breath, Richard sank to his knees next to the table as a wave of nausea hit him. Leaning over, he vomited over and over. As he fell onto his side into the vomit, he glanced at the door. His attacker stood there watching him. His last thought before dying was, *What a fool I am.*

* * *

WALKING OUT OF the warehouse, the assassin removed his mask and pulled out a phone. He punched the number one on his speed dial. "It's done. Simone is headed your way with the laptop and implant."

"Excellent. Good work, Drake. Torch the place, make sure there's nothing left, then head over to the starting point for the new game, as per Anthony's instructions. The Zurich ticket is yours, leaving in three days' time, after the game, from Logan International in Boston. The money is yours to keep. Consider it a bonus."

"Thank you, Janet."

"I reward people for their good work and for their loyalty, Drake. Don't forget that. I'll be in touch in the coming weeks." She hung up.

The assassin removed his gear, destroyed the phone, and threw all of it inside the warehouse.

A little before ten p.m., Dr. Simone Dubois slipped her key card into the slot and opened the door to the penthouse suite she always booked at the The Westin Jersey City Newport Hotel. Janet had not yet arrived.

Dr. Dubois was renowned in France for her work with implants and the release of medicine by computer or phone app. She had made it possible for medicine to be released to patients by doctors remotely or on a schedule without the patient having to go into the office. Patients could sit in the comfort of their own home during treatment and be monitored via the implant as the medicine was released, all due to her expertise.

A little over three years ago, she had spoken at a medical conference in Washington, D.C., and had met Janet Simpson. Janet had been interested in her work and they had enjoyed dinner together that same evening. They had been together ever since and Simone had never been happier. It had not taken much to convince her to become a part of Janet's project. She had taken her implants to a new level with the game and was thrilled at its success. No one would know, but Simone was content in her own knowledge of it. And she had begun to work on a new implant to be used with stem cells on Parkinson's patients. Her improved technology would greatly help them.

Setting her briefcase down, she walked into the sumptuous bathroom, and removed her clothes while enjoying the expansive Manhattan views through the full wall of windows. She loved coming to this hotel with Janet. They had been meeting there for months and she never tired of the view. When dark, it matched the beauty of the Paris skyline at night, in her opinion. Turning on the tub faucet, she walked to the sink and splashed her face. This business, while financially rewarding, had taken a toll on her and she was glad that this was the last game. She was ready to return to Europe.

When the tub was full, Simone turned off the faucet, turned on the jets, and stepped inside. With a sigh of pure joy, she sank to her neck and became mesmerized by the city lights as the stresses of the last few days melted away.

"Hello beautiful," Janet whispered, leaning down to kiss Simone.

"I didn't hear you come in," Simone responded, pulling Janet's head down for a deeper kiss. "Why don't you join me? I am feeling quite energized," she said after the kiss, her voice heavy with passion.

Without saying a word, and not taking her eyes off Simone, Janet undressed and stepped into the tub, leaning her back against the opposite end. "Heaven." Janet closed her eyes in contentment. "How did it go?"

"Except for the agent momentarily waking up, everything went like clockwork," Simone responded as she sat up and scooted closer. Leaning forward, she laid on top of Janet and kissed her neck. "The warehouse should be empty by now and possibly even burning at this point." She rubbed herself against Janet while kissing her way down to her breasts.

"What do you mean the agent woke up?" Janet asked while sliding her hands down to Simone's buttocks and squeezing.

"She was awake for a brief time," Simone murmured. "Checked things out, asked a couple of questions. I told her she wasn't supposed to be awake then I gave her more drugs and she was fast asleep."

"You spoke with her, Simone?"

"Not to worry, ma cherie. I was in full gear, she could not see or identify me. Besides, she won't be alive for much longer."

Janet rolled over in the tub, water splashing over the sides, so she was lying on top making Simone giggle. "I like this aggressiveness, mon amour."

Giving her a lingering kiss, Janet whispered, "I'm so sorry, ma petite."

"Eh?"

Janet's eyes narrowed and her nostrils flared as she simultaneously sat up and shoved a startled Simone underneath the water. Simone tried to buck Janet off but she was much smaller and had no strength to do so. Water splashed out of the tub as Simone continued to fight. Her struggles grew weaker and, in a few minutes, ceased altogether.

When Janet was sure Simone was dead, she climbed out of the tub. Grabbing a towel, she dried herself off then wiped the water off the floor. She dressed, hung up the towel, grabbed a washcloth, and walked into the bedroom. Picking up the briefcase, she put her baseball cap back on, pulling it low over her brow, and used the washcloth to meticulously wipe down everything she had touched.

You shouldn't have talked to her, Simone. She shook her head as she left the room, quietly closing the door behind her.

CHAPTER TWENTY-ONE

FBI Field Office, New York City
Earlier on Friday, May 1st

When Jake arrived at his daughter's school, he was told that there was no emergency and no one from their office had called him. Concerned, he tried calling Mali but there was no answer. Texting produced the same results. Where was she?

After making arrangements for someone to watch Heather, and with growing alarm, Jake called Kirsten and was told about Janet Simpson's relationship to Hunter as well as the identity of the owner of the off-shore accounts. She told Jake that Mali never met Joe to go to the meeting with Hunter.

Jake instructed Kirsten to have everyone remain at the office. He had a bad feeling and was headed back in.

Now back at the office at a little after 5:30 p.m., Jake called Frank and the entire team together for a meeting.

He explained the diversion that got him out of the office. "I spoke with Ron on my way in. He said that

Hunter has been in the office all day. Additionally, they intercepted a phone call from Hunter with Simpson at three ten expressing irritation that Mali had not shown up for their meeting. They also briefly discussed her appointment with their financial advisors before hanging up. Kirsten, what time did Mali leave the office?"

"Two o'clock."

"And what time did you text her?"

She looked at her phone. "The text was delivered to her at two twelve."

"What's going on, Jake?" asked Joe.

"Hoop has been taken and I believe she is going to be the next target for the game."

"Oh my God!" said Kirsten.

Joe was visibly upset. "This is all my fault. I stopped to grab a coffee before picking up the car. I took too long."

"Don't go there, Joe. This was not your fault." Jake paused. "Time is of the essence." He looked at Frank and every other team member. "She was taken somewhere between here and the Hunter offices. Amy, Brad, I want you to work with security to check the camera outside this building. Let's find her and track her steps. Kirsten, Joe, she'll be taken somewhere to have the implant inserted. Let's operate on the assumption that they have stayed local so focus on the two labs here in New York and the one in New Jersey first. Needless to say, no one goes home tonight."

Everyone went to work and Jake joined Frank at the back of the room.

"Son of a bitch," Frank said, rubbing his neck.

"She could be anywhere, Frank. And they could take her anywhere for the game."

"Let's not get ahead of ourselves, Jake. Let's work our way through each lead. We'll find her. I'll get a warrant for the Hunter offices and I'll mobilize all local agents so they're ready to roll when we need them. Update me every thirty minutes or sooner, if needed."

Jake nodded and Frank walked out of the control center.

"Joe." He walked over to Kirsten and Joe. "I need you to get the blueprints to the Hunter building. I want to be ready to breach the facility as soon as we have the warrant. Kirsten, are you okay working the labs alone?"

"Yes, Jake."

"Good." Looking at Joe, he said, "I want those blueprints ASAP!"

"Jake, look at this." Brad put a video on the center screen. The team observed Mali leaving the building from the main entrance and walking toward the curb as she opened her umbrella. She stopped and looked at a limousine before walking over to it.

"Can we get any closer to identify who's in the vehicle?"

Amy zoomed in closer but could not get close enough to identify the person Mali was talking to, her umbrella was in the way.

"Damn," Jake exclaimed. "Whoever she's talking to is being careful not to be seen. He or she is obviously someone Hoop knows. And the rain isn't helping."

They watched Mali step into the limo. It didn't move right away.

"Tell me we can get the plate."

"Sorry, Jake, but that truck is too close to the limo to see the plates." Amy said.

As the limo moved into traffic, they watched Joe pull up to the curb.

"Something else occurred to me, Jake," Kirsten said. "Given the type of vehicle Mali just climbed in to, and her background, could the abduction have anything to do with her family?"

That brought Jake up short. The thought had not occurred to him. After considering it, he responded. "It's highly unlikely that this has anything to do with her family. It's just too coincidental that she was taken now." He turned to Brad and Amy. "Look for any other camera angles of that limo. Perhaps we can see a face or a license plate from a different side." Jake studied the still shot on the screen of Mali stepping into the limo. *Hold tight, Mali. We're going to find you.*

9:00 p.m.

"No luck on the three labs, Jake," said Kirsten.

The team had been working non-stop and running into obstacles along the way. Amy and Brad were able to obtain other camera views of the street at the time of the abduction but there was too much traffic and the plate was unidentifiable. The windows were tinted too dark so no facial recognition was possible. They couldn't even tell how many people were inside. The City Registrar and County Clerk offices, which housed the permits and plans for all office buildings, were closed and Joe wouldn't be able to talk to them until Monday. He was able to track down the name of the architect who built the Hunter building but had been unable to reach him. So no blueprints as of yet.

"Kirsten, I want a list of all businesses and buildings owned by Hunter. Are there any facilities that could be outfitted with a lab? Joe, I want a list of the businesses that are renting space in the Hunter building, specifically those that are directly below and adjacent to the Hunter offices. I want access to them as soon as possible." Jake walked over to Frank's office to give him an update.

"Judge Warren has agreed to sign a warrant allowing us to search the Hunter offices as well as his apartment and Janet Simpson's apartment," Frank offered as Jake walked in. "We'll have them by eight tomorrow morning. I have two teams ready to go to their apartments and I have twelve men assigned to go to the offices with you as soon as the warrants are in our hands."

"Good." Jake sighed, sitting down. "We're having a hard time getting information. It doesn't help that it's Friday night. No one is working. Damn, I want this information yesterday and we'll be lucky to get it by Monday." Jake stood up to pace. "The game will likely start tomorrow, Sunday at the latest. Monday will be too late to get the information we need."

Frank handed Jake a bottle of water, picked up his own, and both drank in silence. "Mali is smart, Jake.

And she has the advantage of knowing the game. That will work in her favor."

Jake nodded and was about to say something when his cell phone rang.

"Jake, Kirsten here. I found a warehouse in New Jersey that is owned by Hunter. Turn on the television, channel four. They are reporting that the warehouse is on fire right now."

Jake signaled to Frank to turn on the television.

"Thanks Kirsten," Jake said.

". . . and we have been told that there are bodies inside, although they have not been identified," the reporter said. "In addition, we have been moved further away due to an odor that concerns authorities. Back to you, Gene."

"Jake, meet me downstairs in ten. We need to get over there," said Frank, switching off the television.

"I'll update the team and be right down." Jake left Frank's office and returned to the control center.

"Quick update. Frank and I are headed to a warehouse in New Jersey. It's owned by Hunter and, as you've probably heard from Kirsten, it's on fire." He rubbed the back of his neck. "We're at a standstill here, so go home. Be here at five tomorrow morning. Thanks everyone." He left without waiting for a response.

By the time Frank and Jake arrived at the warehouse, the embers of the fire were smoldering, smoke billowing up. They walked over to the police officer in charge and introduced themselves. The Fire Chief was called over to join them.

"What can you tell us about this fire and why are your men in hazmat gear?" Frank asked.

"We got the call about two hours ago," said the police officer. "A witness reported a fire and small explosion and reported smelling an odor. So we suspected a presence of chemicals prior to our arrival. The facility was fully involved when we arrived."

Captain Epps, the Fire Chief, added, "The witness was being assessed by EMS after complaining of severe nausea. They transported him to Morristown Medical Center. The New Jersey Poison Control Center has been informed and is making their way to the hospital. They are also sending someone here to help assess and identify the chemicals used. In addition, there are four bodies inside. The Medical Examiner is with them right now."

"When will it be safe to go inside the building?" Frank asked.

"I can't give you a specific time. This is a hot zone until we can identify the chemicals. The M.E. is in full hazmat gear."

Frank thanked the men for the information and Jake and Frank stepped out of the way to wait for the M.E.

A short time later, after safely removing the gear, the M.E. briefly spoke with the police officer and Fire Chief before heading to Frank and Jake.

"Good evening gentlemen. Captain Epps said you'd like to speak with me."

"Yes," Jake said. "What can you tell us about the four bodies?"

"Not much. All victims were male. Three of the

bodies were burnt beyond recognition. The fourth body was protected somewhat by a metal table that had fallen on top of him. His body was not as damaged as the other three. We should be able to identify all of them through dental records."

"Could you identify cause of death?" Frank asked.

"No. There were no visible injuries on the fourth victim. Given the suspicion of chemicals present, it's possible he died of poisoning. I'll have answers when I get him back to our facility and run tests."

"Do you know what chemicals are involved?" Jake pressed.

"Not at this time." Taking off his glasses and wearily rubbing his eyes, the M.E. asked if there were any further questions.

Shaking his head, Jake said, "Check for cyanide poisoning."

The M.E. looked a little startled. "Any particular reason why you suspect cyanide?"

"An on-going case. It's critical that we find out as quickly as possible if this is related," stated Frank.

"My staff and I will work all night and contact you with results as soon as we have anything."

"Thank you. We appreciate that."

Jake handed his business card to the medical examiner and they turned to leave. Another car was pulling into the parking lot. There was a sign on the side of the car, 'New Jersey Poison Control Center.' They walked over to the woman getting out of the car and told her to look for signs of cyanide poisoning. They walked back to Frank's car after a promise from her to call as soon as she had results.

Jake received a call shortly after midnight from the M.E. confirming that the fourth victim, and likely all victims, died from cyanide poisoning. He called Frank.

"Mali was there, Frank, I feel it," Jake said after relaying the information from his previous call.

"That probably means that the game will be local, Jake. Let's focus on ways we can find and help her."

"Hunter and his sister are going to pay for this," growled Jake.

CHAPTER TWENTY-TWO

Hotel Cliff, Washington Heights, New York
Saturday, May 2, 8:50 a.m.

YOU HAVE BEEN selected to play 'The Hunted Ones,' a game of survival—*your* survival. An assassin has been assigned to hunt you down and kill you. You have forty-eight hours to live or die.

Rules of play:

1. You have been implanted with a transmitter/receiver behind your ear. The transmitter provides your GPS location, and the receiver monitors your communications. You are being watched 24-7. Do not try to remove this device or it will release a lethal dose of cyanide.

2. Do not leave the city limits or contact anyone as you try to evade the assassin. If you do either, the cyanide will be released.

3. **Dress in everything that is on the bed. There is a go-pro camera in the front center of your outfit. Do not remove or cover it up. If you do either, the cyanide will be released.**

4. **The assassin is frequently given your GPS location; it's not a good idea to rest for long.**

5. **If you survive the next forty-eight hours, you will receive one million dollars. Go to Battery Park, you will receive instructions on where to pick up your cash and the device will be removed at that time.**

6. **Do not remove this note or the picture from the room. If they are not found sitting on the bed, the cyanide will be released.**

7. **You will have a thirty-minute lead. The game begins at 10:00 a.m.**

Disregard this note at your own peril and that of your loved ones. They, too, are being watched. Good luck!

"So that's how they get the targets to participate." Mali grimaced as she looked at a picture of her family taken at her parent's recent anniversary party. She turned the typed note over and read a handwritten one.

Obviously, rule number five does not apply to you, dearest Agent Hooper. We're watching more than your family. I would hate for harm to come to your fellow agent.

And taped below that was a picture of Jake kissing Mali in the garden at her parent's house.

"How the hell . . ." she exclaimed, shaking her head. She winced at the searing pain and reached behind her ear once more, feeling the stitches.

When she awoke fifteen minutes ago, she was lying on her side in her bra and underwear on a bed in some hotel. Her head was pounding, the cut above her ear was throbbing. She saw the note and had cautiously sat up to read it.

Now, she studied the dark room. There was a television on the wall opposite the bed and heavy curtains were drawn closed. She rose and staggered to the curtains, pulling them aside. She was on the top floor of a hotel, six or seven floors up. She was above the entry to the hotel leading to the street beyond although from her position, she could not read the hotel's name. The two-lane street was congested with cars and businesses lined both sides. She did not recognize anything and was not sure if she was still in New York. It was daylight but she didn't know the day or time. She figured it must be morning, given the ten a.m. start time. But how close to ten was it?

Turning back to the room, she walked to the television, picked up the remote and turned it on. Local news came on. *Good, I'm still in New York.* She learned a few minutes later that it was 9:05, Saturday morning. Glancing at the desk below, she found a binder and opened it. She was in the Hotel Cliff. She read the address. *I'm in Washington Heights? They couldn't have put me much further north and still be in the City.* While she wasn't too familiar with this part of New York, she was grateful to still be in the City.

Heading into the restroom, she saw herself for the first time in the mirror. "Oh my God!" Her hair had been chopped off and dyed black. Blood trickled from her ear, across the middle of her face, and below her nose stopping halfway down her other cheek. It was now a sticky mess. Stepping out of her underclothes, she turned on the shower and stood under a warm, if a bit weak, stream of water. She cupped her hand over the incision to protect it and leaned back to wet her hair and face. The water ran black, with a hint of red, as it slid down the drain. She let the water run down her body, feeling somewhat better. Her headache was now just a dull roar and the throbbing behind her ear was manageable.

Turning off the water, she dried herself and went back into the main room carrying her underwear and bra. She looked at the clothes that had been left for her in distaste. She dressed in her bra and underwear then picked up the white sweat pants, well, they used to be white. They were now a distinct gray with unidentifiable stains on the front as well as the seat of the pants. She lifted them to her nose and sniffed. That was a mistake. Wrinkling her nose in distaste, she stepped into them and pulled them up. She tied the strings in the front as tight as she could. The sweat pants were a few sizes too big.

Since she was not sure if the Go-Pro camera had been turned on, before she finished dressing she crept across the room and looked for anything that might help her. She removed the phone cord from the wall and phone and put it on the bed by the pillow. Next she grabbed some tissues and set them next to the cord. She remembered that there was a pen and small pad inside the binder. She grabbed both. Flipping through the binder, she found a general map with a star annotating where the hotel was located. She ripped it out and set it aside as well. Walking back to the bathroom, she pulled a hand towel off the rack. She snagged the plastic laundry bag from a hanger in the closet on her way back to the bed. She looked at everything she had assembled. After some consideration, she picked up the pen and wrote something on the pad then placed all items inside the laundry bag.

It was nine forty. She reached for the sweatshirt that was still lying at the end of the bed and, not looking too closely at it, opted instead just to slip it on. She gagged when the pungent, rank body odor assailed her nostrils. "I'll be warm at night," she mumbled, trying to look at the bright side of things. After shoving her feet into the tennis shoes that pinched her toes, she placed the grimy black baseball cap on her head. Walking back into the bathroom, she looked at herself in the mirror one more time. She croaked out a humorless laugh. *I've seen better days, but I'm alive and I plan to stay that way.*

At nine forty-five, she left the room with her laundry bag and headed down the stairs. Smelling coffee, Mali followed the scent and observed the remains of a continental breakfast buffet spread out for hotel patrons. She grabbed a few croissants and dropped them in the bag, adding two muffins and an apple. As she reached for bottled water, she noticed other patrons staring at her, a few whispering to each other. She disregarded them and continued on, focused on what she might need to survive. She paused, thinking, then added two bottled waters to the bag and grabbed one more.

She was turning to leave when a hotel employee approached her.

"You are disturbing the patrons of this hotel. Leave right now. And put that food back."

She raised her eyebrows at the last comment but said nothing. She made a move to go past him but he grabbed her arm. "I said put the food down."

Shaking her head, lips pressed tightly together, she shrugged his hand off her arm and knuckle-punched him in the nose with her right hand, pushing him away. The employee fell to the ground grabbing his nose, blood dripping down his face and hand.

"Hey, stop her!" yelled one woman.

"Call the police!" shouted another.

Without wasting any time, Mali ducked out the door behind the buffet table and raced down the street turning south on Amsterdam Avenue. She didn't let up on her pace until she passed beneath I-95. She turned west on a side street and jogged to Saint Nicholas Avenue before turning south again. She slowed to a fast walk and tried to blend in.

It was ten o'clock.

CHAPTER TWENTY-THREE

Hunter's Gaming Room, New York
Saturday, May 2, 10:10 a.m.

"Hey Tony! Look at that agent run!" laughed Ted Springs. "She was smart to grab some food, though. I have to give her credit for that. Did you see her punch that guy? She dropped him! Awesome!!"

Ted, Jane, and Hernando had arrived two hours earlier, via the hidden basement entrance per Hunter's suggestion, so they could enjoy breakfast together and prepare for the hunt. All had paid top dollar to play and the three were now good-heartedly arguing over who should give the first set of directions to the assassin. The assassin's first move was coming up in twenty minutes.

Anthony watched his friends, his lips twisted in a wry grin. They had no clue that this was the last game and that he and his sister planned to be long gone, everything cashed in, prior to the game's end. Anthony was sure the FBI would search the building soon. But he was confident that this room would not be found, *not until I'm out of here anyway.*

The room was fully stocked with food and drink, everything they would need to enjoy the game without having to leave. Anthony and Janet had already planned their escape route; his private jet was ready to go later tonight, and before long the two of them would be up, up, and away to a new life together.

He cackled a little wildly. Janet turned from her laptop, to glare at him, eyes narrowed to slits.

Jane asked, "What's so funny, Tony?" as she moved to sit on his lap.

"Just thinking about how fun this particular game is going to be. Our Agent Hooper is going to give us a good run for our money." He nuzzled her neck and settled her more comfortably in his lap.

"With Hernando giving the first set of instructions, why don't you and I make a pit stop?" she whispered in his ear.

"My thoughts exactly, sweetheart." Anthony helped her up before standing himself. He headed to the bar, holding Jane's hand, and poured himself a shot of whiskey.

Janet's eyes narrowed. "Really, Anthony?" she scoffed.

"Hey, it's five o'clock somewhere." He downed the shot, pouring another for himself and one for Jane. Leaning in close to Janet's ear, he whispered, "Care to join us?" His eyebrows moved up and down as he ogled her chest.

"In the bathroom? No. Besides, I'm finishing our pressing business."

"Ah yes. Better that you stay and take care of that. We want everything to be in order, after all. What would I do without you?" Anthony gave her a quick whiskey-laden kiss and grabbed the two shot glasses, whiskey sloshing over the top. Still holding Jane's hand, they rushed to the bathroom, both giggling like kids who were doing something naughty.

"Amigos, que paso? What about us?" Hernando asked.

As Anthony stepped inside and tugged on her hand, Jane paused. She downed the shot and dropped the glass on the floor. Looking back at Hernando, she unbuttoned two buttons on her blouse with her free hand, reached inside and massaged her bare breast. "You got the remote, I've got something else."

Hernando groaned and Anthony laughed.

"Be sure to wait until ten thirty before pinging Agent Hooper's location and sending the first instruction," Anthony reminded his friends before Jane pulled him in and slammed the door.

* * *

As SOON AS the bathroom door closed, Janet returned her attention to the computer in front of her. The numbers on the screen were lost on her though. She was six years old again. Her mind had slipped back to her childhood, reminding her why she was doing this. Eyes unfocused, she looked back.

Adopted at the age of six, Janet grew up in New Jersey with her new parents and four older brothers. She remembered being so moved to have found a forever family, never thinking anyone would pick someone her age who was not as pretty as the other little girls in the orphanage. She settled in quickly, enjoying the attention she received from everyone. She was the princess and they treated her like royalty. She felt special for the first time in her life. There was never much money to buy things a girl might like to have. She never had dolls or stuffed bunnies like other girls but it didn't matter to her. She was part of a family and everyone loved her. Her brothers nicknamed her Janie, a special name just for her. It didn't mean anything when her brothers patted her on her bottom whenever she walked by. It was just their way of showing affection. Her mom harping on her to study hard and do well in school, because her mousy looks would never get her anywhere, was just her way of showing love to her only daughter. That first year was the best year of her life. She was ecstatic.

Things changed when her three older brothers started to sneak into her room at night to hurt her. The pain was excruciating that first time. She felt like her insides were being ripped apart. They slapped her when she whimpered and promised her punishment if she screamed. She was frozen with fear. They said they'd kill her if she told anyone. She had no reason to doubt them. The pain was so intense that she couldn't go to school for a week. She told her mother that she was sick. Her mother didn't ask any questions and let her stay home.

Her brothers visited her room every few nights, each taking their turn. She learned that if she was quiet and acquiesced, they would finish quickly and leave. Only one other person knew what was going on because he was forced to watch. Her older brother by one year, and the youngest of all the boys, Anthony wasn't there the first time but they brought him in soon after and kept bringing him. He used to cry in silence, the sobs shaking his shoulders, tears spilling down his face and dripping off his chin. His brothers always shoved him into the lone chair in her room for front row viewing, laughing at him, and telling him to sit back and enjoy.

The first time she realized that things had changed for Anthony was on a night like any other, a night she dreaded like every other. They had been 'visiting' her for over a year at this point and they came into her room like they always did, tiptoeing so their parents wouldn't wake up, giggling because of the fun they were anticipating. They woke her and, without uttering a word, she stood up on her bed, took off her nightgown and princess underwear, then laid back down.

Hank, her oldest brother by nine years, now sixteen years old, wanted to try something different and told her to turn over and get on her hands and knees. She wasn't sure what to expect but did as she was told. Her other brothers were watching in fascination and with rising excitement, not quite sure what to expect either. Hank grabbed her hips and shoved himself into her rear. The pain was unbearable and she cried and screamed into her pillow, instinctively fighting him and trying to get him off her. He slapped her hard on her buttocks and told her to shut up then continued his assault, panting and moaning above her as he pounded inside her over and over. She turned her head to the side and, through her tears, watched Larry and Jed move next to the bed and egg on her brother, all while stroking themselves.

What broke her, though, crushed her spirit like no other offense, was seeing her youngest brother sitting on the chair he normally sat on, his nine-year-old eyes full of lust, pajamas down at his ankles, feverishly stroking himself. She had somehow thought that he would save her because they forced him to watch. She knew differently in that moment. He would never help her. She had to help herself. And it was at that precise time, while her other two brothers were taking their turns and her youngest brother climaxed on her chair, that Janet made her plans.

The abuse continued for two more years after that night, stopping only when her two oldest brothers were at college and Jed had a girlfriend. While he never touched her, her youngest brother had continued to watch over the course of those two years, taking his own enjoyment while doing so.

By the time she was ten years old, Janet had a basic plan in place. She worked hard in school, harder than anyone, taking every college prep course she could. Graduating early just after she turned sixteen-years-old, she received a scholarship to Georgetown University and left home, never looking back. She changed her name when she turned eighteen and graduated in three years. Her plan was in full swing.

Shaking off the memories, Janet refocused on the computer and her work, her real work. After years of meticulously planning everything down to the most minute detail, and after carefully executing it, her revenge was near. She could taste it. She could smell it. She was drunk on the feeling.

Unbeknownst to Anthony, not only was her last share of Hunted Inc sold yesterday afternoon just before the stock market closed but so was his. And all money was deposited into her Swiss accounts. As CFO, she controlled it all. She had been regularly selling her shares for the past month or so and small amounts of his shares for many months. He rarely checked his holdings, fully trusting his sister. The fool hadn't noticed anything amiss.

Anthony wasn't even suspicious when his assistant didn't come to the office yesterday. He questioned Janet about the temp hire and was satisfied when she told him about Rebecca's family emergency. But Rebecca was an unfortunate loose end, her knowledge of the hidden elevator her downfall.

As for the three stockholders playing the game, they would have to deal with the FBI. She would be long gone by then so what they told the feds wouldn't matter. She had disappeared before, she could again.

And Anthony? She had something exceptional planned for him.

CHAPTER TWENTY-FOUR

Hunter Inc. Offices, New York
Saturday, May 2, 2:30 p.m.

"NOTHING. NOT A damn thing has been found." A frustrated Jake, standing on the sidewalk by the van, hit it with his fist. First there was a delay getting the warrant so the team was not able to access the building until eleven that morning. Nothing substantive was found in the offices. Ron and John reported Hunter and Simpson leaving together last night. They were tailed to their apartments but hadn't been seen since. When the team showed up to search their apartments this morning, Hunter and Simpson were not there. They were nowhere to be found.

The gray mobile surveillance van was activated so that the team could stay on the streets and possibly help Mali, if they could only locate her. Riding in the back with Jake were Kirsten and Robert, a surveillance van specialist. The van was fully equipped with the latest computer equipment, the fastest Wi-Fi access, four monitors, and various tracking devices and weapons. In front with the driver was a doctor, gas mask resting next to her.

Frank was in constant video communication with the mobile team from the Control Center. Joe and the rest of the team at the center were currently searching the streets of Manhattan trying to find Mali as well as looking at various social media in case anything was posted about the game. Drones were on hand to be deployed, if needed.

Choosing to stay with the van instead of going to the offices, Jake had instructed the lead agent of the twelve-member team that was deployed there to finish crating up the documents and computers, and leave half the team on the premises with the rest taking everything to the control center at headquarters. Hunter Inc was shut down and the few employees that were working on a Saturday had been told to go home.

Opening the door now and stepping into the van, Jake asked, "Where are we?" as the van pulled away from the curb.

Joe's face appeared on the monitor as he responded. "I was finally able to reach the architect who drew up the plans. He was fishing at a lake near Scranton. I was lucky to reach him given his remote location. The plans are in his office safe and he's the only one with the key. He's headed back to his office and should arrive there in two to three hours. His office is in Hoboken."

"Good. Take a car and meet him there. I want those

plans scanned and sent to us as soon as you have them. Any luck finding Hoop, Frank?"

"Not yet. All is quiet on the social media front. We've successfully accessed live-feed cameras from around the city. I've brought in additional agents to help in the search. No sign of her yet, assuming the game has even begun. I just hope she's in Manhattan."

"She has to be, Frank. Hunter is just arrogant enough to believe he can pull it off locally. Not only that, but this happened very fast. I doubt he had time to set up the game anywhere else."

"Frank, Kirsten here. I'm sending you a list of Mali's favorite places. Can you give me all camera links to those areas? She might try to go somewhere that she knows and I want to monitor them."

"Good idea, Kirsten. Send that list to me ASAP and we'll get you set up for all but will highlight the cameras corresponding to your list."

They coordinated efforts for a few more minutes as the van headed north out of the financial district. Jake believed that Hunter would not place her anywhere near the FBI building and, on a gut feeling, was moving the van closer to Central Park.

6:10 p.m.

It had been a long afternoon and the team was nowhere closer to the answers they needed, to finding Mali, or to finding Hunter and Simpson for that matter. Frustration was running high. The van had been parked on the south side of Central Park for the better part of two hours, an accident causing the normally forty-minute drive to stretch to more than ninety minutes. The search of the apartments did not bear any useful information, unless learning about Hunter's proclivity for porn mattered.

Everyone was getting discouraged, including Jake. Shaking his head to free himself from the direction his thoughts were taking him, Jake bit into one of the burgers Kirsten had purchased for the mobile van team. As he reached for a fry, his cell phone rang.

"Jake," said Joe. "I'm still at the architect's offices but I have the plans in hand and I've scanned them into my laptop. I'm e-mailing them to you and to the control center right now. Jake, there's an elevator shaft in Hunter's office."

"What? We never saw an elevator when we met with him." At Kirsten's questioning look and Frank's "What's up?" from the video call, Jake put his phone on speaker.

"The architect says that the elevator shaft went in when the building was first constructed. It goes from his office to the garages. He has no idea if an elevator was ever built. At the time, Hunter said it was a possibility for the future."

"Good work, Joe. We've just received your e-mail."

As both teams opened the file to review the blue prints, Joe told them to focus on the northeast corner of the office.

Jake nodded. "I remember that corner, it looked like a small, enclosed room. There was a door, I just assumed it was a private bathroom. Is Tom there, Frank?"

The lead agent of the mobile team responded, "I'm still here at command control, Jake, with Frank, and I'm one step ahead of you. I've instructed the team to search the offices and determine if there is an elevator."

"Tom, if it exists they are NOT to press any keys or buttons or try to determine where the elevator goes. If it exists, we don't want to alert Hunter, Simpson, or the players of our presence. They could release the cyanide and kill Hoop."

"Ten-four, Jake."

Frank's attention was drawn to one of the team members. Returning to the monitor, Frank said, "#HuntedLives on Twitter is active. Two pictures have been posted and comments are starting to roll in. In addition, another picture was posted on Instagram."

Kirsten quickly brought up Twitter and navigated to #HuntedLives. Everyone read the posts that were stacking up for the first picture.

"All right, another game and so soon after the last one. Rad man!"

"I think I saw her in Hamilton Heights earlier today."

"I hope this game lasts a long time. I missed the last one."

"She looks kind of young. But I like her bazookas!"

"Get a life, jerk. We all have bazookas. What's important is what kind of shape she is in. Can she stay ahead of the assassin?"

"Part of me wants her to survive. A small part, actually (haha). I hope they use a cool weapon to nail her."

"She's not the target, this guy is."

Another stream of comments related to the second picture flew off the screen.

"What makes you think it's this guy? He doesn't look like the target."

"Are you kidding? He's definitely the guy. Look how tired and out of shape he is. And he's not talking to anyone."

"You just described a good percentage of people in New York (haha)."

"Hey, no need to be insulting to us New Yorkers. We all want to find the target so just keep looking."

"Christ," Jake said rubbing his face. He studied the first picture. "Is that Hoop? It's hard to tell from the angle of the shot. And how does the person taking this picture know she's the target?"

"He or she doesn't," Frank said. "We could be in trouble if folks post pictures of people they THINK are the target, as with these two shots."

Kirsten opened Instagram. The picture posted was of the young, scruffy-looking man in the second picture. "Same picture" she said before turning back to her computer.

Two hours later, Kirsten exclaimed, her voice pitched high in her excitement, "I think I've found her!"

* * *

JAKE MOVED HIS chair closer to Kirsten and looked over her shoulder as she shared her screen with the individuals in the Control Center.

"I took a chance on the comments being made about seeing the target in Hamilton Heights and looked for her there and in the surrounding areas. No luck seeing her on the streets live so I requested videos of the past ten hours from businesses there as well as Harlem. Mali doesn't have any friends north of that position, nor does she go up there often, at all really, so I made the assumption that she would head south. Look at this clip from West Harlem."

Kirsten hit the Play button and the team studied the cars driving on the street and the people walking on the sidewalk, intent on getting to their destinations. A woman strode into the frame and Kirsten paused the video.

"You think that's Hoop?" Frank asked from the Command Center.

"Yes, I do. It's hard to tell, the clarity of the video isn't the best and the clothes she's wearing are super baggy. Not to mention the baseball cap, something she would never wear. But that's her walk and look at her left hand. Before she left the office yesterday, was it only yesterday?, she asked me if I had a nail file because two of her nails on her left hand had broken, her pinky and ring fingers. And she was wearing dark red nail polish."

Kirsten zoomed in on the hand as she was talking.

Frank squinted and moved closer to the screen. "Looks too blurry to definitively identify her, Kirsten."

"I know it seems far-fetched but I'm telling you, that's Mali," Kirsten insisted.

"Where is this, Kirsten?" Jake asked.

"The camera is from the West Harlem Group Assistance business, an apartment rental agency located on Amsterdam Avenue and West 141st Street. This video was shot at 3:51 p.m."

"That's less than five hours ago," said Jake.

"I don't like assuming that this is Hoop because of broken or chipped nails," Frank stated. "But we need to chase down all leads so, pursue it and try to figure out where she's going. We need to verify if that's her. I will assign three members of the team here to review tapes from the business and traffic cameras south of that area. The remaining team members here will continue to review the live cameras in case this is not Hoop."

Jake added, "I want a map of Manhattan on the center screen with pinpoints of this location plus any others we find as well as the time seen next to each."

"Good idea, Jake," Frank said. "We'll have one up there momentarily."

Ten minutes later, the team found and watched a video of the same woman passing the Welcome to Harlem Visitor Center on Frederick Douglass Boulevard, south of West 127th Street, at 5:23pm.

Looking at the map with the two pinpoints, Kirsten pointed out that the locations were just a mile apart. "As much as Mali exercises, there's no way it would take her an hour and a half to get from the rental agency to the visitor's center. What is she doing?"

"If that's Mali," Frank said.

"Wait a minute," Jake said, "The woman passes the center twice. Rewind the tape a bit."

The team watched the woman jog past the center and then minutes later she passed the center again, this time walking.

"Joe, freeze the video!" Jake said.

"What do you see, Jake?" Kirsten asked.

"She must have seen a camera the first time she jogged past. She's looking directly at it now. Zoom in on her face, Joe."

Joe zoomed in and revealed Mali's unmistakable face, beneath a dirty baseball cap that, clearly, she had pushed back so her face could be seen.

"Oh my God," Kirsten exclaimed. "Look at her hair. They cut and dyed it, and she was limping. She looks so tired."

"She looks determined, Kirsten," Jake said. He focused on the face in the shot. "To answer your earlier question, my guess is that Hoop is taking a twisting, round-about route to wherever she is going to confuse the players and, with luck, the assassin. Zoom out."

No one said a thing as they all stared at her.

Kirsten said, "What is she holding in her right hand? It looks like a bag. Can you zoom in on it?"

It was a white plastic bag with a drawstring at the top. The drawstring was pulled closed, covering the print except for 'H iff'.

"What kind of bag is that?" Frank asked. "It's not a grocery bag. And it doesn't look like a bag from a retail store."

Jake said, "Could it be something like a laundry bag, from a hotel or dry cleaning joint?"

"You're right, Jake," Kirsten said. "The 'H' could stand for 'Hotel.' Let me look for hotels in the area with the letters 'iff'."

As she searched, Frank instructed Joe to play the rest of the video, in case she walked by a third time.

"Hotel Cliff!" Kirsten interrupted. "And it's only two and a half miles north of the rental agency."

"Frank, can we get a police officer in the area to stop by and check on recent guests of the hotel? That may have been Hoop's starting point."

"I'll make a call. And I'll have the team here move on to other videos and live feeds of cameras south of this latest pinpoint. Let's identify where she's going."

It was quiet in the van as well as the Control Center. Time was of the essence and there was a sense of urgency as well as focus now that they had seen her. They were closing in and Mali was helping however she could.

"I just got off the phone with Deputy Inspector Hank Wilson of the 33rd Precinct," said Frank. "He said that officers responded to a 911 call this morning at approximately nine fifty-five for a disturbance at the Hotel Cliff. A woman was reported to have stolen food and water from the breakfast buffet. When approached by hotel staff, she punched him in the nose and took off. By the time the police arrived, the suspect was long gone. Description fits Hoop. I'll contact the hotel for a copy of their security video from this morning to verify but my gut feeling is that the woman was Hoop."

"So the bag she's carrying has supplies inside," Jake said. "Good."

Over the course of the next hour, the team followed Mali crisscrossing Harlem before heading south on Broadway, west of Central Park. Now that Jake knew which side of the park she took, the mobile van moved north a few blocks to position the team closer to her. Frank dispatched agents north as well to meet up with the van. The delta between the time Mali was seen on each video clip to the current time was narrowing.

Jake called the team together to make final plans.

"Tom, what is the status of your search in the Hunter building?" asked Jake.

Tom said, "The team has confirmed that an elevator is located in Hunter's office. Additionally, they went floor to floor and determined that the elevator goes from the office directly to the basement. No other floor has access to this elevator. In the basement, there is a large concrete wall surrounding the location of the elevator."

"Is it a room and, if so, is there access to it?" Frank asked.

"Yes, given the dimensions of the outer walls. Other areas of the garage look the same but the elevator goes directly into this particular space. We have not been able to find a door or any other type of access to it. Parking spaces surround it. No one has used the elevator to go up to Hunter's office and we cannot confirm that anyone is inside this room."

"Where is the elevator physically at this time?"

"We opened the door in the office, Frank. The elevator isn't there. We assume it's at the bottom."

"Tom, we need a visual in that room. Have your

men repel down the elevator shaft, get inside the elevator and put an inspection scope camera through the elevator door. Let's try to get an idea what we're dealing with. And, Tom, I want to see and hear what they're doing. Call me when your men are ready to go." Frank paused then turned to Joe. "Come over here, Joe, and tell everyone what you just told me."

Joe appeared in front of the camera. "If the game is played in that room, as we suspect, and it's surrounded by concrete walls, then there has to be a minimum of one transmitter and receiver somewhere outside the room for their Wi-Fi and GPS to work. We might be able to jam the signal that allows the players to communicate with the assassin. The transmitter and receiver may be hard to find, considering how dark it is, but they would be fairly close to the room, probably low to the ground."

"OK. We'll get started on both of those tasks, Frank," said Tom, stepping away from the video conference to make a call.

"Look at this," Kirsten said. "The last position we have on Mali is at the Whole Foods Market on Columbus Avenue just north of West 97th Street. That was eighteen minutes ago at 8:48 p.m. She is holding something in her left hand that she did not have at the prior location."

That got everyone's attention. Kirsten zoomed in on her hand.

"It looks like a message, a drawing. Can anyone make out what it is?" Frank asked. Everyone studied it.

Jake exclaimed, "I know where she's going! That's a

horse on a pole. She's going to the carousel in Central Park."

"Are you sure, Jake?"

"Yes. We took my daughter there a couple of weeks ago. Hoop selected a place that's familiar to both of us."

"Okay. We will place agents near the carousel to wait for her."

Jake continued, "Joe, is there any way to cut off the Wi-Fi signal in the device implanted in Mali's ear to prevent the cyanide from being released?"

Joe nodded. "We can jam the entire Wi-Fi frequency spectrum for however long you want."

"Jam?" asked Frank.

"Wi-Fi signals are radio waves. To block the signals we need to block the radio waves. We have a jammer that is designed to cut-off wireless LAN networks in a radius of up to one mile. It transmits white noise signals in Wi-Fi frequencies of 2400 megahertz and 5000 megahertz, the standard frequencies used for Wi-Fi. The jammer needs to be placed within one mile of the network, the closer the better."

"So everyone's Wi-Fi within a mile of the jammer will be down?" asked Jake.

"No. Everyone's Wi-Fi in the area will be down. That also includes police radar and other emergency communications."

"What are you thinking, Jake?" Frank asked.

"Looking at the map, it's obvious that Hoop is traveling south on Columbus Avenue. She has deviated numerous times but always ends up back on Columbus.

I've sent some undercover agents up Columbus from our position here as well as on Central Park West and Amsterdam Avenues which run parallel to Columbus. We're close to having an eyeball visual of her. As soon as that happens, I will rotate agents ahead of her to keep track of her position. Knowing that she is wearing a Go-Pro camera, we need to make sure our agents stay far enough ahead of her so that they are not seen by the players. With one exception. I plan to have two agents, posing as a couple, approach her from the front and pass a message to her. I want Hoop to realize that we are near and working on a solution. The mobile van team will stay with her. Our plan will be synchronized to coincide with entering the room in the Hunter building and jamming the Wi-Fi."

"Good. It's just after nine o'clock now. The team will be in place at the carousel within the hour." Frank turned away for a moment to instruct the off-screen agents. His image appeared again. "We're displaying all live stream camera feeds of the Central Park carousel and surrounding area on the right screen in the Control Center for us to monitor Hoop's progress. In addition, I have instructed Tom to get answers for me regarding that room by ten and Joe will set up the Wi-Fi jam near the Hunter building. I will advise the police in the area of our intent to jam the signal and the approximate time it will be down. We'll make our final plans after that. Hopefully, Hoop will be in our sights soon. Stay focused people and work the game to our advantage."

CHAPTER TWENTY-FIVE

Near Jacob's Pickles, Amsterdam Avenue
Saturday, May 2, 9:15 p.m.

Mali crouched between two cars parked on the street and slowly ate her last croissant. She had one more muffin and a bottle of water left.

After her initial dash from the hotel, Mali had slowed to a walk in order to eat a couple of croissants and drink some water. Afterward, knowing she had to get as far away from the hotel as possible, she had resumed her run. Hunter said she would have a thirty-minute lead time but after that, she had no idea if the players constantly gave directions to the assassin or at pre-determined times.

She had been running for twelve hours. Hours ago, blisters on her feet caused so much pain that she was forced to stop. She had briefly removed her shoes to give her feet some relief. The sock on her left foot was bloody from the blisters. After slipping her shoes back on, she had continued at a much slower pace. *Amazing that I've only gone six or seven miles from the hotel as the crow flies.* She hoped that her strategy of not appearing to go in any particular direction or to a specific destination had worked in her favor. Knowing that the assassin would only follow instructions given by the players, her hope had been to confuse them.

The first camera she had seen was at the Harlem Visitor Center a few hours back. She had taken a calculated risk to circle back to that camera and walk past with her cap pushed back so that her face would be clearly visible. The players wouldn't realize or care that she was back-tracking and she had hoped that she was far enough ahead of the assassin.

From that point on, she had been carrying the pad in her hand with the picture of the carousel horse she had drawn back in the hotel. The pad wasn't visible to the players since she held it against her leg, and she believed there would be more cameras along the way. So the pad had remained out. She only hoped that the team would find it at some point. A needle in a haystack but worth a try.

She couldn't allow herself to count on help from the team. She knew they were looking for her, and they wouldn't stop until they found her, but Manhattan Island covered twenty-three square miles. That was a lot of ground to cover. Not only that but the team had no reason to suspect she was even there.

So she was working her way to the carousel in Central Park, an area familiar to her, and planned to use it to her advantage and circle behind the assassin. The phone cord she brought with her was not much of a weapon, and she doubted she could get close enough to him to use it, but she had to try.

Finishing her croissant, Mali took a few sips of water then prepared to leave. She peeked above the car, watching the area closely.

THWACK! The glass on the passenger window of the car next to Mali shattered. Startled, she jumped to the side, still in a crouched position, and looked at the window then the ground. Lying amongst the shards of glass was a Shuriken, a Ninja star. The blade was as big as her hand and was made from a flat metal plate. It had four double-edge points, forming a shape similar to a Swastika.

A group of people were standing on the sidewalk near the cars where Mali was hiding, laughing and talking loudly. At the sound of breaking glass, they looked over at the car and Mali.

"Hey, that's my car!" Someone shouted. They rushed over to her.

Not wasting any time, Mali stood and pushed her way through the group, amidst complaints of 'What are you doing?' 'Watch out,' and 'Take a shower lady.'

When they recognized the throwing star and understood what was happening, their complaints quickly turned to shouts of glee.

"OMG! This is a new game!"

"Where's the assassin?"

"Get your camera out, Maddie!"

"What is that thing on the ground?"

"Who knows? But I'm grabbing it. It'll be worth a fortune one day."

"Should we follow her?"

Their comments faded as Mali raced up West 84th

Street toward Broadway, ducking and weaving as she went. Heart pounding, she turned up a side street, still running at full speed, not daring to stop. Out of breath, she looked behind her. No sign of the assassin. She slowed to a jog and continued to zigzag through the streets, eventually making her way back to Columbus Avenue. Reaching for her bag to grab the towel, she groaned. *Damn, I forgot it.*

"We just spotted her, Jake," said Agent Jones.

"Where are you Glenn?"

"I'm outside the Shake Shack on Columbus and 77th. She just turned the corner from 78th and is walking quickly this way, albeit with a limp."

"Stay well ahead of her Glenn. I don't want you visible on the Go-Pro camera and I don't want the assassin to spot you. Keep me posted on her route. I'm sending two agents north now." Jake gave instructions to the other agents in the area then removed his headset and opened the van door.

Before he stepped outside to the two waiting agents, Kirsten put a hand on his arm. "I need to be the one who takes the note, Jake."

He shook his head and was about to respond. "Jake, Mali will recognize me. She will be on alert and will realize that I've dropped a note. If she doesn't know those two agents who are waiting outside, she won't even look at them and the opportunity will be lost. I'm already dressed in jeans and I don't look like an agent. Even when I'm IN uniform, I don't look like an agent."

Jake smiled at that. Turning to Richard, he said, "Give

Frank an update and tell him the couple is on the move to intercept Hoop." He looked at Kirsten. "Step outside with me."

As soon as they were outside, Jake gave instructions to Kirsten and Wayne.

"You are a loving couple out for an evening stroll. Kirsten, stay on the inside of Wayne so that Hoop passes by him. Place one hand in the crook of Wayne's arm. Your other arm needs to be swinging at your side the entire time, holding the note. As Hoop approaches, laugh loudly and make a comment to Wayne so that Mali hears your voice, then drop the note. Don't lose your stride, don't pause, just keep walking. And don't look back after you walk past her. Most important of all, and Kirsten this is especially for you, do not look at Hoop, ever. Your focus is on your lover. Wayne will cue you when to laugh and he's wearing an earpiece so we can keep him informed of Hoop's route." He paused. "Are we clear on this?"

They nodded.

"Head north on Columbus. This could take a while. Stay in character the entire time."

Mali had lost track of time. Her feet ached with every step. Her right foot was wet with blood and she thought her left foot was as well now. She didn't dare stop to check. The last stop she had made was at Jacob's Pickles. She wasn't sure how long it had been since she was there but she could not chance stopping again.

After that incident by the car, she had become discouraged. She wanted to stop and rest but had no clue how far the assassin was behind her. She wasn't familiar with throwing stars. Had he thrown it from three hundred yards away or was the range of that weapon closer? She struggled to shake the melancholy mood and stay focused.

She moved to cross Columbus and head down West 68th to make her way to Central Park West Avenue. She was getting close to the carousel and wanted to take cover inside the park. She turned mid-block to check traffic and was about to jog across the street when a familiar laugh caused her to pause.

It can't be! Still facing the street, Mali looked to the side and noticed Kirsten walking arm in arm with a man, no doubt an agent as well. Kirsten dropped something even while talking loudly and laughing with her partner. Mali looked to the left and right, pretending to determine where to go, before glancing back at the couple who were approaching her. They didn't look at her. They just continued walking down the street. After they passed, Mali turned to walk up the street and knelt down when she was a step beyond what she now recognized as a crumpled piece of paper. She reached behind her and picked it up tucking it inside her sweatpants. Looking down, she made a show of readjusting her left shoe. Without wasting any more time, Mali stood and ran across the street and down West 68th.

There was a new purpose in her step as a wave of relief hit her. The team was near. Jake was near.

CHAPTER TWENTY-SIX

Hunter's Gaming Room, New York
Saturday, May 2, 10:40 p.m.

THIS GAME HAS been the most stimulating and challenging one yet, Anthony mused, as he watched with his friends. Agent Hooper was giving the assassin a run for his money, much to the delight of Jane, Ted, and Hernando. She didn't seem to be going anywhere specific but had been running a good part of the time, staying well ahead of the assassin. His friends had tried to guess where she was going and had sent Drake on what they later discovered to be several wild goose chases. It sent them into hysterics each time. They were having a ball.

Over an hour ago they asked Anthony if they could ping her location every five minutes so the assassin could catch up to her. They didn't want to end the game, they just wanted to scare her by having the assassin throw the star close enough to get her attention. He had acquiesced, curious himself to see how she'd react.

Within twenty minutes, the assassin was close enough to throw the star.

Her reaction had his friends jumping and shouting like kids at a ball game. They watched her race away but Anthony made them wait a full thirty minutes before pinging Agent Hooper again and giving the assassin his next instruction.

That little deviation put Anthony behind schedule. He had stayed much longer than originally planned. It was time for him to go. Janet left a little after eight, ostensibly to get a hot meal for everyone. In reality, she was headed for the airport in Newark and would wait for him on his jet. They were supposed to fly to Switzerland at eleven but if they had to leave a little later, so be it. Once he was on the road, he would contact Janet so she could have the pilot submit a new flight plan.

Anthony could barely contain his excitement but wanted to play it cool so his friends wouldn't get suspicious.

"Hey, Tony, where is your CFO with the chow? I'm hungry," stated Ted.

The perfect opening. "You're right, Ted. It's been two hours. She should have been back long ago. Here, let me pour you another shot then I'll step out of the room and find out what's going on."

He walked to the bar, grabbed the bottle of Tequila, which was near empty, and squeezed out another shot for each. After handing them their drinks, Anthony walked back to the bar and tossed the bottle in the trash.

Glancing over at them, he saw that they were engrossed in the game.

"Oooh, I love how she doesn't stay in one place for long. This game is amazing. I'm glad we threw that star to scare her. Her reaction was better than expected. She is definitely more athletic than the last target," enthused Jane. "Here's to a long and electrifying game!" They cheered the game, sharing a toast before downing their shots.

They didn't notice as Anthony walked out the hidden door.

Slipping past the agents was much easier than Anthony figured it would be. *Of course, the tunnel leading from the room to the side of the building across the street helped.* He strode a few blocks to a neighboring parking garage and up the stairs to the rental car that was waiting for him. In minutes, he was on the road.

* * *

JANET HAD SMOKED two cigarettes shy of an entire pack. Anthony was supposed to have arrived more than an hour ago and she was getting impatient. Her jet was fueled and ready to go. SHE was ready to go.

She was standing at the bar pouring herself a drink when Anthony strode up the steps and into the jet.

"Where are Sheila and Al?" he asked, looking in the cockpit. "I want to take off as soon as possible."

"As soon as you called, I sent them inside to submit a new flight plan. That can take a little time. Let me pour you a drink. How was the game going when you left and how are our three friends?"

"Clueless and totally involved in the game. It's an exciting one. Agent Hooper is doing much better than I expected. They didn't even notice when I left to check why it was taking so long for you to get the food." He laughed in glee.

Janet handed him a whiskey neat. "Here's to a successful game and an amazing resurgence of your baby." She clinked glasses with him.

"Yes. To the best experience ever. Better than I could have imagined." Anthony slurped his whiskey while Janet gulped it down.

She had just poured them both another shot when her phone rang. She answered it and listened to the caller. "Get here as soon as you can." At Anthony's questioning look, Janet said, "That was Sheila. They've run into a minor issue and will be delayed. She said it shouldn't take too long."

"Damn."

Taking a deep breath, Janet set her glass on the bar and stepped up to Anthony. Pulling him close, she licked her way up to his ear. "Why don't we start our celebration a little early while we're waiting?"

"I thought you'd never ask" he murmured, stepping closer for a kiss. He absently set his glass on the bar but missed. It dropped to the floor, bouncing on the cream colored carpet, whiskey staining it a dark brown. He walked her backward to the chair when she pulled back. "I have a better idea."

She grabbed Anthony's hand and pulled him to the back of the jet where there was a small room with a bed inside. Pushing Anthony on the bed, to his astonished laugh, she told him to scoot back to the steel headboard. Climbing on top of him, she kissed him while unbuttoning his shirt.

Anthony shrugged out of it.

Janet kissed her way down his chest and stomach and when she reached his pants, she caught and held his stare as she unzipped them and pulled them off. Anthony growled.

Lying only in his underwear and socks, he moved to sit up and pull her to him. She shook her head. "This is my gift to you, Anthony. Your baby came to life in a most unexpected and exciting way these past two years. It's time to celebrate your success." She proceeded to crawl up his body and kiss him while moving his hands up to his head. She kissed his lips long and slow, finally breaking off the kiss to reach over to the small bedside table and pull out two furry pink hand cuffs from the drawer. Shaking them suggestively, his eyes widened in anticipation. She knew Anthony would be shocked that his Janie could be adventurous like this.

When he nodded, she took one arm and pulled it over his head to the headboard, securing his wrist there. She did the same thing with his other arm, making sure the watch she gave him for his birthday was not in the way. Anthony growled again, playfully tugging on the cuffs.

Janet leaned down to kiss Anthony again then slid down his body and stood up at the end of the bed.

"Take your clothes off, Janie. I want to see you." He shifted restlessly on the bed, turning from side to side.

But like a slow-setting sun that turned day into night, Janet's demeanor changed. She straightened her clothes, smoothing her skirt with her hands, and stared down at him.

"I think not." Jaw tight, she crossed her arms and sniffed in disdain. "Why would I want to have sex with a sniveling weasel like you?"

Anthony was still in a sexual haze. "What? What's going on?"

"I've waited a long time for this, Anthony, and I want to savor it."

"What do you mean?" His confusion growing, Anthony uneasily tugged at the cuffs. He swallowed repeatedly.

"My entire life has been leading to this day."

He pulled harder on the cuffs.

"You can't get out of those cuffs, Tony." She opened the overhead bin and pulled out a gas mask.

"What the hell are you doing, Janie? Unlock these things now!"

"For all of these years, I have hated my three oldest brothers for what they did to me. But you, Tony? I loathed you. I still do."

"Janie . . ."

She held up her hand. "Don't bother trying to explain. You enjoyed it as much as they did. I saw it in your eyes. Every time they climbed on top of me, I planned how I was going to kill you."

Anthony twisted his body left and right, frantically trying to remove the cuffs. His breathing was erratic, sweat formed on his brow, and the cuffs tore the skin on his wrists.

"Don't get me wrong. At eight years old, I could hardly fathom exactly HOW I was going to do it, I was just sure that I would. So I studied hard and kept tabs on you over the years. When your game took off and Hunter Inc was born, the opening I was looking for was at hand. You were so eager to have me join the company so we could work together. It was all so much easier than I expected it to be." She inhaled deeply, letting the air out slowly. "Two years is a long time to have to wait for the right time. But now that the moment is upon us, I find that I want to draw it out."

Anthony screamed, "Janie, I was nine years old, a kid. I didn't know what I was doing."

"Oh Tony, of course you did. I was there, remember?" She paused then shook her head in mock regret. "Unfortunately, I can't take too long. The FBI is about to interrupt our friends and stop the game. They'll come looking for us once they discover we're not there. What a shame!"

"Janie, I'll do anything you want, give you all my money. Please . . ."

Janet cackled. "I can't tell you how I've longed for you to beg, especially since I begged you for your help all those years ago." She paused. "By the way, I already have all your money. I've been selling your stock and moving it to my Swiss accounts for months."

She stepped back from the bed and lifted the gas mask. Before putting it on, she looked at him from his feet up to his head, finally resting on his watch. "Your watch was the best gift I could ever have given you two years ago. Even as we celebrated the live game, it never occurred to you that the watch was the perfect length for our device. It was much easier to fit your watch with it than it was implanting the device behind the ear of our targets." Her eyes crinkled at the corners as she grinned, noticing the realization dawn in his eyes. "I will enjoy watching you suffer, Tony."

"No, Janie, No!"

She placed the mask on her face and pulled out a small tin box from her pocket. She held it up, wiggling it in her hand so he wouldn't miss it. Opening it, she made a show of lifting a tiny remote then she pressed the button.

Anthony winced and looked at his wrist, screaming, bucking his body, trying to get away.

"No. No. Janie, no."

He coughed and retched, gasping for air. His entire body convulsed as the cyanide took hold. He was dead in less than two minutes.

Janet relished how he looked in death, vomit all over his chest, foam dribbling down his chin, arms hanging there in those pink cuffs. She was inordinately pleased with herself. Turning, she walked out of the room and off the jet. She removed the gas mask and tossed it inside before walking around the corner of the building to where her jet was waiting. Stepping inside, she said hello to Sheila and Al.

"Are we ready for take-off?" she asked.

"Whenever you are, Ms. Simpson," responded Sheila.

"Well, let's get this bird in the air!" She sat down on a plush leather seat, buckled up, and stared out the window as the jet taxied to the runway and lifted off.

Leaning back in her seat and closing her eyes, she slept for the first time in a lifetime.

CHAPTER TWENTY-SEVEN

Central Park, near carousel
Saturday, May 2, 11:00 p.m.

JAKE AND THE team in the van had a final video conference with the team in the Control Center to synchronize their plans before taking their positions.

As soon as Hoop crossed the street to get to the carousel, Joe would jam the Wi-Fi spectrum, and the team in the elevator at the Hunter building would breach the room and arrest Hunter, Simpson, and the players. The team, led by Tom, would also take control of the remote device to prevent the cyanide from being released, in case jamming the Wi-Fi did not work. Jake and the agents were now in place at the carousel to intercept Hoop and take down the assassin. They were as prepared as possible.

And yet, Jake was worried. His brows furrowed as he acknowledged to himself that the only variable in the plan was the assassin. They had no description and couldn't even verify if the assassin was male or female, although Jake suspected it was a man. And the weapon selected could be hand-to-hand combat or long range. The good news was that the assassin wouldn't move or take a shot unless instructed to do so.

Kirsten reported from the mobile van that Hoop just ran across 65th Street and entered the park. The plan had just been set in motion.

The note that Kirsten dropped was not specific, only telling Mali that they were near, they had a plan, and she should continue to the carousel. After reading it, Mali slowed her pace to a walk as she entered Central Park. She wanted to draw the assassin closer to her, if possible, so he or she could be identified and caught. She was careful to weave in and out of trees and bushes, zig-zagging and ducking low to make herself a difficult target.

The carousel was dark, no music was playing, no colorful horses were bouncing up and down. There were no children jumping and laughing. It was quiet. Even the birds were sleeping. The only lights were a couple of street lamps along the path leading to the carousel, and the sound of cars was muffled as Mali tread deeper into the park. She couldn't see any agents but felt their presence.

Mali rushed across 65th Street and, staying in the bushes and trees on the side of the path, made her way to the carousel. Kneeling next to the building, she paused to get her bearings and berated herself again for leaving the bag behind. She no longer had the phone cord to use as a weapon, meager though it was. She stood up and tiptoed to the back of the building, inching along at a snail's pace, ears alerted to any sound. She wanted to find a better position where her back was protected and she could watch for the assassin.

The softest noise reached her ears. She froze, cocking her head to the side to try to identify the sound. Her heart was in her throat and she could hardly breathe, fear a bitter taste in her mouth.

All of a sudden, she was grabbed from behind. A hand was placed over her mouth before she could scream and a muscular arm wrapped around her waist, pulling her close to his body. She struggled, kicking her legs and swinging her arms, trying to make contact with the assassin. She was easily overpowered.

"Mali, it's me, Jake. Stop struggling, you're safe."

As soon as she recognized his voice, she went limp in his arms, shaking as relief flooded her body.

When he was certain that Mali recognized him, Jake removed his hand from her mouth and placed it on her shoulder, moving her into a crouching position and settling himself beside her. His hand stayed on her shoulder, the physical contact calming her as much as it was calming him.

He leaned close to her ear. "We've jammed the Wi-Fi signal which means no signal can be sent to the device. The cyanide won't be released. A team is breaching the hidden room we found to capture Hunter, Simpson, and his stockholder buddies. We'll have the assassin soon. You're safe and protected, agents are all around. Stay put." When she nodded, Jake left her side, disappearing around the corner.

Mali leaned back against the wall and slid down to a sitting position. She was still shaking. Resting her head on her knees, she wrapped her arms around her legs and let the tears flow.

Jake moved back to his position near the front of the carousel where the other agent was lying in wait.

Tom, the lead agent leading the team at the Hunter offices, informed everyone that they had successfully breached the hidden room and caught the three players who were too focused on the game to understand what was happening until it was over. There was no resistance. One of the players had complained that the hunt wasn't over before being shushed by the other two.

"Hunter and Simpson were not in the room, Jake."

"Damn it."

"And Jake," Tom continued, "We have the game console."

"That's great. We don't have to worry about the cyanide."

"No Jake. We have the console." He paused to let that sink in. "We can direct the assassin right to you."

The take-down of the suspect was surprisingly easy. The last directive given to the assassin by Tom was that the target was hiding behind the carousel in Central Park. After fifteen long minutes of waiting, a suspect made his way toward the carousel. Jake and the others watched him pause behind a tree across the path from the carousel, presumably to assess the situation.

All at once, without any indication, the suspect turned and sprinted away.

There was a lot of shouting as multiple agents pursued the suspect from various locations. The suspect managed to run a half mile before one of the agents tackled him. The others swarmed him. Once the suspect was cuffed and hauled to his feet, he was brought back to the carousel and moved under a light. The hood was yanked off his head.

Jake, now standing in front of him, opened the target's jacket and searched him. It didn't take Jake long to find a specially-designed inside pocket. It was empty.

"There's no console on either wrist and there is no game card," said the agent standing behind the suspect.

"Search the area for the console, a weapon, and a card."

Jake ignored the hubbub of agents searching the area, the radio chatter, and the intermittent glow of flashlights that were trained on the ground. He stood silent, arms crossed, jaw tight, never removing his eyes from the suspect.

"We've got the console," shouted an agent, running to Jake. "Still no weapon," shouted another. "No card yet," from a third agent. The wrist console was shown to Jake. He took it and typed a message to Tom then handed it back to the agent.

"Game over. Get this son-of-a-bitch out of here."

Jake raced to the back to the carousel only to find that Mali had been taken to the mobile van, now on 65th, and was sitting on the floor of the van at the open door. The doctor was looking at the incision above her ear.

". . . I said to cut the device out," Mali's high-pitched voice indicated to Jake that this was not the first time she had made the request and she was close to losing it.

"Agent Hooper, this is not a sterile environment and the danger of cyanide release has passed."

"I don't give a damn! I want it out of me!"

Kirsten reached for Mali. "Mali . . ."

No response.

Jake stepped to Mali's side and touched her arm.

She looked up at him and stepped into his arms, saying, "I want it out of me, Jake, now!"

Exhausted, emotionally and physically, he could tell, as could everyone else, that she was near breaking point.

Staring into her eyes, Jake said, "Remove the implant, Doctor."

When the doctor opened her mouth to respond, Jake said, "Now please."

Mali sighed, calmed by his demeanor.

Without further delay, the doctor, Mali, and Jake stepped into the mobile van and the door closed.

CHAPTER TWENTY-EIGHT

Mount Sinai Hospital
Sunday, May 3, 8:00 a.m.

"Surely I can be released now?" Mali asked the nurse, for the tenth time, who was taking her vitals.

"The doctor will release you soon, Agent Hooper." She never took her eyes off the monitor.

"Mali, you're tired and you've been through a lot," Jake said. "You'll be out of here soon."

"Hang in there, Mali," said Kirsten.

Both had gone to the hospital with Mali and had stayed with her through the night. Kirsten only left long enough to go to Mali's apartment for a clean set of clothes.

"I'm just ready to be home," Mali said, shoulders sagging. "Thanks again for staying with me all night, you two, and for staying with me in the van, Jake."

"Hey, I have circulation back in my fingers now. All is good." Jake flexed his fingers and tried to joke about how hard she had squeezed them when the doctor was removing the implant.

Mali half-smiled, half-grimaced, grateful for her friends.

"The doctor will be in momentarily," said the nurse. "Do you have any residual headaches or nausea? From a level of zero to ten, ten being the most severe, what is your level of pain?"

"Three and a half, four."

"Good. You've been patient through all of our prodding and testing for cyanide as well as the cleaning and stitching of your wound. The eight stitches we put in will need to be removed in seven to ten days. We'll give you complete care instructions after the doctor signs your release."

"Thank you. Can you thank the doctor who removed the device then packed and wrapped my wound in the van? I understand she works at this hospital. I'm so grateful."

"Doctor Hammerstein. Yes, of course. She went home shortly after you were brought here. I'll be sure to tell her when she returns tomorrow."

"Thank you again. It was surreal, not to mention creepy, watching her work in that cramped van while wearing the gas mask."

Frank walked in the door as the nurse walked out.

He smiled. "How are you holding up, Hoop?"

"Hanging in there but ready to go home. I'm told the doctor will be here shortly for a final check."

"Good. I won't stay long. I just wanted to make sure

you're okay and to tell you that you are taking next week off."

Mali opened her mouth to complain. Frank held up his hand to stop her. "No exceptions! I want you to rest. And do not turn on your television, open your computer, or read any news for forty-eight hours. Jake and I will debrief you at your apartment tomorrow morning, ten o'clock. Understood?"

At her nod, Frank said goodbye and left.

It was more than an hour later before the doctor arrived. After reading the updates made on her chart by the nurse, he checked her heart rate, and looked into her eyes, ears, and mouth. He asked a few questions before releasing her.

"Kirsten, can you take me home?" Mali asked.

"Of course." Kirsten looked at Jake, who was leaning against the window ledge. "Let me go ask the nurse for those instructions she was talking about while you finish getting ready."

'Thanks."

"I could have taken you home, Mali," Jake said after Kirsten left.

"I know, and I appreciate that. I'm so grateful for everything you've done for me since I was taken. But you need to go home to Heather and spend some time with her. And I just want to go home and forget about this for a while, if that's possible. Do you mind?"

"Of course not. But I am going to call you this evening to check on you."

Mali smiled her thanks as Jake walked out the door.

* * *

Mali's Apartment
Sunday, May 3, 11:15 a.m.

SARA AND JEN were already in Mali's apartment when Mali and Kirsten walked in. The four of them cried a little and hugged each other for a long time.

Jen was the first to break away from the group hug. She wrinkled her nose. "I love you, Mali, but you need a shower."

That had everyone laughing, as it was meant to do. Mali headed into her bedroom, relieved to finally be able to shower.

She stripped out of the clothes she wore home from the hospital and dropped them on the floor. "Ugh, I don't think I'll ever forget the smell of those clothes I had to wear." She reached the door to the bathroom and looked back at her friends who had followed her into the bedroom. "Kirsten, would you toss those into the washing machine?" She pointed to the clothes lying on the floor. "They carry the stench too."

"Gladly. I'll even start a load for you." Kirsten wrinkled her nose as she lifted the clothes from the floor and walked out of the bedroom.

Mali closed the bathroom door and turned on the hot water, stepping into a steaming hot shower. After relishing a longer-than-normal shower, she dressed and walked back into her living room where her three friends were sitting on the couch, talking.

"I feel so much better."

"Good," said Sara. "Now head straight back into the bathroom. I've brought hair dye and scissors."

All converged in Mali's bathroom where her hair was dyed a soft auburn, closer to her natural color. Her tresses were cut and styled to get rid of the uneven, frankly horrid, chop Hunter gave her for the game. Her BFFs pronounced her chin-length bob beautiful. If the area above her right ear didn't quite match the rest of her hair because of the bandage, her new style would hide it.

"I've got mint chip ice cream in the freezer," said Jen. "Let's go sit on the couch for a while before we let Mali get some rest."

Mali and Sara sat on the sofa while Jen and Kirsten dished up ice cream for everyone. Returning to the couch with the goods, the four friends snuggled and talked about anything and everything except what had happened to Mali. Despite how tired she was, girl time with her friends was exactly what she needed.

"Bed. Now," Sara ordered. Mali was nodding off.

They ushered her into her room and said goodbye, promising to call later.

When Mali woke up, she walked into the kitchen and prepared a light meal. She was amazed that she had slept for more than four hours, crediting her friends for that. She stepped onto her balcony with her plate in hand and gazed at the Hudson while she ate. The boat engines and occasional honking of boats trying to navigate the other vessels soothed her. When she finished eating, she crawled back into bed and fell asleep.

Mali was back at the carousel, walking in circles, around and around. She was looking for Jake. The carousel lit up and moved, playing music. The horses were so bright and colorful, they hurt her eyes. She jumped onto the carousel and held on to a horse. The carousel spun faster and faster and she was getting dizzy. She tried to look up but it was too difficult to hold up her head. The speed of the carousel forced her to her knees. The music played louder and louder. She pulled herself up using the pole of the horse, trying not to get hit by it as it bounced up and down. Jake was calling her but when she looked behind her, a man dressed in black was poised to strike with a raised machete.

Screaming, Mali sat up in bed. Drenched in sweat and breathing hard, she tried to shake the nightmare from her mind. She felt as if she had just run a marathon. Shoving the blankets off of her legs, she reached over to turn on the light that sat on her nightstand and glanced at the clock. Eight ten. She groaned. She had only slept another hour or so.

Dragging herself out of bed, she stumbled into the bathroom. Stripping, she took another hot shower then dressed in a sleeveless t-shirt and shorts. She turned on the lights in the living room and walked into the kitchen. She had just finished making a cup of hot cocoa when the phone rang.

She took a sip, savoring the chocolate on her tongue. "Hello?"

"Hey, I was just calling to check on you," said Jake.

"Aside from the nightmare? Terrific. Just great." She told him about the nightmare as well as her time with the gals.

"Enough about me. Tell me something lighthearted so I can shake this mood."

"Pops, Heather, and I had a great day together. We went bowling." He described in detail all about their misadventures bowling including how his dad held on to the ball when he first swung, the momentum spinning him so that he was facing Jake and Heather, and how both of them ducked behind the chairs. Jake also told her how he threw the ball so hard in the gutter that when it hit the back wall behind the pins, it jumped back and knocked all the pins down giving him a strike.

"Stop," Mali said, laughing so hard her stomach hurt. "That can't be true."

"Well, maybe that last part about the strike was an exaggeration. The ball actually knocked just one pin down."

They both laughed and talked for a few more minutes.

"Will you be able to sleep now?"

"Yes. Thank you, Jake, for making me laugh and for being there for me. It means a lot."

"You're welcome. Now get some rest. Until tomorrow."

"Good night."

"Good night, Mali."

CHAPTER TWENTY-NINE

Mali's Apartment
Monday, May 4, 8:50 a.m.

BUNDLED UP IN her toasty robe, Mali was relaxing on her balcony. She had been sitting there since well before dawn with a cup of coffee and a carafe holding more sitting on the table next to her. Always in awe of the sunrise, she realized that she might not have seen it this morning or ever again.

Pouring more coffee for herself, she sat back in the chair and reflected on what had happened to her. She had never felt such terror, pain, relief, stress, physical exhaustion, hunger, or gratitude, all in the same day, and she was overwhelmed by the efforts of the team to find and help her. They saved her life. She was also proud of herself for how she was able to use the game to her advantage. She discovered that she was strong, stronger than she ever believed possible.

Mali's musings were interrupted when the doorbell

rang. She frowned, not expecting Frank and Jake for another hour.

She walked inside setting her cup on the kitchen counter as she strode to the front door. Eyes round as saucers, her mouth fell open as she stared at her parents. It didn't register that they were standing on her doorstep, so unexpected and out of place it was for them to be in New York.

"Aren't you going to invite us inside, Jasmine?" asked Willow Hooper.

"I'm sorry, of course." She stepped aside to let them in. She kissed her parents on both of their cheeks as they passed her then closed the door.

"Can I offer you some coffee?"

"That sounds wonderful," her father boomed. Her mother nodded.

Mali went to the kitchen and made them each a cup, watching her parents meander through her apartment surveying everything. Was this an episode of the *Twilight Zone*? Both were standing at her windows gazing at the Hudson when she joined them and handed them their coffee.

The three stood there a little awkwardly before Mali finally said, "I'm surprised to see you here. Would you like to sit down?"

"Of course we're here," her father stated, turning to face her. "When we were told that one of our daughters was almost killed by some lunatic in a computer game that was being played for real . . ."

"Something I don't even understand," Mali's mother

murmured, interrupting her husband, still looking at the Hudson.

Charles glanced at his wife before continuing, ". . . we had to come to make sure she was all right. It's a shame we had to hear it from someone else."

"Who called you?"

"Jake Black called us last night," said Willow, a little stiffly.

That was nice of Jake. Out loud, "I'm sorry I didn't call you. I didn't want to worry you. I'm fine."

"You're fine?" Charles asked. "Young lady, I'll have you know that your mother and I have been worried about you. The reports on the news have been harrowing to say the least."

"Father, we were working on an on-going FBI investigation. I couldn't tell you what was happening. And I didn't realize I was going to get abducted or I would have called you beforehand."

"Don't get smart with me, Jasmine Suzanne," he groused, getting red in the face as he did when his emotions got the better of him.

Chastised, and feeling guilty, Mali muttered, "I'm sorry I didn't call. That was thoughtless of me."

Somewhat mollified, Charles sniffed. "Well, we're happy that you're on your feet and moving around."

Willow commented, "You have an interesting home, Jasmine."

Here it comes.

"The security is exceptional as is the view." She paused, glancing at Mali. "Your taste in decor is a little more eclectic than I would prefer though," she said as her eyes continued their perusal of the room. "But it suits you." Facing her fully now, she reached over and touched her daughter's hair. "Your hair is too short for your face structure but it will grow out." She touched the bandage, concern clouding her eyes. "Are you in any pain?"

Were there tears in her mother's eyes? Mali's throat clogged with emotion. This was the most warmth she had seen from her parents as far back as she could remember.

She shook her head. "Not much, Mother."

"Good." She sniffed. "Now, show me the rest of your home."

Willow and Mali proceeded to the bedroom where Willow praised Mali for the excellent coordination of color and decor. Mali smiled to herself. She knew her mother well.

The doorbell chimed and Charles answered the door as Mali and Willow walked out of the bedroom. He greeted Jake and introduced himself to Frank before introducing his wife.

After the typical niceties were completed, Charles and Willow prepared to leave.

"You're going back home?" Mali asked, her voice rising. She discovered that she wanted her parents to stay.

Willow responded. "Darling, we booked a hotel and plan to stay for a few days." At Mali's look, she added, "We might as well enjoy the City while we're here and we want to spend some time with you. If you're feeling up to it, we would like to take you to dinner tonight. Or, if you'd prefer, we can bring dinner here and eat in."

"I'd like that, Mother. Perhaps dinner here tonight?"

"Excellent," exclaimed Charles. "We will take our leave then so you can take care of business. We will return later . . . six this evening?" At Mali's nod, he added, "Why don't you join us, Jake?"

Jake looked at Mali, who smiled. He accepted and, while Jake and Frank walked into the living room, Mali ushered her parents to the door.

She kissed her father on the cheek and turned to do the same to her mother. Willow hugged her instead. "I'm glad you're all right, Darling. We'll see you later this afternoon."

Mali closed the door and excused herself to change as she passed Frank and Jake, who were sitting on the sofa.

"Help yourself to coffee or anything that's in the fridge. I'll be just a few minutes."

"Take your time, Hoop," said Frank.

By the time Mali joined Frank and Jake, there were two steaming cups of coffee on the table in front of the sofa.

Frank didn't waste any time. "Anthony Hunter is dead from cyanide poisoning."

"What?" Mali asked, leaning forward in her seat, shock written on her face. She looked from Frank to Jake.

Seeing her look, Frank said, "I told Jake yesterday that Hunter was dead although I didn't give him details. I asked him not to say anything until we could speak today. Hunter was found early yesterday morning by ground crew at Newark International. The door to his jet was open and they went inside to inspect. A gas mask was on the floor and they found him in the back bedroom. He was handcuffed to the bed, in nothing more than his underwear. They left the plane and called authorities."

"Christ," said Jake, shaking his head.

"My God," Mali said and paused. "Was Janet Simpson on the plane as well?"

"No sign of her. Hunter's plane had been scheduled to depart at eleven Saturday night. But Simpson cancelled it a few minutes beforehand."

"So where is she?" Jake asked.

"A jet took off from Newark at eleven thirty Saturday night, the sole passenger fit Simpson's description. It was scheduled to land in Zurich late yesterday afternoon but never arrived, went off radar somewhere over the Celtic Sea. There's a search party looking for the plane but I don't expect them to find it. She is presumed dead. Why she killed Hunter is a mystery, one that we'll never solve. Nor will we ever have answers to questions like how they picked their targets and who picked them." He shook his head.

Mali mulled over this news, flabbergasted by these developments.

Changing the subject, Jake asked, "How were you taken, Mali? We watched you walk over to a limo from the outside cameras but your umbrella blocked the view of whomever you were talking to. Joe was delayed getting to the front of the building because he stopped to get a cup of coffee on the way out. Traffic was pretty bad too."

"Oh, I hope Joe doesn't blame himself for what happened," she took a deep breath and let it out slowly, shaking her head. "I made a stupid rookie mistake. Janet Simpson was in the limo and called me over. She said she was on her way back to the office after a meeting in the financial district. When I suggested that we go up to our office, she said Hunter had documents that could help our case. She offered to wait with me in the car until Joe arrived and then offered me a bottled water once I got in the car and out of the rain. I didn't realize that the water was spiked until it was too late. By the time I figured things out, the car was moving and I was too dizzy to get away. I passed out shortly after that. Like I said, a stupid mistake."

"Don't beat yourself up," said Frank. "You're not a trained field agent and the weather did not work in your favor."

"The bottled water did not look to be tampered with and the bottle had not been opened. It didn't occur to me that anything had been added to it."

"You were taken to a warehouse in Newark," Jake said.

"Wait, I also remember reading a text from Kirsten in the car just before I passed out. Simpson and Hunter were siblings?"

Frank responded, "Yes. Janet was adopted by

Hunter's family when she was five or six. She graduated early and left home right after, changing her name
sometime later. She joined Hunter Inc as the CFO when
the company took off. There aren't any more details than
that."

"Hmmmm . . . that's bizarre. I could have sworn
something was going on between the two of them."
Shaking that off, she continued, "Back to the warehouse,
I woke up once in a room that looked like a surgery
room at a hospital except the room was enclosed with
plastic. I had no idea where I was. I spoke briefly to a
woman."

Frank's eyebrows shot up as he leaned forward,
elbows resting on his knees. "Really? What did she look
like? Was she a doctor? Would you recognize her if we
brought pictures over for you to review?"

"I have no idea what she looked like, Frank. She was
petite in size but she wore a gas mask. She was French, I
think, although her voice was muffled."

"A woman was found yesterday morning at The
Westin Jersey City Newport Hotel, a French woman,"
said Jake. "She was in the bathtub of the penthouse
suite. Her name was Dr. Simone Dubois and she was
renowned in France for her work with implants and
the release of medicine by computer or phone app. She
was a genius in her field. We believe she designed and
implanted the device in all targets, including you. The
fact that you spoke with a French woman appears to cor-
roborate that."

"My God! How did she get involved in this? And why would she jeopardize her life's work?"

Frank jumped in. "Employees at the Westin said that Dr. Dubois was a regular guest at their hotel, always checking into the penthouse suite. They confirmed that a woman was a regular guest of hers, although they apparently arrived separately and always ordered room service for their meals. No one could give a description of the woman who joined her but we believe it was Janet Simpson. In all likelihood, she had a relationship with the doctor in order to use her skills."

"I'm stunned," said Mali. "It never occurred to me that unassuming Janet Simpson was the mastermind and manipulator of this whole thing."

They took a break and Mali went to the kitchen to get some snacks and more drinks.

Frank and Jake continued to brief Mali about the events of the past few days as well as what was being said on the news and comments that were made on #HuntedLives before it was removed again from Twitter.

The Hunted Inc empire was no more, the doors had been closed and locked while agents scoured the offices for more information. Hundreds of people were out of work with many losing their shirts due to the drop in stock value. The three businesses run by the players, Lakeway Technologies, Enterprise Trading Firm, and Bank of Mexico in New York, were all in a state of flux and losing stock value. The stock market opened more than four hundred points lower and was still falling.

"What about the three players?"

"They've all lawyered up, each claiming that they assumed the targets were fake, that they were only playing a more real-time version of The Hunted Ones," said Jake. "Unbelievable."

Wiping his face from his brow to his chin, Frank said, "We've got too much on them for them to get away with this." He paused. "Technology has made our lives better in so many ways. Even social media has its benefits. My wife has reconnected with her high school friends and some distant family members, something she wouldn't have without social media. The downside is that they have made it too easy to forget that there are humans at each end of the conversation. I am amazed at how easily people forget that. It's all treated like some sort of virtual game. Not only that, there's an addictive quality, a numbing effect like dopamine does for alcoholics and drug addicts. The user has to go back for more. Look at how many people kept returning to #HuntedLives, yearning for more, for another high. The desired instant gratification and this imbalance is a problem from my perspective." Frank shook his head and sighed. "Enough of my soapbox. I'm getting too old for this." He smiled. "By the way, my boys are no longer playing The Hunted Ones. Their choice. They said that they're sorry you were hurt and they don't want to have anything to do with that game anymore. In fact, the boys are spending more time with Carol and I. We're suddenly cool to hang with. Go figure." He chuckled.

"That's wonderful, Frank. I agree that talking

face-to-face is so much more powerful and meaningful than through a screen."

Frank stood up; Mali and Jake followed his lead. "Time for me to get to the office. Jake, take the rest of the day off then meet me in the morning. I want to talk with you about a new program."

They shook hands.

"Thank you, Frank, for everything," Mali said as he opened the front door.

"I'm glad you're all right, Mali. Rest up and no work until next Monday."

* * *

As SOON AS the door closed, Mali hustled back to the sofa and grabbed the remote to the television.

"I've been dying to check out the news!"

Jake laughed and settled himself more comfortably on the sofa.

She turned on her favorite channel, WABC. The lunchtime news hour was currently discussing the weather forecast.

"Breaking News," the lead anchor broke in. "More details regarding The Hunted Ones' live game are coming to light. As was reported yesterday, Anthony Hunter, owner of Hunted Inc and believed to be the mastermind behind the game, was found murdered in his private jet. Details have still not been released. In addition, the bodies of two women were found dead and may be connected to the game. The first victim, Rebecca Smith, Anthony Hunter's Assistant, was killed in her apartment two weeks ago, strangled. No forced entry. She lived alone, no pets, and was never reported missing. Her body was found three days ago when a resident complained of a rancid odor in the hallway in front of her door. The second victim, Dr. Simone Dubois, drowned in a bathtub at The Westin Jersey City Newport Hotel on May first. At first believed to be an accident, authorities at the FBI confirmed that Dr. Dubois was the creator of the cyanide implants in Hunter's victims and they're investigating her death as a homicide. Why both were killed is a mystery. In related news, the three players of the game, Jane Bellows, Ted Springs, and Hernando Gutierrez were arraigned today. All have proclaimed their innocence but are considered a flight risk, given their financial resources. Bail was denied and they will be held until trial. The whereabouts of Janet Simpson . . ."

Jake reached for the remote and turned off the news. "We've watched enough for now. Let's get another drink then enjoy the Hudson for a while."

"I like that idea."

They walked into the kitchen for their drinks then stepped out onto the balcony and sat down. The street and river noises enveloped them.

"Before I forget . . .". Jake reached into his shirt pocket and pulled out an envelope.

"What's this?"

"Another invitation from Heather."

Mali opened the envelope and removed the folded light pink construction paper. Opening it, she read aloud, "Hi Miss Mali. Can you come to our house for dinner? Daddy will pick you up. We can play with my dolls."

She placed a hand on her heart. "I'm touched. Please tell her that I accept." She smiled at Jake before reading the invitation again to herself. When she finished, she placed it back in the envelope and set the envelope on the small table between the two chairs.

Jake took her hand in his and they both soaked up the view, enjoying the serenity of the river. *I could get used to this.*

Made in the USA
Columbia, SC
18 February 2021

32322852R00190